LADY HAMILTON;

OR,

NELSON'S LEGACY.

A ROMANCE OF REAL LIFE.

" Oh, what a mansion have those vices got,
That for their habitation chose out thee !"—SHAKSPEARE

LONDON:

PUBLISHED BY E. LLOYD, SALISBURY-SQUARE, FLEET-STREET,
AND SOLD BY ALL BOOKSELLERS.

PREFACE.

THE Life and career of LADY HAMILTON sounds far more like a romance than many productions ostensibly belonging to the school of fiction; and yet he who would attempt, by the aid of fiction, to make the truth regarding the life and acts of this extraordinary woman more striking or wonderful, would find that nothing within the probabilities of imagination could come near, in strangeness or seeming romance, than the absolute narrative of facts.

In the following pages the reader will find a full, true, and an authentic Life of LADY HAMILTON, certainly the most extraordinary, and as certainly one of the most beautiful and fascinating, of women. Her acquirements and her varied achievements remind us of the Cleopatras and the Vallières of history. Her indomitable resolution made her the companion of conquerors, and her varied charms elected her to be the charm of Courts.

Of her morality, and of the bearing of her life upon the state of public taste and public propriety, any reader will form his or her own judgment. It has been sufficient for us to present to the world the career of a remarkable woman, not as an example, but as a beacon to the young and the lovely of our land.

That LADY HAMILTOM was happy with all her successes, and even as the mistress of the great Nelson, is more than doubtful—that she might have been happy in the serenity of private life is a fact, which, in her last moments, she did not hesitate to admit.

London, Oct. 1849.

GERMAN LOOKS
AT NELSON.

DID LADY HAMILTON LOVE HIM?

LAST WISH.

A CONSIDERED German view of Nelson is always worth having. It is interesting to us to know what our former rivals on the sea think of our greatest naval commander—how the Nelson touch appeals to them. In "Nelson" (Hutchinson, 12s. 6d.) Herr Friedrich M. Kircheisen, the German historian, has no hesitation in declaring the little admiral on the sea the counterpart of Napoleon on the land.

A masterly appreciation of the qualities which made Nelson great is tempered by a restrained criticism of the weaknesses which made Nelson a moody and susceptible hero. The author does not dole out his admiration and we are not surprised to read:

To us (Germans) Nelson is the most popular officer in the British Royal Navy, and the one with whom we are most in sympathy; he is surely the only British Admiral who set his seal on the history of his times. . .

TWO PASSIONS.

Herr Kircheisen points out that when Nelson stood on the summit of his fame he had only two passions—love of country and love of Lady Hamilton. Later a third was added: affection for his daughter.

As for Lady Hamilton, whose supposed sad fate has for years invoked the tears of the sentimental, the German historian is daring enough to disentangle the truth from the myth, and to show up the lady as a very extravagant creature to the last who spent money like water.

She is said to have lived at last in a state of the utmost destitution; but that is not quite correct, for, in spite of all her losses, she still had £200 a year interest on her daughter Horatia's capital.

The statement that she was buried in an old petticoat in a rough coffin made of thin boards is also legendary. On the contrary, she was really buried in a good oak coffin.

FAME THE MAGNET.

Did the fair and wayward Emma love Nelson? Herr Kircheisen thinks not. "In all probability the love was only on his side. Probably Lady Hamilton never loved anyone but Greville, and it was only very gradually that she got over the desertion of her lover, who was glad that his uncle had taken her from him.

"It is safe to say that her interest in Nelson lay not so much in his personality as in his fame."

LADY HAMILTON;

OR,
NELSON'S LEGACY.
A ROMANCE.

NELSON'S INTERVIEW WITH LADY HAMILTON.

CHAPTER I.

"Oh, what a mansion have those vices got
That for their habitation chose out thee."
SHAKSPEARE.

THE HUMBLE HOME.—THE BLAZING THATCH.
THE GIRL AND HER PRESERVER.—THE
FIRST KISS.

How still—how exquisitely calm, as
though a halo of serenity and holiness was
around it, slept the village of Preston, in
Lancashire, on the night of the 10th of
October, 1777. The light dewy mist that
arose from its cottage gardens, and lingered
around the trunks of its majestic trees,
seemed as though by faint and fleecy pressure
it had stilled all sounds; the watch-dog
bayed not to the moon—the sleepy owl
ceased its low hooting cry—the very spirit
of repose was there. And sailing through
patches of deep-blue sky, spangled with
bright stars, was the majestic moon, veiling
its serene face only at moments as some
light island of vapour swept gently between
it and the earth, and then, with silver rim,

peeping out again like a bride that for a time has veiled her speaking charms from those who love to gaze and gaze to love.

In truth, it was as gentle a night as ever Heaven fashioned.

But the repose and the mild glory of the night, with its soft airs, its twinkling stars, its bright moon, and its light fleecy dew-like clouds, was not to last long. Already the change had begun; and in the low crouching figure of a man, who was cautiously making his way through the main thoroughfare of the slumbering village, might have been pointed out the demon that was to work the change. We will watch him.

This man, notwithstanding his stooping posture, might have been seen to be of gigantic height. By the light of the moon, which, even in dark places, sent a reflected radiance, his costume was visible. It was of that hybrid character which goes in the country of England for anything, but which generally in game districts denotes the poacher. Your real poacher always effects, as far as in him lies, the appearance of a gamekeeper, and hence the castoff coat of some such personage in authority graces his crouching form. The individual we have in our eye was no exception to the general rule in such cases. He wore a close-fitting seal-skin cap; and the thick leather leggings that encased his lower limbs, were well calculated to carry him safely through

"Brake, bush, and brier."

The coat—once a green velveteen one, of no small pretensions in the way of sporting cut, and fancy buttons—was fastened round him by a piece of string to the button-holes. In his hand this man carried a stout stick, which from the manner in which one end of it always drooped and sought the ground, was evidently there loaded with lead.

"The old place is still enough," he muttered. "I'll warrant it won't be so long. There will be fuss enough soon, or my name ain't Will Flamborough, that's all."

He had now got to the outskirts of the village, where the cottages were much more straggling, and facing in different directions, according as the fancy of their owners dictated. The little patches of garden-ground, too, were rather larger than in the heart of the village, and the dew seemed to be denser, or it was only so in appearance from the fact that the moon's rays mingled more uninterruptedly with it. There was one cottage with a yellow washed face to it, and a very deep overhanging thatched roof, that stood so far apart from the others, that its garden went all round it; and despite the dew and the night clouds, that garden could be seen to have some amount of attention bestowed upon it of a character essentially different to what was given to the little patches of land attached to the rest of the cottages in Preston.

The skulking man paused when he got to the little inefficient paling that surrounded this cottage garden.

"I wonder if it's really true," he muttered, "that the Lyons don't sleep here to-night. They say at the 'Ostrich' that Sir Gilbert has ordered them to sleep at the Grange till he comes back from London; and it may likely enough be true, after the robberry at the Grange when he went before; and to be sure, old Lyon has been in the service of the family for many a long year. Hang him! He was never the man to say 'How goes it with you?' to a poor fellow like me, who didn't like work while other folks had good pensions; and he all but swore to seeing me about on the night of the robbery. He'd not have been far out if he had sworn it outright."

Will Flamborough, or Will Flam, as he was more generally called, for shortness' sake, upon the country side, now ventured to raise himself up sufficiently to look over the fence into the little garden; and then finding that all was still, he vaulted over, and crept towards the cottage.

"It's all right enough," he said. "They are at the great house, or their dog would be here. Fool-like, they have taken him with them, and left their own house unguarded, while they look after another man's. I should just like to trample on them all as I trample on their patch of garden they are so mightily proud of; and some of these days I'll have my revenge upon that Emma, who is so proud with her pretty face and her fine lady-airs, that she must alarm the whole village, only because a fellow offered her a kiss in the lane at the back of the Grange. This will be a little surprise to them in the morning, along with others, I'll be bound."

As he spoke, he went through the garden as noiselessly as he could, for fear of awakening any of the neighbours, trampling down the flowers, and dashing to pieces any little contrivance for their support and culture. In the course of five minutes he had made that trim little spot of ground a complete scene of desolation.

"There," he said, as he left the place. "Now, Miss Emma, you have your work cut out for you; and it will go hard but I provide you with so much beside to think of before the morning, that you will not know which way to turn."

Creeping cautiously to the fence, he vaulted over it again, and then watching a moment when the moon was behind a cloud, he crossed the principal thoroughfare of the village again; and leaping a stile, was in the domain of Sir Gilbert Radley, the principal man of the village and neighbourhood.

There was an avenue of very beautiful limes that led up to the Grange, as the place of Sir Gilbert was called; and diving amid these trees, Will Flam made his way towards the house. When he got near to it, he took a circuit to the right, so that he avoided the principal entrance to the Grange, and reached one of the sides of the building. Then he paused.

"Let me see," he said. "Yes; all's right. There ain't much wind; but what there is blows this way, so this is the place to begin at; and the long room here will be the very thing. This will be a glorious job, though I am single-handed in it. You may not know it, Sir Gilbert, but that month you got me in the county-jail for snaring your hares will cost you a trifle."

There was a pretty lawn of about a quarter of an acre in extent upon this side of the house; and immediately looking into it through three windows, with casements opening to the ground, was one of the principal rooms of the building. Immediately beyond the lawn there were some farm buildings; and almost touching its light iron fence, was a stack of old hay.

"Now," said Will, "we shall see what we shall see. It's a pity if the noodles of the village don't have a bonfire now and then, and they ought to be much obliged to me for accommodating them with one; but whether they are or not, they shall have one."

After some rummaging in his pockets, the poacher and burglar, who upon that night was about to add incendiarism to his other pursuits, found a glazier's diamond, and then creeping up to the window of the room that faced the lawn, he soon cut out a pane of glass, which enabled him to put in his hand and undo the fastening of the casement. In another moment he was in the room, and then his care was to prop open one of the windows. He held up his hand to ascertain what current of air was in it, and then he muttered—

"It will do. There is breeze enough to set the old Grange in a blaze. I can't do the job just as I should like, but perhaps it will be none the worse on that account."

After listening intently for a few moments, and being quite surprised to find how profoundly still the house was, he left the room, and went across the little lawn to the hay-stack, from which he began to pull as much of the dry combustible material as he could. When he got a quantity, he compressed it as much as possible, and carried it to the room, upon the floor of which he cast it. By repeating this process some eight or ten times, it was astonishing the quantity of hay with which the room was strewn.

"There's nothing like working with a will," muttered the fellow. "How farming would pay if the men only worked as I have for this half-hour! Hang it all! I could always work hard enough for any mischief, but I don't like the regular labour, not I. That don't suit Will Flam. How precious quiet they are in the old place, to be sure; but then, after all, there's nobody there but Lyon and his wife, and old Peter the baliff, and his deaf daughter-in-law, and that little pretty-faced spitfire, Emma Lyon. Who the deuce is she, I wonder, that she can't take a kiss from a fellow when he meets her in a lane?"

The moon, as though grieved to see what was going on in the village of Preston on that night, hid its fair face behind a bank of clouds that crept up from the south-western horizon: and the darkness that crept over the face of nature began to be more black and intense each passing moment. The wind, too, materially increased both in volume and in fury, and at times it had quite a winterly sound, as it swept around the quaint gables of the old Grange.

Once more did Will Flam go into the room, and this time it was to take something from it. He wrapped up a clock that had been upon the chimney-piece in a table cover, and with all the speed he could make, that was at all consistent with caution, he bounded back to the cottage which the Lyon family had temporily deserted.

He hid the clock, still wrapped in the table-cover, beneath the thatch of the house.

"It will hang 'em," he said.

Back then again he went, and he now considered himself so favoured by the darkness that he did not skulk along with the same timid movement that had before characterised him, but ran up the avenue of limes with quite a degree of boldness as compared to his former manner. As soon as he reached the lawn, he began fumbling in his pockets, and soon produced the incendiary's accomplice, the phosphorus box. At this moment a light rain began to fall.

"Well, if I did not think it would turn out a queer night," he growled. "There was a water ring round the moon, a long way off; but let it come, a light rain will do no harm, and it can't damp the hay now. Here goes for a good-by to the old Grange, I only hope."

As he uttered these words, he cast a bunch of lighted splints into the room among the hay. There was for a moment a sparkling blaze, but that subsided, and as the wind poured in at the open window, a low hissing sound came from the rapidly-igniting combustible materials in the room.

"It's as good as done," said Will.

He ran across the little lawn and plunged among the trees, where he watched the result of his diabolical manœuvring.

The soft rain came pelting down upon such of the leaves of the limes as still lingered upon the boughs, in defiance of the close approach of the winter season; and the wind, with a melancholy sighing cadance, made itself heard in the little plantations; and, mingled with that sighing wind, the attentive and expectant ears of Will Flam heard another sound like a low muttered roar. At times it rose and fell like the murmur of the ocean, and sometimes a strange, crackling, hissing tone mingled with it, as though some wild animal was snarling as it scented its prey upon the night air.

"Ha!—ha!" said Will. "I have it now. It is getting on famously. What a merry night's work, to be sure.!"

Through the trees, now, there came a strange light; each moment it gradually increased and became redder; it spread upward to the dim sky, and the roaring noise increased.

"Capital!" said Will; "it's waking now.'

The strange red light increased, and dis

tinct sounds of the cracking of glass came upon his ears. The heat in the room was too much for the windows. The roaring wind did not increase so much as it became steadier and less fitful in its tones. The rain was on the increase; but the wind without did not seem to be quelled by the shower: on the contrary, it seemed as though it were a living thing, sent to sack that deserted home where flame was waging rude war against the sacredness of a home.

"It will do," said Will.

Suddenly, the brightness of the fire became so great, that, in a feeling of momentary alarm, he shrunk back further into the woody copse in which he was. It seemed to him as though, at the moment, the flames had flashed upon him with an audible voice, saying—

"That is the man!"

He fled to a considerably greater distance from the Grange; and when he paused, panting, partly from fear, and partly with the sudden exertion he had made, he wiped the perspiration from his brow, as he he said—

"What a fool I am! It seemed to me at the moment as if the flames were coming after me. I—I didn't think I should have been frightened in this way. Frightened? I —no, no—I am not frightened. Who says I am frightened?—who says I did it? No one—of course, no one. Who saw me?"

He quite involuntarily cast his eyes upwards for a moment as he asked the question, for, hardened and inured to crime as it was, his own heart at that moment told him that God saw him; but such emotions were not likely to be more than transitory with such a man; and as he recovered from his fright, he once more resumed his brutal tones of triumph.

"All's right," he said; "it's doing bravely now, I hear it. They will have need of more than a pail of water to put that out!"

"Fire!—fire!—fire!" cried a voice; and the cry was like three blows upon the brain of the incendiary.

CHAPTER II.

THE RESCUE FROM DEATH.—THE PROMISE AND THE REMEMBRANCE.

"Fire! fire!" Amid the death-like stillness of the night, can any cry be more intensely awful? What volumes does it not speak of terror and dismay—of pain and agony — of desolation — of destruction !— "Fire! fire!" Small wonder that that cry found quickly an echo from the village.

The wind, setting as it did full through the windows of the room where the fire had first been kindled, not only fanned the flame, but sent it into the body of the house. Unfortunately, the walls of that room were of old dry wainscot; and the flames soon laid hold of them, wrapping them in a sheet of brilliancy. When the villagers awoke and rushed to the Grange, the whole build-

ing seemed doomed to destruction. It was then that Will Flam ventured forward along with the others, thinking it safer to do so than to hide himself; and no one was more eager than he in asking what was the matter, and in pretending to lament and wonder at the catastrophe.

In the course of ten minutes at the furthest, the whole population of Preston was on foot. Such hasty measures as upon the spur of the moment could be adopted, were brought to bear upon the fire; but it was like attempting to stem a torrent with a butterfly's wing, to throw pails of water upon the blazing Grange. The parish engine was, of course, out of order, and would not work; and so the fire went merrily on.

It was fully believed that the few inmates of the Grange had escaped; for upon the lawn there stood John Lyon, and there lay his wife in a swoon, and there was the old bailiff and his wife, and his deaf daughter-in-law, with a trumpet at her ear. At first, Lyon had seemed half-stupified at the unexpected event. He gazed upon the flames like a man half-asleep; and it was not until more than one neighbour had shaken him by the arm, saying—"Why, John, man, what do ail thee?" that he shook off the lethargy that had come over him. Then, and not till then, did any one comprehend that there was a calamity impending that was worse than the destruction of the old Grange. Glaring around him eagerly, Lyon suddenly cried—

"Where is Emma? Where is my child, Emma?"

At the question, everybody looked round; and her name was repeated in every variety of intonation. There was no response; and the agonised father was calling aloud upon the name of his child, when a shriek from some one in the house attracted the attention of all. The sound directed the many eyes where to look; and the light of the flames, as they roared and danced out of the lower windows, enabled them to see that for which they looked. At a small window near the top of the house was some form, partly obscured by the rolling smoke, but at intervals to be distinctly seen. It was Lyon who, with clasped hands and a voice of horror, gave a name to that form—

"My child!" he cried, "it is my child, Emma!"

"Father!—father! Save me," cried the girl, as she clung to the sill of the little window-frame, while she looked upon the sea of faces below. "Save me! Save me!"

"Yes," said Lyon.

He would have rushed into tht burning house, but to have permitted him to do so would only have been to have added his certain destruction to the uncertain fate of Emma.

She might yet by some rare chance be saved, for the fire was all at the lower part of the house; but that very circumstance made it death to venture across its threshold.

Two strong men held the father in a vice-like grasp.

"No, John Lyon," said one. "Thee can do no good, and thee shall not go and singe thyself to death afore our eyes."

"Let me go. It is my child I go to save. Let me go. Are you men or devils that hold me when my child calls?"

Emma wrung her hands, and they could see her weeping at the window as she ever and anon cried—"Help me—oh, help me!"

Will Flam watched her with flaming eyes. "It serves her right," he muttered. "Who's she, I wonder, that she should make such a fuss because a fellow wanted to kiss her in the lane?"

"A ladder!" cried one voice. "A ladder!" cried a hundred voices. "A ladder!—a ladder!"

There was a rush of about twenty young men from among the crowd to where they all remembered there was a tall ladder, used for covering hay-stacks. In two minutes it was brought to the spot, and a loud cheer burst from the mob as this means of safety for Emma Lyon presented itself. A dozen eager hands placed it against the house. It reached to within two feet of the window. Emma sprang upon the sill, and seemed about to trust herself to the ladder. A volume of flame from one of the windows below issued out and completely enveloped half-a-dozen rounds of the ladder.

"She can't pass that!" cried twenty voices. "She can never pass that alive. Stop, Emma. Stop—stop."

The girl paused; but now the ladder, with that fire-flame bursting upon it, ran every risk of being burnt to pieces if it were not used quickly. A young man—almost a lad—rushed from the crowd and commenced its ascent.

The cheer that came from the lips of all there present, but one, urged him on. That one muttered—"She had no right to make a fuss at a fellow, for wanting to kiss her in the lane."

And now the gallant youth reaches the part of the ladder which is subjected to the action of the flames. He pauses a moment. He tries to dash onward. Blistered and bewildered by the smoke and the long-tongued flames that play around him, he loses his hold and falls. That hope is past!

And now the flames are creeping up higher and higher still; and only at rarer intervals is the young girl seen at the window. She still cries for help. She calls upon some below by name, some that have been kind to her, to save her; for she can see well the upturned faces by the glare of the conflagration; and more than once she calls again upon her father, but they will not let him go. If youth and strength could not mount the ladder, age and feebleness surely would fail. Yet stay; another attempts it: yes, another; and he is a strong man. He has dipped his handkerchief in water and wrapped it round his head and face; and so he thinks to rush through the flames and save the girl. It is a gallant attempt. God speed him!

Every voice is hushed now to watch that man—every heart beats short and thick—every eye beams with moisture. Even Will Flam shades his lurid-looking eye-balls with his hand, and looks on and says nothing. He forgets at the moment that he was refused a kiss in the lane, for which great offence he thought it was a meet punishment that a young and beautiful girl should be burnt to the death in that blazing house.

Is the ladder firm? Have the flames not yet charred it sufficiently to make it yield beneath the weight of that man? These are anxious questions, but no one utters them, although all ask them of their own hearts during those moments of intense suspense.

The man ascends calmly, but yet with sufficient quickness to carry him past small dangers. It is quite clear that he will do all that any one ought to do with the smallest regard to their own life. Up—up; round after round of the ladder he reaches.

"Save me—save me!" cried Emma.

The man makes an impatient gesture, as though he would say—"Do not speak: you distract me by your cries;" but she does not see him. The flames that still come in a full roaring volume from the window below her, prevent her from seeing the lower part of the ladder at all, so she is not even aware that any one is attempting the perilous ascent, or that any one has already attempted it, and failed in reaching her.

"Help! help!" she cries; "oh, save me."

Again the man makes the impatient gesture, and then he reaches the point of danger. They see him fighting with the flames. They see him driven back a step, and then advance again. He is all but enveloped in the long fiery tongues that seem resolved to lick him into the jaws of destruction.

There is a sigh, and then a groan among the people. The strong man is beaten by fire. He hangs to the ladder with one hand, only for a moment or two; and then, in a struggling manner, sufficiently indicative of broken strength and energies, he comes down. He does not absolutely fall, but he all but does so.

When he reaches the ground he is insensible.

And now it would indeed seem that all hope or expection of saving the young girl is gone. Many turn away, unable to bear the spectacle before them. Rough-visaged men weep, and more than one prayer ascends to Heaven on the fiery wings of the flames for succour for Emma, the pride and the beauty of the village.

Will Flam clasps his head in both hands, and with a cry, more like that of a demon than a man, rushes into the plantation.

Again Emma cries for help, but help comes not. Then she clasps her hands over her face, and sinks upon the window-sill. Her long chesnut ringlets float idly far out into the night air. The fire roars and shouts about her.

Hark! what is that? A horn! Yes—the clear notes of a bugle horn. The mail-coach is passing through the village, and the conflagration of the Grange lights up the vehicle and all its passengers.

"Stop!" cried a sharp, clear voice. "I will alight."

"We can't wait, sir," said the coachman.

"But it is a fire! God knows what good we may do!"

"Can't stop, sir. If so be as the blessed 'varsal world was a-fire, sir, I must keep my time. We has lost a'ready a matter o' two minutes and three-quarters."

A young man sprang from the coach.

"Leave me behind, then," he said. "I cannot go on. Something seems as if it whispered to me that I was wanted here. Go on—go on."

"Werry sorry," said the coachman; "but 'osses is 'osses, and mail bags is mail bags; so, you see, on we goes. Blaze away, Jem."

The guard blew a long, melancholy, wailing blast upon his horn, and away sped the coach, leaving the youthful passenger in the village of Preston. Agile and light, without an ounce of superfluous flesh about, it did not take the young man many moments to reach the scene of the conflagration. The undress naval uniform that he wore, and the little hanger by his side, procured him a respectful passage. He lost his hat in the throng, however, and his light, silky hair was blown about by the wind.

"What is this?" he cried. "Are you all struck dumb? Is a house on fire a national calamity? Ah! that ladder! Stop! Good God! Is she alive?"

"Yes—yes!" cried a hundred voices.

"And you call yourselves men!"

In a moment, before one word of prevention—of explanation—of encouragement or of warning, could be spoken, the young stranger had dashed forward and commenced the ascent of the ladder. With a marvellous agility, that set all the experience of those who looked at him at defiance, he reached the point where the flames caught the spokes of the ladder. With a crash, the ladder parted at that spot. One burning fragment fell to the ground; the other, with the young stranger still clinging to it, fell against one of the window-sills of the house. But one small circling flame was coming out at that window, accompanied by rather a dense body of smoke. He gave but one glance upwards to the young girl at the upper window, and then dashed through the blackened casement that was close to him, and disappeared into the house.

Every breath was suspended. The people looked at the window through which the young stranger had disappeared, and then at each other, as though they doubted the evidence of their own senses as to what they saw. Where had he gone?—what would become of him?—was the inside of the house sufficiently strong yet to hold him up? A wild Hurrah! bursts from every lip. The young man appears at the window, upon the sill of which Emma still lay so still, that many thought death had already claimed its lovely victim. He has found the staircase sufficient to carry him to that height from the floor into which he had plunged.

He touched the girl lightly. With a shriek she turned and clasped him in her arms.

"You have come to save me!" she cried. "God has sent some one to save me!"

"If I can, my dear."

"Yes—yes. Oh, God, you are so good to me. You would not have been sent, if not to save me. I will cling to you—Yes, yes, I will cling to you."

She hung upon his neck and burst into hysterical sobs, mingled with wild laughter.

Another cheer burst from every throat below. He clasped the young girl round the waist firmly with his left hand; both her arms were round his neck; and so they disappeared from the window together.

"Be calm. Be calm," he said. "We shall escape from the back of the house. Hush—hush; don't cry in that way. All's well."

He rushed from the room to the landing, where there were two staircases. Up one of these, flames and smoke were slowly crawling. The other was free, and he at once took it. After proceeding about twelve steps, they came to a window which looked into a garden. The window was about fifteen feet from the ground, and the turf was soft beneath.

CHAPTER III.

AFTER THE FIRE.—THE FALSE CHARGE.—
THE IMPORTANT LETTER.

"THIS will do," cried the young stranger. "What do they call you, my dear?"

"Emma."

"Then, Emma, be so good as to stand a moment, while I make a cradle for you."

"A cradle?"

"Ah, you don't understand that. It's something that we let down or haul up anything with, that holds it quite safe during the process, at sea. But how should you understand it? Can you stand by yourself, Emma, for one moment?"

"Oh, yes—yes. Do you hear the flames how they threaten us?"

"Let them threaten. I have heard the waves threaten louder still, and the good ship on a lee shore the while, and yet no great mischief done. Don't be afraid. You will live to be an old woman yet, Emma, and to talk of the young midshipman who got his hair singed off in the fire."

As he spoke, the young stranger rapidly took off his jacket, and began to place it round the chest of Emma in such a way, that by holding the two arms of it, he could let her down a distance quite sufficient from the window to prevent the possibility of her being hurt by dropping the remainder.

"Now, Emma," he said; "away you go."

Before she could, in the state of confusion she was in, have the least idea of what he was about, he had lifted her up and put her feet out of the open window; and then letting her down gently by the sleeves of the jacket, he cried—

"Away you go. Drop easy."

He let go of the jacket; and as she was not above a foot from the green turf of the garden, she reached it without sustaining the smallest shock. She turned and looked up to her deliverer, saying—

"But you—how will you escape? How selfish I have been. Ah, I wish I was back with you again."

"Don't say that; I shall be with you in a moment. I am like a cat, always safe to light on my feet, and safely too."

Even as he spoke, the young stranger sprung from the window and alighted in safety by the side of Emma. That they were completely saved from the blazing house was now an incontestable fact. Huge masses of smoke rolled over their heads from the burning timbers, because the wind carried it in that direction; but as yet, the actual flames had not laid a fiery hold upon the back of the building.

How deliciously cool the air in the garden was, in comparison with the heat in the house—that heat which, like the hot blast from a furnace, had made the breathing thick and heavy, and laid hold of life's energies with the hand of a giant. But in that garden, facing to the cool north as it did, there was a climate so delightful by contrast to the senses, that both Emma and her young deliverer could have lingered for a long time, breathing that highly vital air. They even forgot at the moment that to those in front of the building their fate was all uncertainty, and that, although they had been seen to disappear in the blazing house, their re-appearance was unknown to all but themselves; and there was some there who loved Emma too well to be left long in such a torturing doubt.

They were looking at each other, that young midshipman and the fair girl whom he had rescued from so awful a death—a death terrible to all and at any time, but how much more terrible to the young and the beautiful. Yes, they gazed at each other; and he held her hand in his, while, despite the pain of some transient scorches he had received, he smiled as he said—

"How happy I am that I have saved you."

There was at the moment an awful crash. They both started, and turned towards the house—the roof had fallen in! Had they been only three minutes later in effecting their escape, they would have been engulphed in the ruins, and nothing could have saved them from absolute destruction. But such was not to be.

That couple were reserved for other things.

Perhaps in that secret companionship they found in each other company, although neither of them spoke much—no one speaks much when the heart is full. They might yet have longer lingered, but in the course of the few moments succeeding the fall of the roof of the Grange, there came up from the burning ruins a dense shower of red-hot sparks, and they taking, of course, the direction of the wind, soon began to fall thickly upon the youthful pair.

"Ah! You see, Emma, the fire has not done with us yet," said the young stranger. "Let us get to windward of it; it's bad seamanship to get on the weather-bow of the house, in this way."

With her hand still clasped in his—that hand which, but for him, would surely at that moment have been blackening amid the flames—he ran towards the eastern angle of the house; there was a light fence to get over; he vaulted it himself, and then lifted Emma clear of the obstruction. In another moment they turned the angle of the house and came in sight of the pitying crowd in front of the doomed building, not one of whom ever expected to see Emma Lyon or the young sailor again in this world.

What a strange thing it would have been if they had both perished in that fire! How the world would have missed them both! But, as we have said, it was not to be. They had not yet by many a long year fulfilled their mission.

And now go with us in imagination, and picture to yourself what the people thought and felt when, like two spirits from beyond the grave, Emma and the young stranger burst upon their gaze. Imagine the glare of astonishment; imagine the silence of incredulity for a moment, and then the glad shout of recognition; but above all, and before all, imagine the feelings of the father and of the mother, when once again they clasped in their arms their much-loved child, after they had began to mourn for her as one of the bright and beautiful things that, with the summer flowers, had passed away.

The glad shouts of the people gave the whole affair now the aspect of a holiday; and one would really have thought, to see the many faces glowing with satisfaction, and ruddy with the fierce glow of the flames, that that house had been lit as a kind of bonfire for purely rejoicing purposes, instead of its destruction being, as in good truth it was, a calamity to the district.

The glad shouts reached the ears of Will Flam; and, starting from his hiding-place, he cried—

"They must have put out the fire! No—no—the sky is ruddy with its flames. What does it mean?—do they suspect me? Do they suspect me, and are they already rejoicing at the prospect of my execution?"

Curiosity led him captive to the spot; and there he soon learnt what had produced the popular effervescence of joy. With a skulking manner and a gloomy brow, after casting one long look upon the young deliverer of Emma, he again plunged among the thickets, muttering—

"Saved her, has he? My curse light on him, and she too! Who is she, that no end of riot should be made because a fellow only wanted to kiss her baby-face in the lane? But my time will come yet. Yes, my time will come yet; and I can afford to wait a little."

That the young stranger should be loaded with caresses and congratulations, may well be conceived; the attentions of old Lyon and his wife were divided between him and their daughter. They felt that they could never make enough of him; and it is something of a wonder that his arm was not shaken off by the many that crowded round him to say something kind to him, and shake him by the hand, if it were only for a moment.

He had at the least fifty invitations to different cottages, to pass the remainder of the night; but he replied to one and to all—

"My good friends, don't take it amiss; but I am off—I shall walk on till I get to the next post town. Remember that I am in the service of my country—I am going to join my ship, and have no time to lose. So, God bless you all, and good-night!"

"No, no," said Emma; "you will stay until daylight? Who knows what dangers you might meet with on the road at such an hour as this?"

"Danger is my profession," he replied, with a smile. "Permit me to go; but I do hope that we shall meet again."

"And I," sighed Emma.

"I shall keep this jacket as a remembrance of to-night," he added; "so now farewell."

"If the young genleman wants any one to show him the way," said a rough voice, "I'll do it with an amazing deal of pleasure;" and Will Flam, with an insolent, ill-put-on ease, pushed himself forward among the throng of persons.

"No," said the young stranger; "of the two, I would rather lose my way than choose you for a guide—for to tell you the honest truth, my friend, I don't like your looks."

"Not like my looks?—What is there in my looks that you don't like?"

"Everything."

"You are right enough, sir, as regards that man," said old Lyon. "Do not have anything to say to him—he is a bad character."

"A bad character!" cried Will. "So I am a bad character, am I? Ha! ha! A bad character!—ha! ha! That's good, old friend; your character won't look very bright soon—soon, I say. Do you hear that?"

"I hear you; but will have no altercation with you. As for you, young sir, if you will go, I myself will go with you."

"No, no," said the young man; "what do I want with any one? The road is clear enough, and see, the moon is now struggling out again from behind the clouds. Look at the scud. We may have a squally, but not a bad night, on the whole: so, good-by once again."

"Ah, you are a nice set," said Will.

"Why are we a nice set?" said one.

"Why, you leave the old Grange to burn down, without ever lending a hand like natural beings, as you ought to be, to stop the flames. All the world knows that Sir Gilbert is no friend of mine, as how should he be? He is a strict game-preserver, and folks call me a poacher; but still it does put me about a bit to see the respectable old house burnt down, that it does."

Old Lyon shook his head.

"Yes," added Will, "and my firm belief is that it wasn't an accident, do you see."

"Not an accident?" cried half a dozen voices. "Who did it then?"

"Mum," said Will. "Mum's the word just now; but who will come with me, and let's see if anything can be saved out of the fire? It's a shame and a sin to let the old house go to the ground in such a way. Why, I've been so used to look up to its old gable ends, and its weather-vane on the clock tower that I shall be ready to cry to-morrow, when I find it all gone."

"Carve it on the pump," said one, "that Will Flam cried once."

"I'll carve you on the pump, stupid. Come, who will try yet to save something out of the Grange? I don't mind a little singeing, not I, though Sir Gilbert and I don't get on exactly like brothers; but where's the odds? Perish the man that bears malice when his neighbour's house is on fire."

The young sailor had listened to all this with amused attention, and he fixed his keen grey eyes upon Will with a scrutinizing glance, that the poacher might well shrink from, as in truth he did.

"Come! Who's coming?" he cried.

"We will all do what we can for the Grange," said one, "but we had rather do it without your company, Will Flam. Mind you, if it was only for the matter of a hare or two that you took out of the preserve, or mayhap a pheasant, their's nobody in Preston would turn their backs on you; but you are a bad one, Will, and you know it, and we all know it, so we won't have anything to say to you."

"A bad one, am I, a bad one? Well, that's a lively idea. We shall see—we shall see. A bad one? Ha! ha! Well, do what you can. Bless you all. Ha! ha! Good-night, old Lyon; good-night, Emma. What a pity such a fuss was made one day about a kiss in the lane. I'm a bad one, am I? Ha! ha! ha!"

With something between a curse and a laugh, Will Flam now darted off, and was soon lost to sight in the gloom of the night. The Grange still burnt, but virtually the fire was over, and the whole of the building, with the exception of about three rooms at the west wing, was destroyed.

What had once been quite a specimen of an old English residence, was now nothing but a blackened ruin. Sad contrast—sad sight, to those who, from many old associations, perchance, loved the old house. But so it is with all the possessions of this world. They will pass away, and

"Leave not a wreck behind."

"And you will go, then?" said Emma, to

the young stranger. "You really will go?"

"Don't say, will. It's a case of must."

He kissed her gently; and then, while the tears stood in her eyes, he turned away. Waving his hand to the villagers, he said—

"If ever I come near Preston again, I will call upon you all, you may depend."

"Farewell! and may God bless you!" said Mrs. Lyon.

"Yes," added Lyon. "He will bless you, for you have done a noble deed to-night."

With another smile the young sailor turned away, and walked briskly from the cottage. He heard a footstep behind him, and a soft voice cried to him to stop. He turned, and saw that it was Emma. She reached him, and laid her hand upon his arm.

"Your name?" she said. "Tell me your name, that I may think of it often when you are far away."

"HORATIO NELSON!"

CHAPTER IV.

THE FALSE WITNESS.—THE LETTER.—EMMA SAVES HER FATHER, AND CONFOUNDS WILL.

THE morning after the fire of the old Grange at Preston, was as fair a one for the season as ever peeped out of the heavens. The clouds which had hovered over the night sky had all dispersed, and there was the clear blue ether only between the world and Heaven.

The birds flew in a wide circle around the still smoking Grange, and from far and wide, parties came to the village to see what amount of devastation the agent of destruction had produced. The state in which the little garden belonging to the Lyon's was found, soon, however, divided the interest of the fire with the inhabitants of the village. Every one had a look at the trampled and broken-down flower-beds, over which Emma shed abundance of tears. Truly, for her, it was a distressful morning, for he, it will be remembered—he, the mere lad—who had tried to ascend the ladder and save her before the arrival of Nelson, was lying dangerously ill and hurt by his fall; and she had loved him perhaps more because she knew how dearly he loved her, than for any passion or feeling of her own towards him. The Grange, too, had been burnt down while her father had the care of it; and it was yet a subject of conjecture how Sir Gilbert, its owner, would view the affair, when he should get the news of it, and come down from London to look at the ruins of his farm and ancient home.

It was the house in which he had been born.

All these were anxieties enough for poor Emma; but she put on her little straw hat, and wrapping her cloak about her, she went to see the wounded Edwin Lee, for such was the name of the youth who had fallen from the ladder, and of whose noble attempt to aid her, and its disastrous issue, she knew nothing at the time of its happening.

Edwin was the son of a widow, and her sole support.

When Emma reached the cottage of Mrs. Lee, she felt so much affected by the accumulation of distressing circumstances by which she was surrounded, that she could not find courage to enter it, but leant for awhile against the little gate that opened to the garden. She was seen, however, by the widow, who, wiping her eyes with the corner of her apron, came out to her, saying—

"Emma Lyon, Emma Lyon, I only wish you had been ever so ugly, and then this would not have happened to my poor boy."

"Alas! Mrs. Lee, you don't know how sorry I am. May I see poor Edwin?"

"Oh, yes; I suppose you had better see him, for he does nothing but rave about you; and he won't believe, unless he sees you, that you are saved from the fire, but will have it that we only tell him that to comfort him and to keep him quiet; so come in, by all means; only I do wish you had been ugly, Emma Lyon, and then my poor boy would not have lost his wits, as I believe he has, all along of you."

Emma did not feel herself particularly called upon to make any reply to these selfish remarks of Mrs. Lee; but she followed her into the cottage. Edwin was in an inner room; and Mrs. Lee, pointing to it, cried—

"There he is. You will find him there. Heaven knows there is trouble enough for poor people in this world, without their neighbours' daughters driving their sons out of their minds by being a deal too pretty. I never knew any good come of beauty, for my part, either among rich or poor."

Emma, the moment she went into the next room, was deeply affected at the reception Edwin gave to her. He burst into a passion of joyful tears, and cried—

"Yes, it is true! She is saved! My beautiful Emma! She is saved from the fire that I could not snatch her from! I can die so happy—so very happy now!"

"You will not die at all, Edwin."

"Come nearer to me, Emma, and let me hold your hand in mine. It is only for a moment. Do not shrink from me. Of late I have began to think you did not really love me, and I have tried to reconcile myself to it; but last night, when the fire was, my only hope and wish was to save you, and to then perish in the flames myself. I thought then that when I was gone, you would sometimes, as you passed through the village-churchyard, where I should be lying so still and so calm, say 'Poor Edwin!' and drop a tear to my memory."

"Do not speak so, Edwin. Do not speak so. There may be many happy days in store for you yet."

"No—no!"

"Why should you say no?"

"You do not love me, Emma."

"Not love you, Edwin? How can I do

otherwise than love one who did so much for me as you did last night? Nay, do not tell me that you did nothing. The attempt was the deed, and not the success or failure. You would have saved me at the sacrifice of your own life, and that you did not do so is a mere accident."

"And—and you will—you really will love me?"

"Hoity-toity!" cried Mrs. Lee, bouncing into the room. "How fine we can talk! We are each of us as if we had a printed book in our hands, that we are!"

"Mother," said Edwin, "how can you speak so, and Emma here?"

"Oh, it's all mighty fine, of course! Because folks have pretty faces—though there's two words to that, perhaps, in some minds—they must not be spoken to, not they! Thank God I was never pretty! I was always plain Martha Brown before I married—plain Martha Brown! I never made folks get up ladders after me, and fall and break every bone in their skins!"

"But no bones are broken, mother."

"That's not the question. They might have been all broken, and so I have a right to say that they are!"

"But, mother——"

"Don't mother me. A nice thing, indeed, and the winter time coming too, and I a lone widow, and you so stiff with all your bones broken, that you ain't able to do a bit of work, and all through somebody having what the folks call a pretty face. Hang all pretty faces, say I! I was always plain Martha Brown."

"And you must have been unpleasant Martha Brown, likewise," said a voice at the door; and at the same moment, Doctor Lukin, the village apothecary, made his appearance. "Why, Mrs. Lee, I heard your voice the moment I got past the pump. I'll tell all the village, if you like, that you are plain and unpleasant Mrs. Lee, who was, plain and unpleasant Martha Brown."

"Well, I'm sure, Mr. Lukin, you oughtn't to join in; I was only saying that I hate pretty faces."

"Then, plain Mrs. Lee, you and I differ most completely, and I love them. They are fashioned by the Almighty, to give us the joy of looking at them; and if I were to say I hate them, it would sound to me like some reflection upon my maker. No, plain Mrs. Lee, you are very wrong, indeed. And now, Edwin, how are you? Ah, Emma Lyon, I did not see you. Is it your pretty face that has awakened the ire of plain Mrs. Lee?"

"I do not know, sir," said Emma. "Will Edwin soon be well?"

"Yes, in a week. There is no harm done. You young folks fall about like cats, without doing yourselves any particular injury. Now, if I or plain Mrs. Lee were to fall down, it would, no doubt, be to the great detriment of our old bones."

Mrs. Lee could stand the raillery of the doctor, as he was called in the village, no longer; but bounced from the apartment in a huff. Emma shook hands with both Edwin and the doctor; and bidding the former be of good cheer, since he would so soon be well, she left the cottage, not very much heart-broken at the reception she had met with from Mrs. Lee, who, as she passed out, said—

"I suppose you are going to carry your pretty face home, now?"

"That is quite *plain*, Mrs. Lee," replied Emma.

Emma could pluck up a spirit when she liked. At the bottom of that young heart lay many slumbering passions. It is not all gentleness that looks soft and engaging in this world.

Emma Lyon had not got many paces from the cottage of Mrs. Lee, when she saw a little throng of persons advancing through the village, in the centre of which was one on horseback. The mounted man was too well known in Preston for her to have a moment's doubt of his identity.

It was the Reverend Jabez Titherleigh, the rector of the parish, and a justice of the peace; a man without humanity—without gentleness—without mercy—a petty tyrant —a gormand and a drunkard. The picture is not overcharged. Fifty years ago the rural districts of England could have presented many such specimens: and there are some now.

As the little throng of persons neared the young girl, she saw that Will Flam walked by the side of the horse, and that the village constable, too, was there. The rest of the persons seemed to be mere spectators. Among them was one who was intimate with her father, and of him Emma asked the cause of the formidable array.

"Why, they do say, Miss Emma, that the Grange was set fire to by some one of a purpose, and that some robbery was committed, too, of some things out of the old place a little before the fire broke out; and so, you see, Mr. Titherleigh is out and about to find out the matter. But where they are going to I don't know, and can't guess."

At this moment Will Flam touched his cap, and in a mighty cringing and affected-respectful manner—his lordship was very fond of lip-service—said something to the reverend justice.

"Oh! where is she?" cried Titherleigh. "Constable, stop that young girl, there. That's her. Oh! yes; I have seen her before. And a pretty creature the little jade is, too," added the justice, in a low tone.

"Yes, sir," said Will, who, notwithstanding the observation was made in a low tone, heard it. "Yes, sir, she is pretty, and fit for any gentleman to take notice of. I wonder you don't take her into your service, your worship."

"Into my service! What do you mean, you rascal?"

"Oh, only that I thought it would keep her out of harm's way. That's all, your worship."

"Oh, ah, to be sure. Well, perhaps I may; but I don't know. This is such an infernal gossiping place."

"It really is, your worship. An honest fellow's character is never safe here."

"You don't call yourself an honest fellow, do you? Ha! ha!"

Will bit his lip; but the attention both of himself and the justice was soon taken up by the proceedings with regard to Emma, whom the constable, feeling that he was acting under the eyes of the justice himself, and, therefore, was bound to be extra vigilant, had laid hold of by the arm. Fortunately, at that moment, Doctor Lukin, who was a sworn foe to the reverend gentleman, came up.

"What's the matter?" he said.

"I do not know," replied Emma. "I have done nothing—said nothing."

"Hands off, Master Constable," said the doctor. "Are you drunk?"

"No, Master Doctor, I isn't."

"Then what have you seized Emma Lyon for?"

"Constable," roared the justice, who saw that his high commands were being disputed by his old enemy the doctor, who upon all occasions, being an independent man, and living upon his little three acres of property, which was tithe-free, despised him—"constable, bring that girl here!"

"Don't be alarmed," said the doctor. "I will stay by you, and Parson Titherleigh would as soon see the devil as me. Ask him if you are in custody, and what for. He is bound to answer to the questions; but stick to the first before you say a word about the second."

"I will," said Emma. "But what can it mean?"

"Oh, nothing but some drunken caprice of his worship, that's all; but I should like to make him smart for it."

They had now reached the justice, who, puffing out his cheeks and goggling his eyes, cried—

"So, your name is Lyon? Ah—eh?"

"Yes. Am I in custody?" said Emma.

"Come—come, no insolence. Constable, look to her."

"Am I in custody?"

"What do you mean girl, by asking ridiculous questions? Hold your tongue, I say; hold your tongue. A pretty thing, indeed, if one is to be questioned by beggar's brats like you in the village."

"Ask him again," said the doctor.

"Am I in custody?" said Emma.

"Oh, so your friend and adviser, Doctor Lukin, puts you up to the question, does he? Then I shall not answer it. I say I shall not answer it."

"Then," said Doctor Lukin, "if this young girl is not in custody, this man, although a constable, has no legal right to detain her; and I, as her friend, will knock him down, as I am justified in doing in her defence. If you give her into his charge, it is quite another thing. That will be an act you will have to answer for."

"I have half a mind to give you in charge."

"I wish you would. You should not disgrace the bench many days longer, Mr. Titherleigh. Again I insist upon knowing if this young girl is given in charge or not?"

"His worship told me to take her," said the constable, who had a very fair notion that Doctor Lukin would be as good as his word, and knock him down in a few moments.

"That is sufficient evidence," said Lukin. "And now, what's the charge? The prisoner insists upon the charge being stated, as you are without a warrant."

The face of the reverend gentleman turned of a purplish hue with rage, and in a voice hoarse with passion, cried—

"Come on—come on. We will soon see what the charge is. Constable, bring her along. This way. We will soon see what the charge is."

CHAPTER V.

THE justice led the way to the cottage of the Lyons, closely followed by Will Flam, whose face was as pale as death itself; and Doctor Lukin walked by the side of Emma and the constable. As they went, he said to her—

"Have you any idea of the meaning of this affair?"

"Not the least," she replied. "I dread everything and know nothing, sir."

"It must be some mistake; and yet I don't at all like the looks of that rascal, Will Flam. Look at him."

Emma did look at him, with a shudder. The expression of Will's face was particularly frightful. A revivified corpse could not have looked more horrible than he did upon that occasion. At moments he seemed absolutely to gasp for breath; and then suddenly taking from his pocket a case-bottle that might hold about half-a-pint of liquor, he put it to his lips and emptied it. After that stimulent, for it was raw brandy that he drank, he recovered somewhat of his usual looks and manner.

The whole party halted at the cottage door, and Emma cried out in a loud voice—"Father! Father! Where are you?"

"Hold your tongue," cried the justice. "Hold your tongue, will you. Here, somebody take care of my horse; I don't know but this may turn out a very serious business. This man, Lyon, never behaved himself very well to me. He was always wanting in respect, because I suppose he thought he had his master, Sir Gilbert, to protect him; but I'll let him and Sir Gilbert both know that I am the commissioner of the peace, and not to be trifled with. Make way—make way."

As he spoke, his worship bustled into the cottage, followed by the whole party, including the doctor, whom he would gladly have excluded, only that he really did not know how.

Doctor Lukin was really a very intractable

sort of personage, and a very particular eye-sore to the reverend justice.

Both Lyon and his wife rose at the entrance of these persons into their cottage, and with feelings of surprise looked at the justice, who, flinging himself into a chair, cried—

"Now, Mr. Constable, if you please, I will trouble you to search this cottage. Circumstances throw great suspicion upon this place; and a very distinct and clearly-spoken witness deposes——"

"A-hem! A-hem!" coughed Will Flam; and then approaching the justice, he said something in a low voice, to which the reverend gentleman replied—

"Well—well. Perhaps so. Let it be then."

"Of course, your worship knows best," added Will; "I only humbly venture to suggest."

"Oh! ah! Yes; to be sure—to be sure —of course. Go on with the search, constable—go on with the search."

"The search for what, sir?" cried Lyon, stepping forward with the flush of anger and insulted innocence upon his brow; "the search for what, sir? If such a villain as Will Flam has said anything to the prejudice of me or my family, I defy him to his teeth —I defy him before you, sir. I only wish Sir Gilbert was at home."

"Perhaps he will be wanted," muttered Will.

"Come, come," said the justice, "we don't want any of that sort of talk here. Be quiet all of you, be quiet. I am in the commission of the peace, and Sir Gilbert is not. But if he should be wanted, I dare say we shall find some means of getting at him, though he is in London."

"He will be wanted," said Will.

"He shall be wanted," said Lyon. "And now, Mr. Titherleigh, I know you have a grudge against me on more accounts than one; but an innocent man need fear nothing."

"Indeed!" said Will Flam; and then, feeling that he had said something rather indiscreet, he added—"Indeed, I hope you are an innocent man, Lyon; for although you are no friend of mine, yet I am not the sort of fellow to bear malice, and I don't wish you any harm of any kind."

"Come, come," said the justice, "it's of no use mincing the matter—I have had information upon oath that a robbery was committed at Sir Gilbert's before the fire, and it's my duty to act upon such information. Come, constable, bustle—bustle, and search the place well. If these people are innocent, they can, of course, have nothing to fear."

"Good Heaven!" cried Lyon, as he shook with emotion, "do I live to see the day when I am suspected of robbing the kindest and best of masters? Oh, wife, wife! Sir Gilbert himself, if he were here, would not, I am sure, listen to this for a moment."

Mrs. Lyon sat rocking herself to and fro upon an old arm-chair that was by the cottage fireside, and weeping bitterly. She suspected that there was more in the whole affair than met the eye. The presence of Will Flam had in it something by far too foreboding to be easily got over.

The constable went on with his search, but found nothing; and then Will Flam rose to help him. To be sure, it was at the suggestion of the reverend justice that he did so, or perhaps he would really not have ventured to show himself so officious.

"It may be a mistake after all," he muttered. "I'm sure I should be quite delighted to find neighbour Lyon was innocent, though he has at times given me some hard words; but hard words break no bones, and I'm one of the best-natured estchaps—that is if I ain't put out of temper."

Will Flam then affected to be quite busy in looking at the interior of the cottage; but after a few moments, he gradually sidled to the door, inducing the constable to accompany him; and when they were both outside, he said—

"Don't you think the thatch is a likely place to hide anything in?"

"I don't know."

"Well, I suppose you have no objection to look?"

"Oh, none in the least. Of course, I shall look everywhere, you may depend upon that."

"Then I need not be with you."

Will Flam then went into the cottage again, for he would much rather that the discovery that was to be made should be made by the constable alone, than by himself. He had now put the constable upon the right scent in the matter, and he felt certain that, in the course of a very few minutes, the discovery he wished for, and looked forward to, must ensue;—the discovery of the clock, wrapped in the rich table-cover, which he, Will Flam, had taken from the room in which the fire broke out at the Grange, and hidden in the thatch of the cottage.

When he reached the interior of the humble abode again, he found that something like an altercation was going on between the justice and Mr. Lukin. The latter was speaking.

"This seems a most outrageous affair," he said. "It does not require any great penetration for any one to discover by whom you have received this information. I do not mean to attribute to you anything but harshness. Only, I do say, that I would not convict a cat of stealing cream upon the evidence of such a man as Will Flam."

"I am in the commission of the peace, sir," said Titherleigh, "and I shall do my duty. It's nothing to me whether Sir Gilbert will be pleased or angry, or wish or not wish to carry out this case. I will do my duty; and, if needs be, I will force Sir Gilbert to prosecute."

"Mother!" whispered Emma, "mother, do not cry; all will be well. We know that we have none of us done anything wrong, so what have we to fear?"

"He who will bear false witness against his neighbour," said Mrs. Lyon, solemnly; "that, my child, is what we have to fear; and there is the man."

She pointed to Will Flam, who, indignant and wild at the accusation in proportion to its truth, was nearly bursting with passion. In a loud and screaming voice, he said—

"Who dare say it was me? Who dare accuse me? I—I am—"

The constable rushed into the cottage, and laid upon the table before the justice the clock, wrapped up in the table-cover, saying, as he did so, in faltering accents—for he was not altogether a bad man that constable, and he pitied the Lyons—

"Found under the thatch, your worship."

"Ah!" said the justice; "there's a pretty piece of business. If this is not enough to hang anybody, I don't know what is. This is a pretty kettle of fish, indeed. Why, this clock was never made for you, John Lyon; and this brocade table-cover would look rather out of place on your table, I think."

"Good God!" cried Lyon, "these things are the property of Sir Gilbert—"

"He confesses," said Will Flam.

"Hold!" said the docter. "How much does he confess? Simply, that these two articles are the property of Sir Gilbert. Mark that, constable, if you please."

The justice shook his head, as he said—

"John Lyon, this is a sad affair, a very sad affair. I do not ask you to say anything to criminate yourself, but I leave it to you to explain, in any way you may think proper, how those two articles, which you say belong to Sir Gilbert, came under the thatch of your cottage."

John Lyon was very pale, and his lips quivered as he looked around him, and felt the full danger of his situation. Will Flam had retired to a dark corner of the cottage; but Lyon raised his hand slowly, and pointed to him.

"Yes," he said. "Yes; I can account for how the things came under my thatch."

"How?" said the justice.

"He placed them there! He, Will Flam, placed them there! Drag him forward! He placed them there! He knows it! He is afraid to look me in the face! He knows that at this moment the eye of God is upon him! He is guilty! He placed them there, and it is he who has destroyed the garden; and if Sir Gilbert's house has been burnt down by an incendiary, Will Flam is the man!"

"Lies! Lies all!" cried Will, as he rushed from his hiding-place into the middle of the room. "Lies all! He wants to hang me! They all want to hang me!"

The distorted features of the man—his blood-shot eyes, and the fearful attitude he assumed, with his arms elevated above his head, struck terror into the hearts of all there present. Even the justice started from his seat, and said—

"Constable—constable, look to that man! What is the meaning of all this?"

"Nothing—nothing," said Will, suddenly letting his arms drop to his sides. "Nothing. I—I—that is, it is a sad thing for a poor, honest fellow to be accused of enough to take away his life. That's all—that's all!"

"Well, I have nothing to do with all this," said the justice. "Constable, you will take John Lyon into custody. I don't know but what I ought to take the whole family; but that can be thought of afterwards. At all events, John Lyon is in custody; and perhaps his great friend, Doctor Lukin, will find out how to clear him of a charge that to me looks about as transparent a thing as can possibly be."

"If you mean by transparent," said Doctor Lukin, "that any one may see through it, I fully agree with you. I advise John Lyon to say nothing at all just now upon the matter, and I promise him that I will take care Sir Gilbert shall know all about it in good time, and that he shall not fall for want of means to hold him up against this most foul and false charge against him."

Emma crept to the side of Doctor Lukin, and taking hold of one of his hands, kissed it. The action spoke volumes. All the eloquence in the world could not have expressed the amount of grateful feeling that that one simple but significant action gave utterance to.

"Fear nothing, Emma," said the doctor, turning to her. "Fear nothing. Remain at home, and keep up your own and your mother's spirits as well as you can. This is only a cloud, and it will soon pass away from before you."

Will Flam had left the cottage, and was pacing to and fro in the front of it like a sentinel. When the party came to the door, and he saw Lyon in custody of the officer, he started on quickly in the direction he knew they would take; so he did not see the frantic embrace which Mrs. Lyon gave her husband on the threshold of their humble but virtuous home, and he did not see how Emma walked up to her father, and spoke freely to him, saying—

"Father, fear nothing—you did not do it. You know, and they all know, you did not do it; and you and we have a friend in Doctor Lukin; so all will be well. I will not cry because a bad man has made a false accusation against you, father."

This was the first indication of that bold daring spirit which, in after years, enabled Emma to rise superior to circumstances, and in many cases, to mould them to her will.

The old man embraced his child; and then, with a look of as much serenity as he could command, he allowed himself to be gently led from his cottage in custody.

CHAPTER VI.

THE commotion in the village at the arrest of Lyon was most intense. Every one not engaged in labour at a distance was in the little street—that might be called both the

High Street and the low one, inasmuch as it was the only one in the little village of Preston.

There was one universal feeling of sympathy with the prisoner; and if the people had only known accurately, which they did not, that the accuser of such a man as Lyon was such a man as Will Flam, some exhibition of popular feeling might have taken place, that would not have been very agreeable to Will. As it was, however, Lyon was taken off to the justice's house before the good folks of the village knew much of the affair; nor did Doctor Lukin think proper to be very communicative upon the subject. He was himself satisfied of the innocence of Lyon, and he hoped that by regular and fair means that innocence would soon be made apparent.

The justice was resolved to go through the form of hearing as much evidence against the prisoner as would suffice to remand him until the arrival of Sir Gilbert, who must, in a formal manner, swear to the property found beneath the thatch being his, before the prisoner could be committed.

The evidence adduced was just this:—

Will Flam said that he was tired, and he thought of having a sleep under the calm side of the hay-stack at the end of the little lawn of the Grange, facing the room where the fire seemed to commence first. He had not been there long, he said, and had by no means composed himself to sleep, when he saw some one coming across the lawn, carrying a small bundle. He hid himself round the corner of the haystack, and he saw—but to this he was so remarkably conscientious as to decline swearing point-blank—he saw John Lyon pass him.

What John Lyon carried he, Will Flam, had not the least idea of, only he saw that it was something bright, and John Lyon—if it were John Lyon—carried it as though it were heavy.

Then, while the person—whether Lyon or not—was gone, he stated that he saw Emma come to one of the windows of the room, and look out. He heard her call "Father!—Father!" twice in a low tone, but John Lyon had not come back. He did so, however, in a few seconds, and then Emma called to him again, saying—

"Is there hay enough?"

What this meant, of course, he, Will Flam, could not have the least idea; and after waiting some time to see if anything would come of it, he fairly fell asleep, and was not awakened again until he heard a cry of fire.

"And what did you do then?" said the justice.

"Why, your worship, Sir Gilbert is no friend of mine, and I did not like to see the old Grange burnt to the ground, so I did my best to put the fire out; and if the people had helped me as they ought to have done, it would have been put out."

The constable, then, upon oath, formally deposed to finding the clock and the table-cover under the thatch in the cottage of Lyon, **and to his, the prisoner's,** own admission, that **the two** articles were the property of Sir Gilbert. **The old bailiff** and his wife had both sworn to the clock and the table-cover having been **in the** long-room, as it was called, of the Grange.

"Well, prisoner," said the justice, "what have you to say to all this?"

"Nothing, but that it is all false, with the exception of the testimony of the constable, and Sir Gilbert's bailiff and his wife. I was never out of my bed until I heard the cry of 'fire' from my wife, and the manner in which my child nearly fell a victim to the flames, ought to be enough to convince any one of my entire innocence."

"Well, the facts are strongly against you."

"I beg your pardon," said Doctor Lukin. "The evidence may be, but the facts are not. A statement may be against a man, but that statement may or may not embrace facts."

"If you interrupt the court," said the justice, again, "I will order you to be turned out. You would not have been admitted into this, my house, only that this room in it is a public court of justice."

"And you may depend," said Doctor Lukin, "that I should not have been beneath this roof under any other condition."

"I shall remand the prisoner until this day week," said the justice. "Clerk, make out his remand; and gaoler, you see that he is well taken care of in the cage."

"Yes, your worship."

The reverend justice then hastily broke up the court, and Doctor Lukin feeling that at that time nothing more could be done for the prisoner, took his departure home, for the purpose of writing immediately to Sir Gilbert an account of the whole affair. He knew perfectly well that the baronet would immediately come to the village, and that Lyon would find a friend instead of a persecutor in him.

While all this was going on, the utmost distress prevailed in the cottage; and we may truly say, that throughout the whole village there was but one feeling, and that was of sympathy with Lyon, with the single exception of plain Mrs. Lee; and she intimated her opinion that it was all in some indirect way owing to the supposed pretty face of Emma.

Poor Edwin was in a perfect agony when he heard of the affair; and after making an ineffectual effort to rise, and go to comfort Emma and her mother, he lay in a fever of apprehension waiting for any one who would be kind enough to bring him any news upon the subject. This his mother was not backward in doing: for a more inveterate news-monger than plain Mrs. Lee was certainly not to be found for many miles round Preston.

Emma took the advice of Doctor Lukin, and kept within doors; but about an hour after her father had been taken away, a prisoner, there came a gentle rap at the cottage-door.

Emma opened it herself, and saw upon the step a gipsy-woman with two brown, ragged, miserable-looking children—one of the children was crying bitterly.

The woman pointed to the children, saying—

"Our tribe is poor. We are unlucky, and the little ones cry in the wilderness for food. Sickness is among our men, and they"—she still only alluded to the children, and said nothing of her own wants—"and they are starving."

Emma stepped across the threshold, and took one of the children in her right-hand, and the other in her left.

"Come in," she said. "What we have you shall share."

The gipsy-woman sat down upon the door step, and huddling round her her many rags, she sobbed as though her heart would break.

"Be of good cheer," said Emma. "We are poor, but we are not so poor but that we can spare something to destitution. Come in?"

"Are you an angel?" gasped the woman, as she removed her tattered mantle from before her face—"are you an angel, that you can speak words of comfort to such as we are? We have been spurned from door to door, and more than once the dogs have been called to hunt us from the face of the land; but you look upon us with the dove-like eyes of pity!"

"I will do what I can."

"And how shall I thank you?"

"Nay, I ask for no thanks. Take freely what poor fare I can set before you. Come in—come in."

The gipsy-woman would not cross the threshold, but she sat sobbing by it, and looked in at her children, who were soon in the full enjoyment of a substantial meal of bread and milk, to which they paid the most ravenous attention.

It was a deeply-affecting sight to see the starving mother, heedless of her own pangs and wants, looking with joy beaming from her countenance at her little ones, as they satisfied those cravings which she herself felt, but was better able to endure than they were.

But Emma would not allow the poor wanderer to depart in hunger; and as she would not cross the threshold for food, she took her an ample meal to the door. The gipsy-woman thanked her by a look; and then taking one of the young girl's hands in hers, she said—

"Thy mother weeps. Is there woe beneath this roof?"

"There is, indeed."

"Dare you tell me what it is, maiden?"

"Alas, it is no secret. My innocent father is dragged from us on a charge of theft from the Grange that was burnt down last night"

"The Grange? They do not say he lit the match that destroyed the old house?"

"They do. At least, there is one who does."

"His name, maiden?"

"Will Flam, they call him."

The gipsy-woman recoiled a few paces, and then burst into a wild laugh, which, at that moment, made Emma think that her reason was affected; but when the woman spoke, she corrected that opinion, for her language was too coherent to sustain it.

"Will Flam the accuser?" she said. "Will Flam accuse any one of such a crime? And who will take his testimony?"

"It is taken," said Emma, mournfully. "It is taken."

"Look at that child," added the gipsy-woman, pointing to the youngest of the two little tattered wretches she had with her. "It is lame—perhaps for life Will Flam gave the kick that wantonly did that deed."

"Kick a child? That is worse than accusing my father of crimes he never dreamt of, and which are most likely his own."

"His own?" cried the woman. "Most likely his own, do ye say? Ha! ha! We shall see that. I have taken a solemn oath, at the hour of midnight, to be revenged of that man, and I will keep my vow, maiden. Let me look well at you."

She fixed her gaze upon the countenance of Emma for a few seconds with an intenseness that was particularly painful to the young girl; and then she said—

"Yes, there is courage and rare perseverance. It will suffice. If, for your father's sake, I ask you to come to-night at the hour of midnight to the Monk's Hollow, you will not refuse?"

"At midnight?"

"Yes. Is your God asleep at midnight, that you hesitate to say that you will trust yourself abroad at such an hour?"

"No, no;—but the hour, combined with the place, which has an evil reputation, made me hesitate."

"Do you still hesitate?"

"Not if it will save my father."

"It shall do so. Some of our people are encamped now in the Monk's Hollow. Take this whistle; and when you come near enough to make yourself heard by blowing a low note upon it, place it to your lips and do so. It will insure your safety. I will then meet you, and you shall find that that milk and that bread which you have given to my children has been the price of your father's freedom and of my revenge. You will come?"

"I will."

"Tell no one. Tell no one. Swear that to me."

"I do."

The woman called to her children; and then huddling her rags around her, and taking the younger of the two upon her back, she walked hastily away from the cottage-door, without saying another word, leaving Emma quite lost in wonder at the singular words that had been spoken to her.

Before this strange colloquy had taken place between Emma and the gipsy-woman, Mrs. Lyon had retired into the back room of the cottage, for she was too much affected by what had occurred to her husband, to be able even to take part in relieving the distress of the gipsy-children, which, under the circumstances, she would have found abundant pleasure in doing, so that she heard nothing of the strange appointment that had been made between Emma and the wanderer.

And now Emma found herself bound by an oath not even to tell her mother of the appointment she had made; and without regretting the appointment for one moment, she began bitterly to regret that she had been so hasty in promising to keep it a secret from every one.

After a time, however, she got more reconciled to that state of things; and, to her imagination, the idea of being able, perhaps, by her own unaided courage, in visiting such a spot as the Monk's Hollow at such an hour, to save her father, became very delightful to her. She almost began to be glad that she had bound herself to tell no one, inasmuch as if reproached afterwards for her want of confidence, she could easily plead the oath she had taken.

CHAPTER VII.

THE VISIT TO THE GIPSIES.—A NIGHT OF HORROR FOR EMMA.

THE after-occurrences of that day presented no feature of particular consequence, so we may at once hurry on to the projected meeting of Emma with the gipsies.

The little whistle which had been left with her by the gipsy-woman, and which was merely shaped out of a piece of bone, she took great care of.

She was afraid that her mother, being alone, would, perhaps, require her (Emma) to share her bed; but Mrs. Lyon made no such proposition, so that Emma was relieved from that difficulty which might have been an unsurmountable one. Doubtless, her mother, with more of worldly prudence than Emma could possibly, at her age, possess, would have strongly opposed, had she but had any idea of it, the appointment in the Monk's Hollow; but then, how frequently it happens that all worldly prudence is at fault, and that from some act of rash dependance springs important results, which in no other way could have been brought about.

This strange appointment of Emma's with an unknown, nameless wanderer, was one of those pieces of lucky heedlessness.

She and her mother had talked over the position of her father in every shape and way; and it was, at times, a sore temptation to Emma, when she saw how full of woe and dread her mother was, to tell her that she might be more hopeful. She, however, for sheer dread of any obstacle being thrown in the way of her midnight adventure, kept it to herself; and no one ever waited more impatiently for daylight than did Emma for its departure.

At length, the village of Preston once more sunk into repose. The smouldering ruins of the old Grange still sent forth, at times, faint blue wreaths of smoke; and all was still around the now dreary remains of what had, but a short time before, been a home, full of the luxuries and amenities of civilized existence.

Mrs. Lyon retired to rest, if rest she could find with such a weight upon her mind, at an earlier hour than usual.

"Close the casement, Emma." she said, "and go to rest."

"Yes, mother, I will soon."

She kissed her mother, and bade her good-night. Then she did close the casement, and she affected to close the door, too, for the night, but she only latched it; and then, sitting upon a little stool by the rapidly-expiring fire of wood and turf, she waited for the hour of midnight.

The old clock, an heirloom in the family, ticked lazily in its accustomed corner; and a huge tabby-cat, a great favourite with Emma and the whole village, excepting the boys, and boys are the enemies of anything and everybody, dozed opposite to her upon an old rush-bottomed chair.

Cats always like to be the last up in a house, and in this case the old tabby seemed resolved to wait out Emma.

The old clock struck eleven. There was yet a whole hour to wait until the appointed time of meeting with the gipsy-woman; but the place called Monk's Hollow was a good half-mile from the village; so Emma had not to wait in the cottage much longer. She resolved to start when the blackened hands of the old clock indicated the half-hour past eleven.

But what a long half-hour that seemed from eleven to the half-past. The clock seemed to pause for an enormous length of time between each tick; and more than once Emma could hardly persuade herself but that upon that night of all others, the old timepiece was going to stop altogether.

But if time winged its way slowly, it winged it surely, and the long-looked-for half-hour came at last.

Emma rose gently, and put on her little hat and cloak. She gave a kind word to the old cat, which put up its back with dismay at the idea of its mistress venturing abroad at so late an hour; and then Emma, opening the door gently, stepped from the cottage.

For the last twenty minutes that she had sat watching the slow and steady progress of the hand upon the dial, she had heard the wind sighing without, and at times sweeping past the cottage with a sudden rush, as though it was gathering strength to be more boisterous; and now, when she was fairly in the open air, she shuddered at the keen blast that in a moment seemed to wrap her up in its cold embrace.

It was one of those cold autumnal nights that speaks to us eloquently of the coming winter.

The young girl drew her cloak more closely.

around her, and more securely tied her little straw-hat upon her head. Then, despite the cold wind, which had a touch of the east in it, she turned in the direction of the Monk's Hollow.

Now, this Monk's Hollow, as it was called, where she had to go, was a place which, in the soft and gentle summer-time, was full of beauties. It might be called one of the lions of the place as regarded its natural advantages. It took its name, doubtless, from some old monastic legend.

It was a remarkable place, whether you chose to view it with relation to any old associations, or to look at it merely as some freak of nature.

Almost all around the hollow rose an amphitheatre of small hills crowned with verdure; but it was in the hollow itself that vegetation appeared to have played its greatest game, for there was to be found a specimen of any known tree that the surrounding country could supply; and the effect of the different coloured and different shaped leaves and trunks of the trees was very beautiful. Probably the hollow owed its varied fertility to the beauty of its position. Being rich in alluvial soil, no doubt the seeds of many distant plants, borne upon the wings of the wind, had reached that spot, and there germinated, producing the variety in its vegetation which made it so remarkable; and as the taste of the old monks, in hitting upon pleasant spots for their habitations, is not for one moment to be doubted, the hollow had been seized upon quickly enough by some of those ecclesiastical gormonds. Here was it that a ruin, magnificent in some of its proportions, yet was to be found in the hollow, amid the cool shadows of which, even in the hottest days of summer, you might find shelter and a cool deliciously-refreshing breeze.

The place had for many years been the favourite resort of gipsies, and although the hollow was private property, it was not enclosed; and there was a kind of tacit agreement between the proprietor of the spot and the gipsies, to the effect, that if they behaved themselves with all imaginable propriety, they would not be molested in their brief occasional occupation of the place.

Yet various stories found credence among the village gossips of strange sights and sounds coming from the Monk's Hollow. Old legendary traditions of deeds of violence done there were told by the firesides in the depth of winter, when the wind was moaning without, and all nature was sterile and dreary. Then, it was said, that spectres grim and terrible haunted the hollow, and flitted about the old trees, shrieking their information of their fate in life, and the whereabouts, in some unhallowed spot, their remains were to be found.

No wonder, then, that after nightfall, the gipsies for the most part had the Monk's Hollow to themselves, and were fully clear of ordinary intruders. A chance poacher might certainly visit the encampment, and for the use of the camp-kettle, share the produce of his night's labour with the rude denizens of the ragged tents; but of such a class only were the visitors of the wandering tribes.

A young girl, such as Emma Lyon, might well have shrunk from going alone to such a place at any time; but at the solemn hour of midnight, when crime stalks abroad uncloaked by the foreseeing eye of justice, and when superstition has peopled the air with strange fancies, it did indeed require no ordinary courage upon the part of Emma to go upon such an expedition.

But then, Emma was no ordinary personage; and we shall find that as years rolled on, she developed a moral courage that, to look upon her childish beauty at this period, no one for a moment could have supposed her to possess. There was, indeed, a something that pleased her adventurous spirit in the whole expedition; so that, if she had not been impelled by the strong motive of doing what she could for her father, she would, upon a very small amount of inducement, have been inclined to visit the Monk's Hollow.

We have already had occasion to state that the cottage, inhabited by the Lyon's family, was upon the outskirts of the village, so that Emma had not, in fact, to pass any house before she got fairly into the road. All she feared was, that her mother might awaken and call to her before she got out of hearing; for in such a case she would not have liked not to go back, although it would sadly have annoyed her to have had to do so.

Such, however—fortunately, as she considered—was not the case; and as she went at a quick pace, she was very soon sufficiently far away from the village to be out of the sphere of any influence from that quarter.

It was by no means a road that led to the place for which Emma was bound. That is to say, it was not a made road, nor, in point of fact, an established footpath. She had to cross a straggling place called the Warren, and then, upon going through a little wood, she had to make her way to the summit of one of the little hills that surrounded the sweet romantic spot, and from which she could easily descend to it. In fact, the whole route was full of the wild and the beautiful.

Emma was, however, in no mood to expend either time or attention upon the beauties of nature. She was only intent upon reaching the Monk's Hollow, and upon hearing the mysterious communication which, from her deep gratitude, the gipsy-woman had promised her; and so she fought her way against the wind.

Yes, she had to fight her way against the wind—for the night was raw and blusterous. More than once she had to pause to gather fresh breath for the struggle, and more than once she felt a dash of rain in her face, and feared that the night was about to be one of those stormy ones so incidental to the fall of the year; but, despite all her forebodings — despite all her anticipations of storm—she struggled on.

"It is for' my father," she said; "it is for my father I am doing this—it is to save him ; and oh, if I can but succeed in so doing, what joy it will be to me to say—' it was I, father, who rescued you !'—and then —and then some day, perhaps, who knows but I may live to see *him* again !"

Who the "him" that she wished to see was tolerably apparent, by her soft pronunciation of the name of Horatio Nelson ;— that name which, from the moment of its pronunciation by the young midshipman, found a home in her breast, which in this world it was never to have.

"Yes," she added, "it will be great joy to me to see him once again. How poorly I thanked him for what he did for me—how defficient I was in gratitude to him —and what hundreds of kind and grateful things I could say to him now, if I could but see him ; but he is far away now, and soon he will be upon the sea, and exposed to all the dangers of an occupation that, by night or by day—sleeping or waking—is full of peril. Oh, if it could but be permitted to me some day to stand between him and some great danger, so that I might say to him, 'I saved you, Horatio Nelson !' what joy that would be !"

By this time she had reached the little wood, which she had to traverse before coming to the top of the hill, at the foot of which was the hollow ; and in this wood she found that the wind was, if possible, more intense and cold than in the open Warren.

By some accident, blowing from the quarter that it did, the gale went completely through and through this wood, howling among the half-denuded branches of the trees, and making such rude riot, that Emma more than once paused, half-stunned and bewildered by the uproar of the little tempest.

But still she struggled on, and occasionally she felt for the little bone-whistle that the gipsy-woman had given her, and which she had had the precaution, for fear of losing it, to suspend from her neck by a piece of ribbon. She had it safely ; and in the course of two minutes more, she emerged from the little wood and stood upon the top of a grassy mount, looking down upon the hollow, in which there was not the least vestage of any living thing. She had hoped and expected to see some light that would have let her know where the gipsies' tents were, but all was the most profound darkness in the hollow.

CHAPTER VIII.

THE WILD PROPHECY.—EMMA'S TERROR AND DANGER AMONG THE GIPSIES.

FROM where she was, about half-a-dozen steps would have led her clear of the trees, and then her figure, descending the hill-side,

might have been seen by such watchful eyes as the gipsies. She thought the best plan she could adopt was to advance a short distance, and then sound the whistle so that simultanously with observing some one approaching their encampment, they should know who it was that at such an hour sought that strange place.

With this determination, she stepped boldly on ; and when she was quite clear of the trees, and felt that, in all likelihood, she could be seen, she blew two faint notes upon the whistle.

In an instant they were responed to, and a man sprang up from the ground, upon which he had been lying, so close to her, that to all appearance it seemed as though he had actually risen out of the ground.

" Who comes," he cried.

Emma found it dfficult to reply to this question. She had fully expected to meet the woman, and not to be roughly questioned by a man ; so she naturally enough shrank back a pace or two.

" Speak," he cried again ; " I can't see you for the trees behind you. Is it you, Will Flam ?"

" No," cried Emma.

" Ah, a female voice ! Come on, and let us see who you are, my girl, for a young one you are, by your tones. Have you ventured here at such an hour as this, to have your fortune told ? and yet no, you are not of that sort, or you would not have one of our whistles, if it were you that blew it just now ?"

" It was," said Emma.

Suddenly, up the declivity from the hollow, there came some one with great rapidity ; and in a moment Emma heard the voice of the woman, crying—

" Ahab, Ahab, that is my friend. That is a visitor of mine, Ahab. Let her pass, I tell you."

" A visitor of yours, at midnight ?" said Ahab. " Why Zulta, what is the meaning of all this ? Your man must be in a much gentler mood than usual, if he make any one not belonging to the people welcome beneath his tent."

" It matters not," said the woman, who was named Zulta by the gipsy scout. " It matters not. This is, as I tell you, a visiter of mine ; and I answer for it, she is a friend to us all —such a friend as I looked in vain for many hours in Preston and its neighbourhood this morning, and found not, until I found her. Come, maiden, come. May the blessing of Him, who is both yours and the gipsy's God, be upon you. Come, come."

The woman laid hold of Emma gently by the arm, and led her down the declivity to the hollow.

" Are many of your people here ?" said Emma.

" Fear nothing," was the reply ; " if there were thousands of them, you are as safe as if you slept in your mother's arms."

" I do not fear, or I should not have come at such a time alone here. I am only anxi·

ous to know how I may save my father, and then begone again."

"Yes. It shall be so. Come this way, this way."

Emma abandoned herself implicitly to her guide, and suffered herself to be led right down into the hollow; and the deeper she descended the darker it became. The faint light of the night, which—like a dim-remembrance of daylight, or rather of the last ray of twilight—yet lingered on the heights, did not reach to the deep shaddowy depths of that valley. It seemed almost like descending into the very bowels of the earth; and the delusion was further strengthened by the rippling sound of a little stream that ran through the lowest portion of the hollow.

"Are your people really here?" said Emma. "I see nothing."

"Yes; our tents are in darkness; but you will be among them in a moment. Now, see you nothing?"

Emma looked earnestly before her, and then she did dimly see the dark, dusky outlines of some of the gipsies' tents; and the woman, still leading her by the arm, suddenly stretched out her hand towards a tree, and lifting aside a piece of faded drapery, she said, in a low voice—

"Enter."

Emma did so, and found herself in a place that was dimly lighted only by a piece of cotton being immersed in some fat and ignited at one end, that was allowed to project over the edge of the rough earthern-vessel that contained it. It seemed as if advantage had been taken of the position of some tree to hang over its pendent branches some blackened, well-worn sail-cloth, and so to make a tent of much larger dimension than the ordinary ones appertaining to the wandering race.

By the dim light, Emma could see the woman's face now. It had upon it a look of deep anxiety and restlessness. This appearance upon the face of the woman, could not fail to give some uneasiness to Emma, for it looked as though the path to the atttainment of her wishes was not quite so easy as it might have been; and she said—

"Tell me if anything has happened to prevent you from doing what you promised. Do not keep me in suspense."

"Nothing has happened."

"But you look sad and anxious."

"I am sad and anxious, because what I promised has yet to be done; and I warn you that it has to be come at through danger. I hope it will only be through danger to me, and not to you; but you must remain here, and keep a firm heart. I implore you, let you hear what you may, that you will not stir from this spot."

"I will not."

"'Tis well. You will, from this place, soon comprehend in what the trouble and the danger consists; but I will overcome both. I have sworn to do so, and I will yet overcome both; and, be well assured, that whatever threats you may hear of personal injury—even unto your death—I say, be well assured that you are, notwithstanding, perfectly safe from all harm. I will stand between you and the avenger; I will stand between you and the wild bursts and impulses of passion. Sit you down upon this rude seat; it will rest you.

It was a small upturned tub that the gipsy-woman proffered to Emma for a seat, but she threw over it a gaudy scarlet robe before she would permit her to sit upon it; and the young girl was grateful for the opportunity of so resting; for, what with the walk to the hollow, and the excitement she was thrown into by the sudden discovery that the means by which her father was to be rescued from the false accusation that had been brought against him were difficult and dangerous, she was really scarcely able to stand.

"And if you should not succeed!" said Emma. "If you should not succeed!— What will happen then?"

"I will succeed! By the force of my own indomitable will, I shall succeed.—Rest you content."

The woman retired to the farther end of the strange apartment, if apartment it could be called, in which Emma sat; and raising a small portion of the canvas, she, in a moment, disappeared. For a few moments, the stillness in the place was so intense that it was positively painful, and Emma would have given anything to hear some human sound. The repose of the gipsy's tent, however, did not last long, for suddenly a harsh voice from the compartment of the tent into which the woman had gone, burst upon the ears of Emma.

"What is it now?" cried the voice. "Is one's sleep to be slaughtered by you at all times, and at all hours? What are you mumbling and prating about, woman?"

"Seth, I must and will speak to you," said the woman, in a soft yet determined voice. "I must and will speak to you. It is my duty so to do; and you shall hear me."

"Shall and must!" said the man. "What do you mean by all that? Are you mad, that you use such words to me, woman, as shall and must? Do you know your own danger?"

"No, Seth; but I know my own safety. You are a ruffian, folks say; but you have not yet dared to raise your hand against me, Seth, yet, and you dare not; therefore, there is no danger to know. You did a good and a noble deed, Seth, when you refused to join Will Flam in setting fire to the Grange, and then in putting the guilt upon the shoulders of an innocent man."

"Bah! Have you roused me up, Zulta, to say that?"

"Not wholly, Seth. You must go further than refuse to do that which is wrong; you must go a step further than that, Seth."

"What the devil do you mean?"

"I mean that you must, now that Will has done the deed without you, now that he has really burnt down the Grange, and accused an innocent man of robbery, and of the fire-raising—you must, Seth, save that innocent man."

"Ha!—ha!" laughed the gipsy, loudly and scornfully. "Ha!—ha! So you would have me turn accuser, and saviour of innocent men? What is it to me, Zulta? Let them all hang together, innocent or guilty; what are they to you or to me? Are they of our people, that we need care the turn of a stone if they are condemned of one another or not? What matters it to us if fire rooted them out of the land? The gipsy don't know them—at least, not much; and that much only teaches him to hate."

"Not all, Seth."

"Yes, all—all. Disturb me no more, wife, by such ravings. Let me sleep. Let them scorch each other from the land, if they will. Let them hang each other. It is all one to me. I am weary."

"And yet, Seth, it must be done."

"Must?"

"Yes. When Will Flam first projected this burning down of the Grange, and this accusation of an innocent man, he could not find you; and one day he sat down here and wrote to you the proposal. You have that letter still."

"Well?"

"I want it."

"You want it?—You want it? Why don't you say you want the heart out of my bosom? Why don't you say you want the brains from my skull? No; I may refuse a bad job that I don't like, but I am not an informer, Zulta. Will Flam is a bad man. He is worse than a thief—worse than a murderer, if you will. I don't want to see him again;—I don't want to breathe the same air with him. He will have my company no more in his night-prowlings. Call him what you may—and keep him, how you may, at arms-length in time to come—but for the past I cannot—I will not—betray him if he were ten times the villain that he is. No more—no more—I say I won't do it. Let me sleep. A plague upon you!"

"Seth, Seth, listen to me. You have had this day but one piece of bread—I this day have had but such another piece of bread. Our children—our little ones—have gone to rest happy, and not with hunger gnawing at their souls. They did not shriek to us to-night for food."

"Well, you say a young girl, as beautiful as an angel, gave it to them: God bless her!"

"Amen! Seth, amen! Well, well—we won't speak of that just now, Seth. Give me Will Flam's letter."

"Ten thousand furies, woman! do you want to drive me mad, that you continually harp upon that letter? Confound you, and the letter too! I will keep it, for it gives me a hold on Will, in case he should turn out treacherous; but I will not set him the example."

"I must have it, Seth, for some one is waiting for it in the outer place, and that some one has heard every word that you and I have said now. She comes on behalf of the falsely-accused man. She can already swear to your own admission, Seth, that you have such a letter; so give it to me. Its further possession is of no use. It is no longer a secret, Seth."

Emma heard the man spring from the ground, upon which he appeared to have been lying. She heard the most frightful oaths come from his lips; and then he shouted—

"A knife! a knife! Abel, where are you? Abel, boy, where are you? My knife! my knife!"

"Here," said a voice close to where Emma was sitting; and from amid the dark folds of the old sail-cloth there sprung up a youth of some seventeen or eighteen years of age. His long disordered coal-black hair, and his sparkling eyes, sufficiently denoted his origin.

"Here, father. Here!" he cried.

"Who is in the place, Abel?"

The ferocious-looking lad sprang to the side of Emma, and seized her roughly by the arm. He stood aside to let the beams of the lamp fall upon her face; and then he cried—"It is a girl, father. It is a young girl!"

"Take your knife, Abel, and cut her throat if she attempts to get away before I come to you."

Emma saw the gleam of a knife which the lad took from some portion of his clothing; and then crouching down close to the entrance to the tent, with his wild eyes fixed upon her, he seemed only to be waiting, like some beast of the forest, to take a spring upon her and destroy her.

CHAPTER IX.

THE ESCAPE OF WILL.—EMMA'S FIRST SITUATION IN LIFE.

THE situation of Emma was, indeed, a most alarming one. She began to be fearful that the gipsy-woman had far over-rated her influence over her violent husband, and that the expedition would not only utterly fail in bringing the expected succour for her father, but possibly enough end in her own destruction. At that moment she bitterly repented not having gone to Doctor Lukin for advice upon the occasion.

Leave the place she could not, for the youth at the door, if he might be so called, no doubt would have been unscrupulous enough to have opposed her passage out with the knife that, by the faint light of the lamp, she saw glittering in his hand. His eyes and the knife were all she could see of him in the intense darkness of the tent; for the darkness out of the sphere of the immediate rays of the little lamp was, indeed, intense.

She fancied she heard a struggle in the inner portion of the canvas-house. The voice of the man who was named Seth rose in loud and boisterous accents.

"I tell you, Zulta, if she had twenty lives they are all lost. What devil brought her here? What fiend induced you to bring spies to my home? But die she shall! My knife! My knife! Where is my knife?"

"No, Seth, you shall kill me first. Injure but a hair of her head knowingly, and I mysel will denounce you for the crime! I, the wi e of your bosom, Seth, will cast you off! I, the mother of your children!"

"You are mad!"

"No, Seth, 'tis you who are mad! 'Tis you who, with a mad idea of right to such a fiend as Will Flam, would do a deed that you would repent of while you lingered on the earth!"

"My knife! My knife! Ha! 'tis here!"

The woman uttered a shriek of dismay; and clinging to her husband, they both rolled into the outer portion of the tent together.

"Help! help!" cried Emma.

The youth, who had played the part of a sentinel at the door, sprang upon her, and tried to stop her mouth.

"Seth!" shrieked the woman. "Seth, she it was who fed your children to-day! She it was who sent you the only piece of bread which has given you strength to fight against her life! She it is who was and is the angel that said to the little ones—'Be comforted!' Look at her!"

Breaking away from her husband, the woman snatched up the lamp; and kneeling by the feet of Emma, she held it up, so that the rays fell upon that fair face, now pale with terror.

"Look upon her, Seth; she is the angel of mercy. Will you be a devil, and kill her who fed our little ones?"

The man dropped the knife from his hand, and stood trembling before Emma and his wife.

"It is not true—it is not true," he gasped.

"No, no. How shall I know that it is true? Ah, I know—I know how."

He darted back into the inner portion of the tent, and returned in a moment with the half-awake and terrified youngest child, that one who had been hurt by Will Flam, and was lame in consequence of the injury. The child's looks expressed affright, and the father, pointing to Emma, cried—

"Who's that?"

In an instant the features of the little gipsy relaxed into a laugh.

"Ah," it said. "That is the dear girl with the milk and the soft bread. More, more. Oh, give me more!"

The child sprung from the father's arms and rushed to Emma in a moment. With a deep groan, Seth let his arms fall to his sides, and stood like a man soul-stricken with the deep consciousness of guilt. His wife burst into a flood of tears; and while she sobbed hysterically, she clung to the knees of Emma. The lad with the dark flashing eyes and the knife, shrunk back trembling and terrified. Passion, in its stormy aspects and violence, were no novelties to him; but tears and the subdued effect of the finer feelings of humanity, he for the first time saw something of,

Seth slowly retired again to the sleeping place of the children; and then, before the wife could recover from the hysterical sobs that came from her overchanged bosom, he was back again, and this time he brought with him the elder of the two children, who had partaken of the humble in reality, but to them luxurious, cheer of the cottage.

The father pointed to Emma.

"Who is that?" he said.

"Ah," cried the child, "it is the good angel that mother told us we must always love. It is, indeed, the good angel that took us in and fed us, and fed mother, and said kind things to us all."

"It is over," said the gipsy.

He clasped his hands upon his breast; and after a brief struggle with his feelings, he shed tears. He crept to the feet of Emma, and in broken accents, he spoke to her.

"The milk and the bread," he said, "were but small things, but you gave them to my little ones when they were famishing. I bless you for it. You are our mistress. What will you have from me?"

"The letter," said Emma, "that Will Flam wrote to you."

The gipsy took it from his breast, and handed it at once to her. "It is there," he said. "It is your's."

"From my heart I thank you," she said. "I do not know how to tell you how much I thank you. By this letter I shall be able to release my father from a prison. Yes, more than that I shall be able to do, for I shall be able to prove that he should never have crossed the threshold of one; and all this I owe to you."

'Tis nothing. What do we not owe to you? Wife, can we do no more—can we say no more to the angel?"

The gipsy-woman looked up with streaming eyes. "We may some day," she said. "Who shall say? His humblest instruments are fashioned for high uses. Who shall say?"

"I will leave you now," said Emma. She kissed both the children, and rose from the seat with which she had been accommodated.

The lad, who had kept for a brief space such a watch upon her, crept forward and laid the knife upon the ground at her feet. She did not know exactly what he meant, but she held out her hand to him, saying—

"I am friends, I hope, with all here?"

"I will place it here," he said, touching his breast lightly with his finger; "I will place it here, if the fair one tells me."

"No—no!"

"It will be buried there."

He immediately set about digging a hole in the floor, in which to bury that knife, which doubtless, if not so got rid of, would have called forth to those imaginative people, disagreeable recollections whenever they should chance to look at it.

"I will see you to your home, maiden," said the woman, who had now recovered her usual composure, although her face bore yet traces of the storm of feeling that had passed over it so very recently,

"Only to the brow of the hill," said Emma. "I can find my way perfectly well after that."

Some sort of commotion was at this moment discernable at the entrance to the tent, and some words were spoken in a strange language. Both the gipsy and his wife started as if amazed; and she, in a voice that sufficiently exposed her astonishment, cried—

"It is Retila. Surely her last hour has come."

There was the flash of several lights; and the canvas door-way being opened, several dark figures appeared, heaving about a something that looked more like a walking corpse, than anything human. Emma was transfixed with astonishment as she beheld this object—woman she could hardly call it, although woman it was.

From a mass of apparel, that in many places had upon it strange cabalistic characters, there certainly did peer forth the face and hands of something human; but it would be impossible for any language to convey the impression of how very, very old that face was. It was miserably old—unutterably old. It seemed to be a dead face with two living eyes, and belonging to a yet living heart.

The gipsy family bent reverently to the ground before this singular being, who, in a deep sepulchral voice, spoke.

"Where is the child of the new race?" she said; "I saw her in my dream, and she should be here."

The torches, which seemed to have been hastily lit for the purpose of escorting this piece of the animated past, began to burn more clearly, and their light fell upon Emma, The old woman raised one of her skinny fingers, and moving slowly forward, she placed it upon the heart of Emma.

"This is the link," she said, "that unites two creatures. More than one hundred and twenty years ago I was what thou art now, daughter of the new people. My step was light—my eyes were bright, and the laugh and the jest were upon my lips. My destiny was to be what I am. The mother of mothers. The remnant of an age. The living tomb of the past. I am what I am. You will be what, in your wildest dreams, you cannot imagine, for we only dream of what we know. You will be what you look not to be. Linked with the cannons roar, and with the surging waters, will be your fate. The sun of fairer climes than this, where orange-blossoms and myrtle-groves scent the soft air, will shine upon you; and you will be worshipped by many hearts. You will be the divinity of a season; and the star of your destiny will be brighter to one who will wear a star of glory, than all his vast renown; and then the winter of your fate will come, and in darkness, and in misery, you will sigh to die."

She turned, and with the same strange, automaton-like movement, she made her way again to the opening of the tent. No one presumed for a moment to stop her —no one questioned her. She went as she came, with those around her, who, with deep reverential aspects, attended upon her footsteps.

When she was fairly gone, the spell that seemed to have fallen upon the faculties of the gipsy family was broken, and the man spoke—

"This is more than strange," he said. "She has not moved from her tent for many months—but she has dealings with things that we know not."

"She is very old," said Emma.

"None know her age. But she has told you what no one else can tell you."

"And do you think that she really possesses the power of reading the secrets of the future?"

"Those secrets must be known to one," said the gipsy, pointing upward; "and that one may think proper to communicate them to some of his creatures. Who shall say nay?"

To such a proposition it was impossible to oppose any amount of scepticism; and, to tell the truth, the imagination of Emma was strongly excited by the solemn manner in which she had been addressed by that aged woman, who, as she had truly said, was a link between the past and the present ages.

Intense anxiety, however, how to get home with the precious letter that was to save her father, soon began now to supersede every other feeling in the mind of Emma; and she moved towards the opening of the tent, saying—

"I bid you all good-night, and pray that you may be happy—and again I thank you for the precious favour conferred upon me, which will save my father from disgrace, and perchance from death."

"It is done," said the gipsy. "Farewell!"

Emma now, accompanied by the gipsy-woman, who certainly had done much to prove the sincerity of her gratitude, left the tent, and they proceeded together towards the little hill which Emma had descended. As they ascended its grassy slope, the clock of the village church struck one.

Emma started at the sound; and the idea, that, during the hour and a half that she had been away from home, her mother might have missed her, came most painfully across her mind. And yet, what had she not accomplished during that hour and a half from home? What to them all was not the inestimable value of the document she had in her bosom?

"We shall soon," said the gipsy-woman, "be far from this spot; but we shall not forget you; and we shall hear the end of the affair, which will do you and yours no harm."

"You have saved us," said Emma; "if it should ever lie in my power to be a friend to you, I cannot tell you how much gratification it would give me."

At the pace Emma went, they soon cleared the little wood. The wind had somewhat abated, and the rain which, more than once, she thought she had felt upon her face, was now descending in a drifting kind of cloud.

"Now," said Emma, "I am all but at home."

"Then, I will leave you," said the woman, "and may Heaven shower blessings on you. Beware of Will Flam, if this affair should not terminate in his death or banishment."

She turned away, and was soon lost to sight in the wood upon her return home. Emma, at a fast walk—almost a run—made her way towards her own home. Just as she got within sight of the door, she heard a rapid foot-step behind her upon the road-way.

CHAPTER X.

A SUDDEN EVENT.—THE GREAT WORLD IS BEFORE EMMA.

"Stop! stop!" cried a loud voice.

The voice was that of Will Flam. Emma knew it in a moment, and terror added wings to her speed, as may be well imagined, when it is recollected how important a document both to her father and to Will Flam she had in her possession. It seemed to her that by some means he must have found out that she had the letter, and that he came determined to kill her, rather than allow her to escape with it.

Of course, this idea was quite a thing of imagination, for it was not possible that under the circumstances Will Flam could have any idea of the sort. Still, the mere dread of such a thing was more than enough to induce Emma to fly, as though it were for her life, towards her humble home.

"Stop! stop!" cried Will Flam again. "Stop, I say."

. She still made near to the cottage, and reached the little gate of the garden. She heard him coming after her with furious speed, and she cleared the distance from the garden-gate to the cottage-door almost at a bound.

"Stop, fool!" he cried. "It is for your own good I want to speak to you; stop, unless you would have your father hung without a chance of saving him from the gallows."

Emma felt that to avert the calamity, her only plan was to do anything but stop; and gaining the door, which remained upon the latch just as she had left it, she opened it in an instant, and dashing into the cottage, she closed it again, and flung the wooden bar across it, which, when they retired to rest, they were accustomed to place up as a protection to the cottage.

Almost at the same moment Will Flam rushed violently against the door. Emma sunk exhausted upon the floor of the cottage.

"Open, open," he cried.

"No, no," said Emma. "No, no."

"Open, I say; I will come in—I will speak to you. It will be the worse for all of you, if you keep me out. Keep me out, do I say? You can't do that. There is no shutter to the window, I know, and I'll pretty soon find my way in."

She heard him fumbling at the window without, and the idea that by that means he could, as he said, easily get into the cottage, at once roused Emma from the state of exhaustion into which she had fallen. She sprung to her feet in a moment; and rushing to the fire-place, she took down her father's gun from the two hooks upon which it was always placed over the chimney-piece, and presented it at the window.

"Force your way in here, Will," she cried, "and you are a dead man! I swear to Heaven that I will shoot you!"

"You shoot me?"

"Yes. I have the means here!"

From his pocket he took a dark-lantern, from before the bull's-eye of which he removed a slide, so that he got a stream of light from it; and then opening the little casement, which there was no difficulty in doing, he saw Emma standing in the middle of the floor of the cottage, with the gun in her hand, presented full at him.

"Begone, or I will fire!" she said. "You are warned, Will Flam!"

"A plague take the girl!" he cried. "What do you mean by that? I came as your friend; and this is the sort of reception I get, is it?"

"We want no friendship from you!"

"But I can tell you how to save your father!"

"I know how!"

"The deuce you do! Perhaps, then, you have made up your mind to be a little cruel to me? I tell you that I have interceded for your father with Mr. Titherleigh, and he is willing to hush the affair up; and he even says he should not mind taking you into service at the Parsonage House, and he'll be quite a father to you if you behave yourself properly."

"Go away, Will Flam, or I will fire upon you! Go away! I do not wish to listen to anything from you or from Mr. Titherleigh! Go away before I count three, or I will fire the gun at you! One!"

"Don't be a fool! Do you want to see the old man hung?"

"Two!"

"Why, I tell you Mr. Titherleigh will be the making of you and all your family!"

"Three!"

Will popped down his head from the casement in a moment, and ran across the garden with great quickness. Emma had a great mind to fire after him, but she feared she might miss him, and in that case he might, knowing the gun not to be charged, return and overpower such other feeble resistance as she could make to his entrance into the cottage; so that, upon the whole, she thought the charge was a greater protection to her while it remained in the gun than as though she should heedlessly scatter it to the night air after Will Flam.

She quickly lost sight of him completely in the night air.

It was hardly to be supposed that Mrs. Lyon should fail to be disturbed by this disturbance below; so that Emma was not at all surprised to hear her mother calling to her. She had hardly time to ask herself the question if she should show the letter to her mother or not, before down the stairs, in her night-clothes, came Mrs. Lyon.

"Why, Emma," she said, "are you up and dressed?"

"Yes, mother; I heard some one in the garden, and it was Will Flam; so I have been threatening him with the gun, and he has only just gone away."

"Will Flam!" exclaimed Mrs. Lyon. "Oh, my child, my child! we shall be murdered yet in our beds by that man—I feel assured that we shall."

"No, mother, I think we shall see nothing more of him to-night. Let us do what we can to keep the window fast—are there no means of making it secure?"

"A nail, my dear, will do it. Get the hammer—where did your poor father put the hammer? Nail it up, my child, and then, if he should come again, he will have to make sufficient noise in opening it to warn us of his approah."

This was, indeed, the only thing that upon the spur of the moment could be done with the window; and accordingly, Emma nailed it up, while her mother, at her earnest persuasions, went to bed again, and without asking her, Emma, to go with her, as the young heroine fully expected she would.

Emma was, to tell the truth, exceedingly anxious to be alone, that she might read Will Flam's letter, and come to some judgment herself regarding its completeness or otherwise to procure the exoneration of her father from the charge that had been so industriously and so basely brought against him.

She continued to light the fire again, for the air was now bitterly cold, both within and without the cottage. When a few logs blazed up into a cheerful blaze, she drew the curtains across the latticed window; and lighting a candle, she proceeded to read the letter, which she had gone through so much trouble to procure.

That its contents, for good or for evil, were to her of the first importance, may be easily conceived.

The letter was torn and rumpled, but the writing was quite legible; and without any difficulty, Emma succeeded in deciphering it as follows:—

"Keep it snug, Seth, whatever you may do, my boy. You and I have been in many a preserve together, and had many a laugh, old boy. So, we won't quarrel now, if we don't agree. I only wish I could have seen you, because if I had, I could have made the thing plainer than I can do it upon paper, as I ain't any good fist with the pen; but time and tide wait for no man, they say, so I am obligated to write it to you, and here goes. I am going to light a bonfire for the Preston people, not a hundred miles off the Grange—you know it. It's where the dogs were set on us one night, when we were after them pheasant-poults that you recollect, of course, all about. Well, that I want you to have a hand in, and I want you to give a fellow a help in another little bit of business. There's a man in Preston of the name of Lyon I hate him; and if I don't put a spoke in his wheel, it will go hard with me. Only, you see, Seth, he knows me, and he knows I ain't any friend of his; so I want you—and I'll make it well worth your while—I want you to do that job. It's only a trifle. I mean to get something out of the Grange, and hide it in his crib, and I want you to corroborate, as the infernal lawyers have it.

"Meet me at the old stunted oak, where we hid our snares so long, and we will set about the job; but whatever you do, put this in the fire. It will help to keep your pot a-boiling. Mind you come not later than an hour after dark to the oak, and you will find me there. So no more at present from your old pal,   "WILL FLAM."

"Don't let the missus know a word of this. It's always well enough to trust women-folks in the way of a hare, or a rabbit, or mayhap a pheasant or two, but this is another piece of work."

"It will do," said Emma, as she ceased reading, and looked up from the letter; "it will do."

A creaking sound came upon her ear; and as she looked towards the casement, she saw that the curtain visibly moved, and at times it appeared as though a current of cold air was coming in at some opening in the window; and the creaking noise as of something slowly breaking, continued.

It is Will again, thought Emma; and she gently blew out the light, by which she had read the letter. Carefully then folding up the letter itself, she placed it upon the upper portion of a cross-beam, that was across the roof about six inches from it, and bound together the outer-walls of the little building.

The ominous creaking noise still continued at the window; and then suddenly, a small pane of glass shivered to atoms. The noise ceased, and all was as still as the grave. This stillness lasted about a minute, and then a voice, tolerably well disguised, but not sufficiently so thoroughly to impose upon Emma, said—

"Emma Lyon, Emma Lyon, I am come to warn you about Will Flam. I am a friend of your father's. Are you there?"

Emma neither spoke nor moved; and after another brief pause, Will Flam said, in his natural tone of voice, "it's all right; she is gone to bed. I will know what she went to the hollow for, or I will cut her throat. They think to keep me out do they, by putting a rusty nail in the window: but I rather think this little iron Jemmy has overcome greater obstacles than that."

Everything was now explained. The villain had, by chance, seen Emma, no doubt, upon her return from the gipsies' encampment, and he was now burning with curiosity, not, perhaps, unmingled with some uncomfortable suspicions, to know what it was had taken her there at such an hour of the night. With a small crow-bar, he was making an effort to force the frame-work of the window from its hold. Emma felt all the danger of her position in a moment; and now she was indeed thankful to Heaven that she had not fired the gun upon the former occasion, when she would have been almost certain to have missed Will Flam; but now she held his life in her power if she choose.

She trembled at the idea of what, in self-defence, she might have to do. There was something awful in the idea of taking the life even of such a man as Will Flam; but what was she to do? The feeling of self-defence—that great law of human nature—rose up in her mind, and she took the gun from its place once again.

She well knew that it was kept always scrupulously and carefully in order. In early life, her father had well known the use of the weapon, and he had an old attachment to it. She felt that she might depend upon that gun. And what a friend it was at such a moment!

Several more panes of glass cracked as the crow-bar bent the frame-work, and compressed them.

"Confound the old window," said Will. "Who now would have thought it had one-half the strength that it has in it! Ah, I shall have it now."

There was a sudden crash, and one-half of the window fell into the room; some jagged pieces of the glass and frame-work caught the curtain, and tore it down in its descent. Emma stepped forward a pace, and presented the gun at the moment that he held up his lantern, and peered into the room.

He saw her.

To drop the lantern was the work of one moment, and to make an ineffectual attempt to force his way, despite the gun, into the cottage, was that of another. A thrust with the barrel of the piece sent him backwards into the garden. He arose and fled, but the finger of Emma was upon the trigger.

"I will hang your father," cried the ruffian, "if I swing for it myself."

Bang went the gun; and by the broad momentary flash, Emma saw two figures in the little garden.

CHAPTER XL

THE MORNING, AND THE EXCULPATION.— SOME STARTLING EVENTS.

"HILLOA! hilloa!" cried some one: it was not Will. "What is all this about?"

"Speak again," cried Emma. "Who are you? Speak again, and assure me that you are not Will Flam. I do not think you are; but speak again?"

"You do not think I am Will Flam, Emma?" said Doctor Lukin, for it was indeed that worthy personage; "I am very much obliged to you for not thinking so. Don't you know me by my voice in the dark?"

"Oh, yes—yes, I do now. You are Mr. Lukin, and I am so glad to hear you speak. Oh, come in, sir, come in."

"But what's amiss?"

"Stop a moment, I will unbar the door. I will tell you all, sir; and I have in truth much to tell you. Come in, sir; I am safe now. Did you see the villain? Did he pass you, sir?"

"Some one passed me, certainly, and that rather roughly too; but in the dark, I will scarcely take upon myself to say if he were a villain or a true man."

"It was Will Flam."

"Then, my dear, the difficulty vanishes, for a villain he certainly is, to all intents and purposes; and he would have been no loss to society if one of those slugs, that I think have gone through my hat, had found a lodging in his skull."

"Through your hat, sir? Was I indeed so near injuring you, who are so good a friend to us?"

"Why, Emma, guns in the dark are rather dangerous things. It is not everybody that can use them with discretion in the daylight. But here is your mother, and I daresay the whole village will be astir in a few moments. But tell me how all this came about. I was just passing the cottage, from visiting Edwin. I wanted to see how he was at the turn of the night; and seeing a light, and hearing voices, I just turned into the garden, when I was nearly knocked down by some one leaving it, and then nearly shot by you."

"And if I had really done you any injury, sir, I should never have been able to forgive myself for it. I was so wishing to see you. Oh, mother—mother! father will be saved; but I ought not to tell you how, just yet, until I have spoken to Doctor Lukin about it."

Mrs. Lyon, who had started out of bed upon the shot being fired, and come down stairs again, looked from one to the other with an aspect of the greatest alarm. She found it difficult to convince herself that she was as yet awake fully. Doctor Lukin spoke to her.

"Do not be alarmed, Mrs. Lyon; there was some danger, but it is past now. The dawn will soon come; and until it does, I will take a seat here by the fire, which I see is not quite out yet. Do you go to rest again, Mrs. Lyon. You can trust me with Emma, I think?"

"Oh, yes, Doctor Lukin. But can it be true that there is any hope of saving Lyon? He is innocent, indeed he is, Doctor Lukin.'

"There can be no doubt of that, Mrs. Lyon, upon the mind of any-one who knows him as well as I do; but you are shivering already with the sudden change of temperature between this room and your bed; so let me give you some advice, gratis, which is, that if you wish to avoid fever, you will go to bed again."

After two or three more fruitless questions, which Emma evaded, for she wished to have the advice of the worthy doctor before she said anything to any one concerning the letter, Mrs. Lyon was persuaded to go to bed again; and the doctor said—

"Emma, you have something to tell me? There is some mystery in this night's proceedings which you can explain. I beg of you to be perfectly explicit with me."

"I will, sir. Read that letter. It has been given to me by a gipsy named Seth."

"Indeed."

Emma had re-lit the candle; and as the draught from the broken window was anything but agreeable, she and the doctor went into the little room adjoining that which had been the scene of so many events that night. This little adjoining room was at the back of the cottage, and looked into a part of the now dilapidated garden; and as its aspect was towards the east too, from its casement the faint rays of the dawn could be seen.

Then, while Emma watched his countenance with the greatest interest, to note what effect the epistle had upon him, Doctor Lukin read the letter, so imprudently written by Will Flam to the gipsy. But when is guilt prudent?

The doctor got through the epistle in a minute; and then looking up, he said—"This is indeed a godsend."

"It will save my father?"

"Most certainly. In the face of such evidence, even Mr. Titherleigh dare not, with all his wish to do so, detain him a moment. But the most extraordinary thing to me is, how you became possessed of such a letter? How did you get it from the man, Seth, to whom it is written?"

Emma then related to Doctor Lukin the whole of the incidents of the night, with the sole exception of the prophetic greeting she had had from the aged woman in the gipsy's tent. The words of that decayed piece of mortality, had sunk deeply into her heart —so deeply that she could not bring herself to share her thoughts concerning them with any other person.

When she had concluded, the doctor said, "This is certainly a most extraordinary circumstance, Emma but no one can doubt the absolute truth of it for an instant. I can, for my own part, only admire the courage and determination, not to say the ability, you have displayed in the whole affair. It yet wants some time to the morning. You go to bed, and leave this letter with me We don't know exactly how much. Will Flam may suspect his danger; so I will sit up here until the morning, for I would not let him get this letter back, and destroy it, on any account. Go at once, and rest yourself; for if you don't, unused as you are to these nocturnal disturbances, you will be unequal to what you may have

to go through in the morning; for, of course, you must appear before the justice, and if needs be, detail to him the mode by which you got the letter. Be assured that your father will sleep again beneath this roof on the night of the day that is now creeping on so fast."

The joy of Emma upon hearing the doctor, in whose judgment she had the greatest reliance, speak so confidently, was so great that she could hardly refrain from tears. Indeed, her heart was too full to permit her to speak, and she could only thank him and bid him good-night by a look. That look had, however, in it a world of eloquence.

In another moment she had ascended the little staircase of the cottage, and the doctor was alone.

"That girl," he said to himself, "has no common genius. Her intellect is as rare as her beauty. Heaven only know whether she will employ her rare gifts for good or for evil. They are capable of great results in both courses. It really seems incredible that she should be the child of these poor homely people; and yet I never heard of any mystery being in any way attached to her birth. No, no—she is Emma Lyon, and none other."

The doctor stretched himself upon three chairs, but he did not sleep. His profession had pretty well accustomed him to night-vigils; and the east was one glow of yellow light before he thought of moving from the cottage. He felt certain that when once the village was up and awake, there would be no longer any danger to be apprehended from Will Flam, who, like the owl, was only bold and venturesome at night; but who, in the light of day, always had a skulking look and manner about him.

Both Emma and her mother were soon down stairs, and they insisted upon the doctor breaking his fast before he left them; and Emma bustled about to prepare the homely but wholesome morning meal for him.

The doctor saw that the curiosity and anxiety of Mrs. Lyon were both very great to know what had taken place that could give so very favourable a turn to the affair which had temporarily consigned her husband to a prison; and he at once told her all about it. The good dame, held Emma in her arms and kissed her fervently, at the same time that she deprecated the visit to the Monk's Hollow, as by far too great a risk to run by one so young and inexperienced as Emma, although, certainly, the good woman's arguments lost much, from the fact, that the adventure had resluted so favourably.

"And, now," said the doctor, "let us go to Mr. Titherleigh's at once, for, no doubt, John Lyon will be not sorry to see his own cottage again, and the Justice dare not refuse to liberate him upon this evidence.

Upon this intimation both mother and daughter hastened to get ready to leave the cottage; and they were soon with Mr. Lukin on the road to the justices. Hanging about the gate, close to the Lodge entrance to Titherleigh's house, they saw Will Flam.

His eyes were bloodshed, and his whole appearance was that of a man at war with himself, and with every one else. The fact is, he had been now up for two nights, and Will Flam was likewise not one of the most temperate men in the world.

He looked, or affected to look, quite astonished to see the party that was proceeding to the justice's; and bending a scowling glance upon them, he said,—

"What now? The remand was till Sir Gilbert came down, and he has not arrived yet, I know."

"Don't answer him," whispered the doctor. "Take no more notice of him than as though he were a stick or a stone."

Acting upon this advice, Emma and her mother passed on, and the doctor followed them about half a dozen yards behind, for he could not say but that in his desperation and dread at what they were about to depose to, Will Flam might attempt some violence. The ruffian lounged after the doctor; and after passing through the lodge-gates, he spoke to him.

"What's it all about, doctor? I am sure you are not the sort of man to listen to anything against a poor fellow."

"I will trouble you, Will Flam," said Doctor Lukin, "to keep as far off from me as possible, and I beg to decline any conversation with you upon any subject whatever."

Will Flam would fain have resented this rebuff; but then it was broad daylight; and besides, he knew that the doctor was not a man to be trifled with; so he hung back, only muttering curses between his clenched teeth; and really lost in wonder as to what the errand of the three to the justice could mean.

That it was, however, something in which he had an interest, he could not very well be off imagining; so he followed in a dogged, morose-looking manner, determined to oppose by any amount of false swearing, whatever might be urged by the Lyon's, or their friend, the doctor, in favour of John Lyon.

It was well known to the establishment of the justice that nothing but business would bring Doctor Lukin to the house; and accordingly his worship's clerk was ready to meet him, which the doctor was not sorry for, as the clerk, independently of the fact that he had, for his living's sake, to do some of the dirty-work of his master, was by no means a non-intelligent man. To him, then, the doctor had no hesitation in stating his business, and showing him the letter; saying, in conclusion—

"There can be no doubt of the innocence of John Lyon; so he ought to be brought up and liberated."

"I doubt if his worship would do so much," said the clerk; "and the best way is for me to give the order without consulting him; and then, when the prisoner is actually here, he must adjudicate upon the case in some way or another."

"I am much obliged to you," said the doctor. "Do so at once, and I will wait the result in the justice-room. This Will Flam must, of course, be apprehended."

"I should say so But it is better to leave that until the other affair is settled. I will send an order for John Lyon at once. I'm afraid you will find it very cold in the justice-room."

"Never mind. It is the only room in th s house that I would willingly wait a moment in. I look upon it as not belonging to the house at all."

His worship was not up while all this was going in, or he would probably have been not a little indignant at it. Little did he imagine that Emma and her mother were quite comfortably bestowed by a roaring fire in the kitchen of his house, and that Doctor Lukin was keeping up the circulation by rapidly walking to and fro in the long room that had been devoted to the purpose of hearing cases while his clerk had taken upon him to send for a prisoner.

When his lordship was informed of what had taken place, by the clerk, he was at first rather furious; but the said clerk used sufficient arguments to convince him that it would not do to keep John Lyon an hour longer than the facts and statements warranted him in so keeping him; and as his worship had a perfect horror of being struck out of the commission of the peace, he soon succumbed to the urgent reasoning of the clerk.

The prisoner soon arrived at the house; but being quite ignorant of why he was sent for thus again so early, he thought in his own mind that it would be on account of the sudden arrival of Sir Gilbert, his master, from London; and the difficulty of exonerating himself from the charge brought against him by Will Flam, appeared to him to be so great, that he was most miserably depressed in spirits. To look at him, one would have supposed that ten years had been added to his age.

The scowl of disappointed malice that was upon the brow of the justice, was by no means calculated to reassure John Lyon, although, if he had translated it the right way, it ought to have done so.

CHAPTER XII.

A PETTY TYRANT.—EMMA'S DETEMINATION TO SEEK HER FORTUNE IN LONDON.

EMMA would have gone up to her father and spoken to him when he was brought into the room, but the justice cried roughly—

"Officer, keep every one away from the prisoner."

Upon this, she was not rudely—for who in Preston, besides Justice Titherleigh, would be rude to Emma Lyon?—but firmly kept back, so that poor John Lyon had no means of knowing what was about to take place.

"Now, then," added his worship, "what is all this about? Do you mean to tell me that this fellow is to escape the gallows?"

Emma stepped forward. There was a flush, partly of modesty and partly of indignation, upon her countenance.

"For shame, sir," she said to Titherleigh. "for shame, sir. If my father were guilty, it would be the act of a coward to speak to him in such a way; but being innocent, it is base indeed."

"I'll commit you to prison, my girl, for insolence to the bench, if you don't mind what you are about. Swear this girl, clerk, and let us hear what cock-and-a-bull-story she has hatched up now."

Emma was duly sworn; and the state of indignation into which she had been thrown by the remarks of the justice, no doubt, had fully the effect of getting her over the nervousness that otherwise might upon this, her first public appearance, have materially injured the effect of what she had to say.

She, however, told her story with the greatest clearness; and then, the doctor produced the letter, which was read by the clerk. At that moment, the sudden revulsion of feeling was too much for John Lyon, and he fell to the ground.

Reckless, as they might well be, at such a moment, of whether it was pleasing or displeasing to the justice, both Emma and her mother flew forward to the relief of the prisoner. Doctor Lukin followed them.

"Father! father!" said Emma, "you are free—you are saved! Speak to us—you are free to come home to us now——"

"John! John!" said his wife, "do you not know me? Why do you not speak, John? You are free, now."

"I don't know that," said the justice.— "Don't be in such a hurry."

"But, I know it," said Doctor Lukin, "who had torn open the vest of John Lyon, and listened for a moment or two, with his ear placed upon the region of the heart. "But I know it."

"What do you mean, sir, by addressing the Bench in that way? I shall remand the prisoner again. He shall come before this court to-morrow morning."

"He will not."

"Will not?—will not? I will make him."

"You cannot. He has carried his case to a higher court than is to be found in this world—the court of Heaven. John Lyon is dead!"

"Dead?"

"Yes; the sudden shock of finding he had escaped you, has brought on a crisis in a disease of the heart, to which he has been long subject; and he will never breathe again."

Mrs. Lyon fainted upon her husband's body, and Emma, as she knelt by the side of her parents, the dead and the insensible, clasped her hands and looked so despairing, that every one but Titherliegh was deeply moved at her distress.

"I—I did not expect this," said the justice, who was frightened, if not affected. "I—don't—like dead people here. Break up

the court at once, clerk; break up the court!"

"Stop," said the doctor. "Will Flam is guilty, if John Lyon be innocent. He is now hanging about the grounds. It will be necessary to give him into custody."

"Well, well, do so then," cried the justice. "Only break up the court, and take the dead body away. I—I will pay the expenses of the funeral in a plain way. Dear me, what do those low people want with such fine feelings, I wonder!"

Emma burst into a passion of tears. His worship hastily left the room; and as the news of what had happened was bruited about the place, some of the female servants came in to take charge of Mrs. Lyon and Emma, and offered to them such consolation and assistance as they could. The doctor would not leave the room until the clerk had given orders for the immediate arrest of Will Flam; and as the servants said he was only just outside the house, the constables, accompanied by the clerk and Doctor Lukin, went at once to take him.

They saw him leaning against a tree; and upon the constable going up to him, and saying —"Will Flam, you are my prisoner, and you had better go gently to jail, my man," he looked the picture of astonishment.

"Why, what's become of Lyon?" he cried—

"Oh, he's proved to be innocent, and it's found out you did it all."

"Catch me who can, then," he cried; and knocking down the constable with one blow, he darted off towards the lodge-gates at great speed. But the clerk and the doctor pursued him.

Now it had happened that the wife of the man, who had kept the lodge, had seen the attempted capture of Will Flam, and the knock-down blow that he gave to the constable; so she thought her best plan was to close the gates, which she did, calling to her husband, who was at work in the little patch of garden-ground adjoining the lodge, to come and help to capture Will.

The ruffian saw the woman shut the gates, and when he arrived at them, his first act was to strike her a brutal blow, which felled her to the ground, as though she had been struck by a thunderbolt. Her husband had heard her call to him, and was just in time to see this. He was an old man, and would have had no sort of chance for a moment with Will Flam in a scuffle, but he had a gun always loaded over the mantel-shelf in the lodge.

To take down the gun was the work of a moment, but that moment had been sufficient to enable Will Flam to open the gate again; and crying—"Catch me who can!" he rushed out into the open road-way, and made for a copse immediately opposite.

The old gatekeeper levelled the gun. "I can't catch thee," he said; "but here's something that flies faster than thee, my mon!"

He fired, and with a loud yell, Will Flam

fell to the ground; and after rolling over twice, he lay quite still.

"How dost thee like that, my mon?" said the old gatekeeper. "That will teach thee to leave my old woman alone another time, thee wagabone! I be thinking I had thee then; and if that be'ant enough for thee, my mon, here's t'other barrel with a couple of slugs for thee!"

No such argument as the other barrel, cogent as it was, was required for Will Flam. The contents of the first one, although they had only been good-sized shot, had been quite sufficient to stop his career for some time. Upon the doctor and the clerk getting up to him, tkey found that he was quite disabled, while the expression of his countenance was so perfectly demoniac, that they turned away from contemplating it in disgust.

"Mark me," he said, as the constable came up, and ordered a cart to be brought for him. "Mark me! I will, sooner or later, have my revenge!"

"I cannot attend upon this man professionally," said Doctor Lukin. "You must get another medical man, constable, for him. He can wait, for I can see the shot has only, after all, hit him in the legs."

What immense changes the last half-hour had produced! Poor John Lyon was lying dead upon one of the benches in the justice-room, and his accuser, bleeding and wounded, was being conveyed to prison in a cart like a load of rubbish. Emma and her mother were still in the justice's house. Mrs. Lyon was only slowly recovering from the fainting fit that had taken possession of her, and Emma was weeping in the housekeeper's room.

She had not been there very long before she heard a heavy footstep on the floor behind her, as she was sitting near to the window, and upon turning, she, to her astonishment beheld the justice.

She started to her feet.

"You need not be alarmed, Emma Lyon," he said, in a tone of voice that was evidently meant to be wonderfully conciliatory.— "You need not be in the least alarmed, for no one, I'm sure, can be more sorry for your bereavement than I am."

Emma was silent, for she did not know to what this prelude might lead to; and after pausing a sufficient time to see if she meant to say anything, and finding that she did not, the justice proceeded by adding,—

"I sincerely pity you, and am quite desirous and willing to do something for you. I will take you into my service; and if you are a good girl, you will find yourself very comfortable indeed."

The words that Will Flam had uttered the night before to her, and which were so nearly similar, at once recurred to the memory of Emma; and with a shudder, she made a movement towards the door.

"May I suppose I may expect an answer?" said Titherleigh, placing himself fully in her way.

"I reject your proposition, sir, with the contempt and scorn it deserves."

"Contempt and scorn! Upon my life those are fine words for a pauper to use.— Why, girl, you don't know what you are saying! You are destitue now, and my offer was no common one."

"Let me leave this room, sir."

"Nonsense! Come, be a little rational, and don't spoil that pretty face by a frown; you shall have a gold watch by your side, and more fine clothes than you will know what to do with.—Come; will that content you? Only say what you do want, and you shall have it—I will provide for your old mother, too, who is past work, I dare say, at her time of life."

"Oh, this is too much," cried Emma; "and my dead father, too, beneath this roof."

"Stuff! stuff!—don't be a fool, girl. You may carry your pretty face to a worse market. Nobody need know anything about it. Don't be a fool, and stand in the way of your own interest. Why, I will make a complete lady of you, I tell you. You surely cannot understand me, girl?"

"Oh, too well—too well. Let me go, sir!"

"Will you consent? Come, only say you consent.

"Never! never!"

"Then you will think of it? Say you will think of it, and call here again to-morrow, and let me know. I'm sure the more you think of my offer, the more you will see what a good thing it is for you. Only say you will call again to-morrow, and you shall go at once."

"I will not say it—I will not say it. Stand aside and let me pass, I implore you—I command you."

"Pho! pho! You have been reading all these heroics out of some book; but beware, I say—beware! I have power in this parish, as you all know. My enmity is as much to be dreaded as my friendship is to be courted. Think better of what I have said to you, Emma, and I will forget anything offensive that you may have said. You are a charming girl, indeed you are. Of course, I will, in time, make you Mrs. Titherleigh; for you know I am a single man, and can do just what I like. But there's one thing that nobody knows, and that is, how rich I am · so that you may have a coach to yourself at once. Yes, you may go to your father's funeral in your own coach like a lady."

"Oh, Heaven, must I endure this?"

"Why, what is there to endure?"

"I will cry for help, and the consequences of the scene that will ensue, be upon your own head."

"You dare not. Why, you little slut, what do you mean by such conduct? Am I not a gentleman? and do I not condescend to tell you that you are beautiful? Yes, you are beautiful. I have had an eye upon you for this last year, Emma, and determined to make a lady of you. Of course, if your father were alive, he would see the great advantages I offer you in a moment."

"If my father were alive," said Emma, "he would strike you to the earth for this insult. It is worse than ungentlemanly, sir. It is unmanly to detain me here against my will."

"But I want you to listen to reason."

"I will listen to nothing that you can have to say. You are the murderer of my father!"

"What an absurdity! If that is your only objection, I am sure that your own natural sense will soon put an end to that. I will, indeed, be very kind to you."

He advanced, and would have clasped her in his arms; but with a cry of horror and dismay, she eluded him, and flew to the other end of the room. Her head touched something, and, upon turning round, she saw it was a bell-rope. To seize it, and pull it vigorously, was the work of a moment; and both she and her assailant heard the peal upon rather a loud-toned bell that it produced.

Anger—fierce and uncontrollable anger—now took the place of every other feeling in the breast of the justice. Even he could not but feel quite assured that Emma's rejection of his infamous proposals was indeed final. As is always the case where there is mere passion without real love, it turned to hate.

"Very well," he said; "be it so. You reject my offers; and I will take good care that, before many days are over your head, both you and your mother shall feel the weight of my displeasure. You may think to save yourself by mentioning this interview and this threat; but I will deny both. Oh, Mrs. Brown,"—to the housekeeper, who at that moment made her appearance—"I insist upon having this girl turned out of the house for insolence. She wanted me to take her into my service, and actually threatened me if I did not. Turn her out!"

CHAPTER XIII.

EMMA'S SITUATION.—THE ROAD TO LONDON. MORE PERILS.

It would probably have been perfectly futile upon the part of Emma, if she had stated the real facts of the case to the housekeeper, who, upon the instant, began a long tirade upon what she called the "horrid insolence of the lower classes." Emma walked without a word from the room, and made her way out of the house as quickly as she possibly could.

It was not until she reached the cottage and shut herself in, that she began really to feel how desolate the death of her father had made her, and to reflect upon the probable poverty that was before her and her mother. She began to think how much better it would have been if, after all, she had been allowed to perish in the flames of the old Grange; but then, with that thought came likewise the remembrance of him who had rescued her so gallantly and nobly from the burning house; and she said to herself—

"Ah, yes, I am glad that I was saved, for I may see him again. Who shall say that fortune may not again cast us together? I shall never—never forget him. Will he remember, and at times think of me? Alas, I fear not."

She leant her head upon her hands, and sobbed bitterly. This was the first time in her young existence that Emma had felt so truly wretched, and she gave free vent to her tears. She felt that she might many times in after life shed tears, but she thought none could be so bitter as those that now came from her overchanged heart upon that melancholy occasion.

She was aroused by her mother being brought home by the good doctor. Poor Mrs. Lyon was only partially recovered from the severe shock which the sudden and most unexpected death of her husband had given her, and she looked extremely ill. By the joint efforts of Emma and the doctor, she was conducted to bed; and then Doctor Lukin drew a chair to the side of Emma in the lower room, and spoke to her kindly.

"My good girl," he said; "what do you think of doing, now?"

Emma could not reply to him for some time, for her tears; and then when she could command her voice sufficiently to speak, she could only say that she did not know; but she recounted to the doctor what had taken place in the housekeeper's room at the house of Mr. Titherleigh; and he was so moved with anger at it, that he was compelled to rise and pace the cottage to and fro for some minutes to recover his ordinary state of composure.

"You did quite right, Emma," he said, "to reply to Titherleigh in the way you did. He is a scoundrel, and wholly unworthy of a thought. Let me advise you to tell this story to no one. It will only expose you to remarks if you mention it; and in the minds of many, to doubts of your veracity. Forget it, and the wretch who spoke such words to you."

"I will forget him."

"Do so—do so, Emma. And now it will be necessary to think of what is to become of you, seriously; and there is one thing that I would advise of all others."

"What is that, sir?"

"It is, that you remain in Preston no longer than will suffice to pay the last homage of respect to the remains of your deceased father. It is a matter of necessity that you should seek a subsistence in the great world; but do not begin your career in Preston. You have here friends, it is true, but you have likewise enemies."

"Alas, sir, where can I go?"

"It is in my power to recommend you to a situation, with a Mr. Thomas, of Hawarden. I do not say that Thomas is just the sort of person I would wish you to be with; but his wife, I hear, is an amiable woman enough:

and, at all events, you can stay with them until you can better yourself."

"But my mother—What will become of her?"

"I will promise you that she shall not want. Recollect, Emma, that I am a bachelor; and although I may be of great assistance to a woman of your mother's age, I must not expose you to any misconstruction which might arise were I to keep you here in Preston, and support you. In this world, it is not only necessary to be honest and virtuous, but one must take care to seem so likewise. Remember, however, that you will always find a friend in me, upon any and every occasion; and I beg that you will never scruple to apply to me, if you should be in any trouble or difficulty."

"I will do so, sir."

"Very well, then, we will look upon that as all settled, Emma, if you please; and now I will leave you to comfort your mother, as I am quite sure only you can comfort her."

The doctor took his leave, and Emma was soon by the bedside of her mother, breathing to her words of consolation, which in their echo had likewise an effect upon her own grief.

We need not pursue the events of the succeeding six days. They were productive of nothing but a dull routine of tears and woe to the bereaved wife and child. The remains of John Lyon were placed in the little village churchyard, there to rest until the fiat shall be issued by the Almighty for the dead to rise again.

News of Will Flam's recovery from his wounds, and his daring escape from the county jail, arrived in Preston on the evening of the day of the funeral of John Lyon.— Emma and her mother both trembled when they heard it, for well they knew the implacable character of the man; and they firmly believed that he would not rest until he had taken vengeance upon all concerned in his late mishap.

Mrs. Lyon was sorely troubled by her fears; but Emma spoke cheeringly to her, saying,—

"Be comforted, mother, upon that, by recollecting how little, if anything, you have had to do with the whole affair. It is against me, no doubt, that the anger of Will Flam is alone directed; and I shall be out of his reach soon by going to Hawarden. Indeed, I do not, for one moment, consider that he will interfere with you; and as for Doctor Lukin, although I know he has awakened the revengeful feelings of Will Flam, he is well able to protect himself; and his position in life places him out of the mode of small persecutions."

Mrs. Lyon was not able to reason so closely as her daughter Emma; and although she could not gainsay her reasonings, yet she retained very much of her fear of Will Flam, notwithstanding.

There was one person whom Emma thought herself bound to take something more than a mere general leave of, and that was Edwin Lee, who, although able to get up, had not left his mother's cottage since the disastrous night of the fire. If her heart had whispered to her nothing favourable to Edwin, gratitude for the attempt he had made to save her would at last have dictated some special farewell to him.

Much as Emma disliked crossing the threshold of Mrs. Lee's cottage, she did go to it, on the evening prior to her departure from Preston to Hawarden.

Edwin was sitting upon a chair in the garden, and he saw her coming. With difficulty, and assisted by two sticks, he rose to welcome her; and oh! what a world of joy was in the boy's face as he looked at her.

"You have come to see me, Emma?"

"Yes, Edwin; but sit down. I do so hope that you are better. Come, lean upon my arm, and I will help you to the chair again, which you should not have left upon my account."

"And you will let me touch your arm, Emma?"

"Oh, yes—yes!"

"How soon I should be well, dear Emma, if you would come often to see me. No—no; perhaps I ought not to say often, dear Emma; but once, only once in the day, if you were to pass the garden and look at me, and give me one smile. Ah, I should be well and strong then."

"Edwin, I should have come to you oftener, indeed, but I have had many, many griefs."

"Yes—yes, dear Emma, I know all—I feel all that. They told me all; and how I wept and prayed for you. It was very selfish of me to ask you to come to me oftener. You had your poor mother to comfort. Will you forgive me, Emma?"

"There is nothing to forgive, Edwin. Indeed, there is not."

"Yes, yes, Emma—I have pained you."

"Not at all, Edwin. But—but——"

"But what? Your eyes are filled with tears. Ah, Emma dear—good Emma, what are you going to say to me?"

"I was going to say, Edwin, that I feared, although you had not pained me, that I should have to pain you much."

"Oh, no—no, you cannot pain me, Emma —I am sure you would not."

"I would not if I could help it, Edwin; but you must keep a bold heart, and learn to think that the best of friends must part."

"Part, Emma?"

"Yes—I am going from Preston tomorrow."

For a moment or two poor Edwin could not speak. The very breath of life seemed to have deserted him, and he could only look in her face to see if, by its expression, he could note that she was really not in earnest; but he saw nothing but a grave and solemn regret, while a tear trickled down her cheek slowly. He was convinced then that she was really going from Preston. Oh, what an agony of grief did that conviction give to him.

"I *must* go, Edwin," she said; and she said it rather for the purpose of breaking the awful silence that had ensued, than that she thought there was now any necessity for impressing the fact upon his attention.

"No—no, Emma. Oh, no!"

"I must, Edwin, I must, indeed. But be of good cheer; for some day we may meet again."

"Some day!" gasped poor Edwin.

"Yes, Edwin. You will be glad to see me I am sure. Good-night, Edwin. Good-night now. You will soon be well again."

"No—no, do not leave me in this way, Emma. Oh God! do not let her go away from me in this way. Emma, Emma, I have not yet wholly told you how much I love you. You shall not go from Preston. I shall soon be well; and I will work for you, day and night, my Emma. Oh, say that you will stay. Do say only that you will stay in the old cottage!"

"I cannot, Edwin. Farewell!"

He clasped her hand in his; and in a shrieking voice, he again implored her to stay while he only told her how he loved her; and she was fain to linger by him a little while, for she really feared he would go mad. She held his hand in one of hers; and she spoke long and kindly to him; she promised that she would write to him—very soon.

At length he was calmed a little; and he was able to speak in a different tone to her, saying—

"You will go, Emma; and you will not come back again to the old dear village; but you will tell me where you are going; and when I am well enough to do so, I must walk and see you, be it as far as it may be."

"No, Edwin, you must not even ask me where I am going to—for I must not tell even you."

"Not tell me, Emma?"

"No. I have made a solemn promise to tell no one but my mother; and you would not have me break that promise, I am certain; but be assured that you shall hear from me; and Doctor Lukin will always be able to tell you if I am well."

"Ah! how often I shall ask him; but the good doctor will not be angry. He will always answer me kindly, for he knows that I love you, Emma, and he loves you too; so I shall ask him after you very, very often."

"And be assured that he will always tell you; I will make it a particular request with him, that he should do so; and then, for my sake as well as for yours, Edwin, he will always give you correct information of me."

"Yes, yes, he will."

Edwin still held her hand clasped in his. How could he make up his mind to let her go? The twilight was deepening. Long shadows were creeping over the little garden: but how could he resign that little hand that he held in his?

"Edwin, good-night!"

"Not yet. Oh! no, not yet!"

He sobbed convulsively. He held her hand to his lips, and kissed it; and she felt the hot tears fall upon it.

"Good-night, Edwin."

"No, no. Do not leave me; I cannot live when you are gone. Do not leave me, Emma; something tells me now that we shall meet no more in this world."

She stooped over him for a moment, and kissed his brow; and then she made a slight effort, and disentangled her hand from him, and at once walked rapidly from the garden. He did not attempt to follow her, but he stretched out his arms, and when she got near to the gate of the little garden, he cried out to her—

"Emma—my Emma."

She turned a moment or so, and waved her hand. "Farewell—farewell, Edwin," she said.

"For ever," gasped the boy, as he fell from his chair to the ground.

Emma did not see him fall, and she went rapidly home.

CHAPTER XIV.

EMMA'S PROSPECTS AT HAWARDEN.—A HARD PLACE.—HER RESOLUTION.

THE feelings of the young girl were much more touched by the simple affection of Edwin, that she would let him see; but as she left the cottage her eyes were full of tears. Mrs. Lee encountered her before she reached home.

"Well, I am sure, Miss Emma," she said, "some folks would have called to see poor Edwin before now, in spite of these mighty pretty faces, I think."

"I have been," said Emma.

"Oh, you have been, have you? Well, to be sure, that is wonderfully kind, and condescending, of course, on the parts of such pretty folks. As for me, I am plain Mrs. Lee, and, of course, my feelings aint quite so fine. Oh dear, no. We plain folks is very common in our ideas, in course, and I dare say it's quite fit and proper as we should be so. Thank God, I was plain Martha Brown before I got married, and now I'm plain Mrs. Lee."

"You trouble me, madam," said Emma; and she walked briskly past plain Mrs. Lee, leaving her perfectly transfixed with astonishment at being treated in so cavalier a style by a mere chit of a girl, as she called Emma.

"Very good!" exclaimed Mrs. Lee, bridling up, and giving a toss to her head, as though there had been something particularly disagreeable on the end of her nose, and she hoped to jerk it off that way. "Very good. I feel confident she will come to a bad end, that's one comfort. I always thought she would, and now I'm sure of it."

With this christian consolation, Mrs. Lee went home, to inflict upon her poor son a series of remarks, that were almost enough to drive him quite distracted.

Emma was soon at home. She found her

mother asleep; and barring and fastening up the cottage, she strove, for that last night she was to pass under its roof, to compose herself to a calm sleep, in the little bed she had occupied from the earliest of her childhood's recollections.

At an hour in the morning when but few persons would be up in the village, she was to meet the doctor, who, with his chaise, was to take her far upon the road to Hawarden. By him she was already provided with the letter of introduction that was to procure her the situation at Mr. Thomas's; and by his kindness she likewise had two guineas in

THE ATTEMPT TO CARRY EMMA OFF AT CHORLEY.

a little purse that he had brought to her, and made her a present of. Her state of mental excitement, and the many painful subjects of thought she had pressing upon her, effectually prevented her from sleeping; and the eastern sky was already tinged with the coming dawn ere Emma found repose on that her last night beneath the roof of the cottage in which she was born.

When she did sleep, she enjoyed that deep, dreamless slumber which only youth and innocence can possibly hope for in this world. When she did awake she found her mother by her side.

"Ah!" she said, "I have slept too long."

"No, my child," said Mrs. Lyon; "it is yet time. I was awake, and watching the old clock, so as to rouse you up; and it is yet good time, Emma."

The young girl rose at once, and hastily performed her simple toilette, during which her mother said—

"I have had so strange a dream, my dear; but I don't know if I ought really to tell it to you."

"Why not, mother?"

"For fear it should fill your head with fancies that had better, by far, find no place in it; particularly as you are to get your living by service. You must not think now of anything that is above the condition to which you will belong; and that, I understand from Doctor Lukin, is——"

"A nursery-maid," said Emma, "at present; but be assured, mother, that I shall not be a nursery-maid all my life. I feel a sort of confidence that such will not be the case. I am born for something better than that."

"Alas, my child, such thought will be the ruin of you."

"Not so, mother; I will always strive to be content with the situation in which I may be placed; but yet I believe that mine will alter greatly; and I will not refuse such advancement as fortune may throw into my hands."

"Alas! alas!"

"Why do you cry alas, mother?"

"I am thinking of my dream, my child; and I do believe I must tell it to you; but that I can do as we go along to meet the good doctor—for I must see you off, and soon I must take a journey to visit you, and see how you look; for my thoughts will be always with you. I am, but for you, alone in the world."

Emma made a hasty and simple breakfast of milk and bread, and then was ready to leave the cottage. As she stood upon the threshold of it, she took a long regretful glance at it and its contents—she seemed to have a sort of presentiment that she should never see that cottage again, although she did not say so to her mother; yet Mrs. Lyon could perceive that she was much affected at leaving it.

As she passed through the little garden—that garden which, at the hands of Emma, had received for many a year such abundance of care, and such abundance of love—she plucked a late rose-bud from a tree, and placed it in her bosom.

It was not for show that she plucked that rose—it was to keep as a memorial of the place where she had been very, very happy in the soft pearly days of infancy and childhood. Even she had a thought or an ambition beyond the precints of that little garden-paling.

In other lands, and in far other circumstances, she at times looked at that faded rose-bud, with its brown, cankered leaves, and sighed for the little garden at Preston!

"You have got your little purse," said Mrs. Lyon, "and the two guineas in it, my dear?"

"Yes, mother. It is a deal of money; but Mr. Lukin would make me take it. I thought the gold would be more useful to you; but he said that he would always be at hand to succour you, when he might not be able to reach me; and he advised me to keep the money, in case, from any circumstances, I should require to come here, and be far away at the time, with no friend but these two guineas to help me on my way; 'and then,' he said, 'you will find that gold a friend who will not be false to you, Emma.'"

"He is right, my child. He is right. Gold is, indeed, a friend to all, when rightly used; but oh! what a foe has it not been to many!"

"It may be so, mother; but you have not yet told me your dream, and the time is passing quickly."

"I have promised to tell it to you, and I will keep my word, although I do, in my heart, think it is better untold. I thought I was in a large room, the walls of which were covered with rich hangings, and the roof full of gold; and there was a fine company there, and such music as one might only expect to hear in Heaven; and all of a sudden there was a kind of bustle, and some one said—'Make way for her ladyship!' and then who should come in but you, with an elegant dress of white satin on, and such a row of bright diamonds round your neck, as I never thought there were the like in all the world."

"And what did you do, mother?"

"I thought that I ran forward, saying, 'That is my Emma;' but at that moment I awoke."

"And it was only a dream?" murmured Emma.

"Only a dream, my dear. Why good-heart, you don't think it could ever come to be true, Emma?"

"I don't know, mother."

"Heaven preserve the child's wits. She don't surely think anything serious of a mere dream?"

"I say, that I don't know, mother."

"The idea that poor Emma Lyon, the daughter of John Lyon—God be good to him—who is dead and gone; and of Dame Lyon, of Preston—should ever be a great lady, with jewels round her neck!—ah, no. We may hear of such things in fairy-tales, and we may dream of them; but that's all—that's all."

"Yes," said Emma, musingly, "that's all. It would be something like a fairy-tale, indeed."

"Well, well, we will forget it; and don't you let such fancies lay hold of you now, or you will be quite unfit for your work; and remember, my dear child, now that you are going out into the world, all you have to do is to be honest, and diligent, and respectful to your superiors; and say your prayers every night; and don't be led away by any idle vanities."

"No, mother, I will not."

"And, above all things, mistrust any-one

who praises you for beauty; for beauty in a poor young girl is only a pitfall and a snare; so mind, Emma, that you don't listen to anything of that sort from any one."

"I will not, mother."

"Then, my child, you will do well; and God will bless you, if you keep a contrite and humble heart."

"Humble," said Emma, to herself; "no, I shall never be very humble." She would not, however, hurt the feelings of her mother by any one word which would look like a disregard of those homely precepts of wisdom that Dame Lyon thought it necessary upon the present occasion to instill into her daughter's mind, now that she was, as it were, about to be launched into the world; Emma did not at that time want for feeling.

They were a few minutes before their time at the place of appointed meeting with Doctor Lukin; but he very quickly drove up to the spot in his little yellow gig, that was as well known in that part of the country as he was himself.

"A pleasant, healthful morning," he cried. The air is full of life and vigour on such a morning as this. Ah! Emma, it has lent, already, a deeper tinge to the roses on your cheeks."

"I have just been telling her," said Mrs. Lyon, "that she must never listen to anything concerning her looks."

"Oh, but you must not mind me," laughed Doctor Lukin; "I am a privileged old bachelor."

"I did not mean to say anything about you, sir," said Mrs. Lyon. "Indeed, I did not, believe me "

"Never mind if you did, Mrs. Lyon; I certainly thought you meant to snub one a little about these same roses I spoke of in Emma's cheeks, and no great harm if you did, either; and as far as the sentiment goes, I quite agree with you, that if she listens to flattery, she is lost."

"Lost?" said Emma.

"Yes, my dear," added her mother, "quite lost, so, now, good bye, and may God bless you.'

"Hallo!" cried the doctor, "what is all this, at such an hour of the morning? Why, to be sure, it's a gipsy family on the tramp; let them go by before we start. There is a large party of them. Why, they must be the lot that have been for some time in Monk's Hollow? There are more of them than I thought."

The doctor drew up close to the road-side, while from a meadow, there came the gipsies, with all their bag and bagggae, evidently packed for a long march. They were proceeding in that slow and somewhat dignified manner which is a peculiarity of their rate of movement. It would seem that they had so much experience, as wanderers in the wilderness, that they considered themselves, as by far too much at home, to bring in their movements.

"Your friends," said the doctor, to Emma, "should be among these people, surely."

"Doubtless they are," replied Emma.

The question was soon set at rest; for suddenly, at a word of command being given by some one, the whole of the cavalcade stopped, and Seth, with his wife, and their children, came towards the chaise in which Emma was sitting. They all knelt upon the road, and stretching forth their arms towards her, they said something in their own peculiar language or dialect; and then, without waiting for any words from her, they joined their friends, and at another word of command the cavalcade again proceeded onwards.

"They are, in truth," said the doctor, "a singular people; but it is time for us to be off, so now give your mother an adieu, and then away we will go. Recollect your journey is a long one, and that this short distance, I can take you upon the road, is as nothing compared to the distance you have to proceed before you see Howaden, in Flintshire."

"Is it, indeed, so very far," said Emma.

"Yes. But you will find, no doubt, conveyance by waggons, and as Mr. Thomas knows how far you have got to go, he will not expect you soon. Come, Mrs. Lyon, don't impede Emma, for she must be off, now, at once, and really there is, I assure you, no time now for me to lose, I shall be wanted in Preston."

CHAPTER XV.

HOWADEN.—THE LIFE OF A DOMESTIC SLAVE.—THE BROKEN SPIRIT.

MRS. LYON hung upon the neck of Emma.

"My child," she said, "if you can leave me, I cannot leave you. No, no, Emma, you and I are alone in the world, now. Your poor father is laid low in his grave, and everything I see and everything I hear in the village would now put me in mind of him. The cottage has already become hateful to me.

The very ticking of the old clock, and the look of the familiar things in the kitchen drive me mad. I cannot—I cannot, my child, remain any longer at Preston. We two are alone in the world, and where you go I must now go."

Emma was certainly totally unprepared for this strange burst of feeling from her mother, and she looked all the astonishment that she felt upon the occasion; and Doctor Lukin, too, was rather amazed, not that Mrs. Lyon should have those natural enough feelings, but that they should only then, at the last moment, as it were, manifest themselves.

"Do not look at me, my child," continued the mother, "in such a way as though you wished to say nay to my words. Do not, I implore you; I cannot stay at Preston, I meant to follow you to night, and to walk all the way, for as it is, I will live near you, and with a mother to come to appeal to for advice and aid, you will be more happy."

"There can be no doubt of that," said the

doctor, " and if you, Mrs. Lyon, choose to settle in Howaden, I do not see anything that can be said against it."

" Ah, Heaven bless you, Mr. Lukin, for those words."

" And do you think, mother," said Emma, " that I could do otherwise than joy to see you always by me. Oh! why did you not say that you would leave Preston before; I thought how few charms it would continue to have for you when I and poor father would both be gone; but I did not like to ask you to leave the old house you had been in so many, many years."

" It is no longer the same home that it was to me my child."

" In truth, mother, it is not; and the little garden which we all loved so much—that, too, is gone; for the despoiler has left behind him but few traces of its former beauty."

" All is changed," said Mrs. Lyon, bursting into tears. " Yes, all is changed, and the happy old times will come back no more."

" But there may be happy new ones," said the doctor. " What is that bundle you have with you, Mrs. Lyon? Is it for Emma to take with her?"

" No, no—she has her things," sobbed Mrs. Lyon, " but—but the truth is, I did not intend to go back to the cottage at all, but to follow Emma on foot as best I might, and these are the only few things I should be unwilling to part with that were in the cottage. I have left a letter on the table. It is addressed to you, sir, and it begs that you will let some one have, for what they may please to give, all the furniture that the cottage contains, and send the money to Emma at Hawaden. I thought to do all this in the way, I say, but my feelings have overcome me, and I have now told all."

" And much better is it, Mrs. Lyon, that you should so tell all. I am quite convinced that you would never be happy in Preston again in such a lonely condition as you would be reduced to; and as you have made all your arrangements to accompany Emma, get into the chaise at once, and do so. I daresay for once in a way, as Emma is not very big, and I am not the fattest of mortals, we can make room for you easily."

" Yes, mother," cried Emma; " you don't know what a weight it has taken off my mind to have you with me."

Poor Mrs. Lyon was so delighted to hear what the doctor and Emma said, that her countenance was expressive of the first gleam of joy it had worn since the arrest of her husband. She did not need to be asked twice to get into the doctor's chaise, which, to tell the honest truth, was not very well adapted to hold three persons; but it is wonderful how well people can pack themselves together where they have a mind so to do, and so somehow or another they all found themselves seated.

" Now," said the doctor, " I can take you no further than to where you will meet the waggon that goes to Clitheroe, and so you will reach the place comfortably enough; and after that, you must make your further progress as comfortably as you can towards the place of your destination."

The doctor's nag stepped out, notwithstanding its additional burthen, and the fresh morning air, although rather cold, as might naturally enough be expected at that season of the year, was nevertheless specially fine and invigorating. Half-an-hour's drive brought them to a high road, where the waggon for Clitheroe was sure to put up at a little inn called the Travellers, and there the worthy doctor drew up, and Emma and her mother alighted. They were duly informed by the landlady of the inn, in answer to their enquiries, that the waggon had not come up, but was momentarily expected; and then the doctor, after shaking hands with them both, and ascertaining that Mrs. Lyon had enough money to pay all the expenses of the journey, left them.

It was strange what a pang his departure gave to Emma. She was further from home than she had been for years, and notwithstanding the presence of her mother, a great feeling of insecurity and lonliness crept over her. It was quite a relief when the waggon came up, and there was something like a sense of bustle and animation in getting into it. A bargain was soon struck with its driver to take Mrs. Lyon and Emma to Clitheroe; and he informed them that they would find plenty of accommodation in similar conveyances to carry them on their journey, until they came to the water, which they would have to cross.

Just as Emma was getting into the waggon, two gentlemen on horseback rode up to the inn door, to bait their steeds for a few moments; and Emma heard one say to the other—

" By Jove! there is a rustic Venus for you! Did you ever see a prettier girl than that is who is now getting into the waggon? She is a perfect paragon!"

" Handsome decidedly," cried the other.

" Handsome do you say?—she is more than handsome. I tell you what, I have half a mind——"

The rest of this sentence was lost in a whisper; and then a laughing conference ensued between the two gentlemen, the subject matter of which was a mystery to all but to themselves. Emma had felt the blood tingling in her cheeks, while she heard such remarks made concerning her. That she was pretty, her looking-glass, as well as the opinion of the villagers of Preston, had made her fully aware; but this was the first time that she was fully aware of how perfect strangers were likely to be affected by her charms. It was doubtful if she were more pleased than displeased at the little occurrence. She looked in her mother's face to see if she had heard what had passed; but the good woman seemed quite unconscious of anything of the sort.

In five minutes more, the waggon, with its rather motley assemblage of personages, was in motion. The bells at the heads of the horses kept up a jingling noise, that, after awhile, the ears got so accustomed to it that it was completely forgotten, and so Emma might be said to be fairly launched into the great world to seek her fortune.

The personages in the waggon consisted of several women and some men and children, most of whom seemed, from the heavy monotonous movement of the machine, to be half asleep. They were none of them deserving of particular notice; and Emma, after a conversation with her mother for a few moments, about the cottage and all that they were so familiar with in the village of Preston, which it was doubtful if they should ever again see, propped herself up with the straw in the waggon as well as she could, and began herself to experience that sensation of drowsiness which such a mode of travelling was sure to engender.

She had dropped into a light sleep, which the rumble of the wheels, nor the noise of the bells at the horses' heads, could not disturb; but which the sudden cessation of those sounds at once put an end to.

The waggon had stopped.

"We want a lift," cried a voice. "We are tired of walking, and will pay you your charge for a lift on to the next place you stop at."

"Sartinly, gentlemen," said the waggoner, "proud to have you in the vehicle, gentlemen; and, if so be as you is going on as far as Clitheroe, you won't get there nigh so comfortable, though I says it as perhaps shouldn't, any way as in my waggon."

"Not a doubt of it," said the voice again; and then there got into the waggon the two identical gentlemen that Emma had seen on horseback at the door of the inn, and who had bestowed such praise upon her beauty. That they had left their horses somewhere, and had come after the waggon solely upon her account, was the idea that at once took possession of Emma; nor was she wrong in such a conjecture, for such was the precise fact.

The one who had spoken to the waggoner was the same one who had passed such encomiums upon her beauty. She knew him perfectly well by his voice again; and of the two, he certainly was by far the most vivacious; although from the slight glance that Emma got of them, before the waggoner started from the "Travellers," she thought that the other was decidedly the handsomer of the two.

By the glance they both cast round them when they got into the waggon; and the satisfied look that they both wore when they saw her, she was yet more convinced that it was entirely to her presence that the waggoner owed his two unusual customers. The dress and appearance of these persons proclaimed them to be moving in a very different sphere of life to the usual travellers by such a humble conveyance; and their appearance exited looks of great surprise among the people in the waggon.

The younger one of the two gentlemen.

That is to say the younger in aspect and manner, for there could not have been much difference between them as to age, being both under five and twenty, at once made his way to the part of the waggon where Emma was seated, and pushed himself into a place by her side. This was the one who had spoken to the waggoner. His companion took a plac where he happened to see a vacancy.

The corner in which Emma and her mother sat, was the darkest in the whole waggon, being the furthest removed from the door or entrance, so that those who had taken up a position near the entrance, could only distinctly see what was taking place at the further end of the vehicle; and Emma soon found that the audacity of the young gentleman was fully equal to taking any advantage of any circumstance that was favourable to a manifestation of his admiration of her charms. He had not been seated by her five minutes, when he slily took hold of her hand. She drew it away quickly, but that did not abash him for he spoke to her at once.

"I hope, miss," he said in a low tone, "that you will have a pleasant journey."

To this Emma made no reply; but he added almost immediately. "My friend and I have been travelling over the country in search of the picturesque and the beautiful. Yesterday we found much of the picturesque, but to day we have found more of the beautiful than we ever yet beheld."

"Sir," said Mrs. Lyon, who only heard the word beautiful, and thought that it was more directly applied to Emma than it had been, in the well wrapped up compliment that had been paid her.

"Madam," said the young gentleman.

"I thought you spoke to my daughter, sir."

"Certainly, Madam. I hope you are quite well."

Mrs Lyon did not know exactly whether the occasion called for any exhibition of anger or not, so she was silent, but she resolved to keep her ears open to what the young spark might say to Emma; and she blessed her stars heartily that she had accompanied her on her journey, almost for the first time; for Mrs. Lyon began to consider what a perilous possession that beauty of Emma's was, and into what snares and pitfalls it might lead her. The good woman soon became so completely immersed in such speculation, that the young gentleman had a better oportunity than ever of speaking to Emma; and in the same low tone that he had before spoken in—a tone that had quite a friendly and confidential-like sound about it, continued—

"Nothing can be further from my wish than to appear to you curious or impertinent, but permit me to ask you who you are, where you come from, and where you are going to, and what you are going to do when you get there?"

Emma was so much amused at the cool effrontery of this mode of questioning, that she replied to it by saying—

"For a person who does not wish to be

either curious or impertinent, you certainly, sir, ask some extraordinary questions."

"Ah! what a sweet voice," said the stranger. "Pray speak again, that I may have the pleasure of saying that I heard finer music in Lancashire than in Italy. Pray speak again, my dear!"

CHAPTER XVI.

EMMA ENCOUNTERS SOME DANGER AT AN INN.—A NIGHT ADVENTURE.

EMMA was silent. The tone of flattery and adulation in which these last words were spoken, was too new to her not to be rather revolting to her former taste. She was not yet sufficiently used to the world to have got up a spurious appetite for compliments.

"I hope I have not offended you," said the young gentleman.

"No—no—but—"

"But what? Say what you please to me. I give you free leave to be as unkind as you like in words.

"I would rather not have anything more to say to you; and I would rather that you would sit somewhere else in the waggon than by me."

"Then you don't like me? Only say that you don't like me, and I am off in a moment. Say the words, and away I go."

Emma hesitated for a moment, and then she said, "I don't like you."

"Very good," said the young gentleman, "that's quite sufficient. Mind, I don't believe it a bit; but that is not the question. I said I would go, and go I will. Herbert, my boy?"

"Yes, Charles," said the other gentleman.

"Will you change places with me?"

"Certainly, with pleasure."

The change was rapidly effected, and to her chagrin, Emma found the other gentleman squeezed into the little place close beside her and her mother. But, at all events, she was rid of the talkative and certainly impudent younger one, and she did not expect for a moment that this quiet looking young man would venture to say one word to her.

Emma was very much mistaken.

In such a whisper that it was impossible it could reach the ears of any one, but herself, he spoke to her.

"My charming girl," he said, "I hope you have sufficiently repulsed my friend, that he will not dare, again, to raise his eyes to your lovely face. From the first moment that I beheld you I loved you, and although I am of a quiet, retired disposition, and rather timid in the expression of my sentiments, and decidedly object to strong measures, or any out-of-the-way proceedings, if you will only condescend to give me a little encouragement I will upset the waggon, and run off with you in spite of all the world."

"You are too modest, sir," said Emma.

"Ah! How, dear one?'

"You deprecate your own abilities."

"Indeed, do I, my rose of Lancashire."

"Yes, sir, your friend has a tolerable amount of assurance, but you certainly throw him completely into the shade; I only hope, that like him, you will be gentleman enough to take a dismissal."

"But you wont dismiss me. You cannot."

"Can I not?"

"Certainly not; how is it possible? Only look at me, I am one of the modestest fellows the sun ever shone upon; the sunlight of your eyes, I mean; and so I can truly say that being so decidedly good-looking as I am, I don't see how you can dismiss me."

"Really, sir, if to have a good opinion of oneself is to be a happy mortal, you must be at the height of felicity. Your friend, when I told him to go, went."

"And I, by our agreement, for we made one concerning you, on honour, and I shall be obliged to go likewise, if you say you don't like me, and bid me go."

No one could possibly help being amused at this odd agreement which had been entered into by Emma's two admirers, and she had great difficulty to keep herself from laughing; but knowing that the eyes of her unfortunate lover were upon her, she controlled the impulse, and with as much coldness as she could assume, she said,—

"Go, sir, I do not like you."

"Very good," he said; "you will bitterly repent of this when I am gone; for you certainly will not meet with many like me in this world. However, as you tell me to go —go, I will."

He rose on the instant, and cried out to the other one,—

"Charles, I think we will get out of this waggon."

"As you please, Herbert," said Charles.

In a moment, without troubling the waggoner to stop his team, they sprang out of the vehicle, and having paid him munificently, a fact which might be sufficiently assumed from the profusion of thanks which he returned to them, they walked arm in arm along the road again in the direction from which the waggon had come.

"My dear," said Mrs. Lyon, "what did they say to you?"

"Nothing particular, mother."

"But they said something."

"Yes, mother, you may conclude that they did not call me ugly."

"Ah, my child—my child, that was what I feared."

"Why, surely mother, you would not wish me to be called ugly, or to be so in reality?"

"Yes, but I would; I only wish you had not such a pretty face; but it can't be helped, now."

Emma might have asked her mother in relation to that, and now at what time it could have been helped, but she said nothing, for the interior of a waggon was not a very excellent place for a family discussion of that character. Nothing of any moment occurred now upon the road, and Clithroe was fairly reached at length, after about six hours travelling, which upon the whole, was considered very quick work, indeed. There the mother and daughter partook of some simple refreshments, and hearing that from an Innyard in the town, another waggon would, in the course of an hour, go on to Chorley, they became anxious to secure places in it, as at Chorley they could pass the night as well as at Clithroe, and it would be so much further on their way. They soon came to an agreement with the waggoner, and being, with the exception of a man and woman, the only passengers, they had plenty of room, and were on the road to Chorley by two o'clock in the day.

They hoped to reach it by six or half past, at the latest, as the waggoner praised himself and his horses mightily for the speed they intended to make.

The whole distance from Clithroe to Chorley was traversed without incident or accident of any importance; but darkness had been upon the face of the land for more than an hour before they reached their destination. At the Inn in Chorley, where the waggon was put up, Mrs. Lyon and Emma engaged a bed; but when they came to look at it, it was nothing more than the framework of an old couch, with a few bed-clothes upon it, and besides, it was in a room at the top of the house, the sloping roof of which did not permit any one to stand upright.

"Can we have nothing better than this to sleep upon?" said Mrs. Lyon, with a look of disappointment.

"No," replied the landlady: "our only two best beds are taken, but your daughter can have a shake down by the kitchen fire for the night, while you sleep here, for two, of course, it won't hold."

"No," said Mrs. Lyon, "I will lie by the kitchen fire, since some one must, and you, Emma, can sleep here."

This was finally arranged, and after it was all settled, the landlady grew wonderfully gracious, and asked them both to a dish of tea, during the consumption of which, it was difficult to avoid telling her who and what they were, and that they were going to Hawarden to live permanently, if the situation that Emma had been recommended to should be found to suit her well enough to induce her to stay in it.

All this the landlady listened to as she would to any ordinary gossip; and so, at about nine o'clock, Emma being really fatigued by her journey, she was shown to her little attic-room by the landlady, who burst out into quite an eulogium upon the bed, which she declared was at the very least a thousand times better than it looked.

"Fatigue," said Emma, "will, no doubt, make me sleep well."

"Ah, to be sure, my dear," said the woman, "and what's more, you may sleep safely here, for there isn't so much as an impudent mouse in this house, to disturb any one in the night."

About half an inch of candle was left to Emma, by the fading light of which she had to undress and get into bed; but before she did so, she fastened the door, as well as she was able, with a miserable old rusty bolt that was on the inside, and which certainly could not be a very efficient protection. But then, what had she to fear?

Had not the landlady told her what a safe house it was? and surely she ought to know; and yet that was the first night that Emma had slept from home—home she felt that she should always call that little cottage at Preston, home, let her be where she might. Could she ever forget the little garden, any particular flower in which she could have gone to with unerring accuracy, on the darkest night than could be conceived? Ah, no—no—no.

In such thoughts and reflections as these, Emma, upon whom the slow monotonous movement of the waggon had had a most wearying effect, soon fell fast asleep, and for her the world, with all its joys, and all its sorrows—all its hopes—its despairs, and its aspirations, was forgotten.

*　　*　　*　　*

How long she had slept she had not the smallest idea, but a something—she knew not what—suddenly aroused her. It must have been some noise, for the dim echo of it seemed to linger on her ears after she was awake. The room was most profoundly dark.

Emma listened intently. The beating of her heart—for she had awoke in a fright from the sound, whatever it was—became perfectly fearful for a few seconds; but as she heard nothing, and began to reason herself out of her fears, that subsided, she began very much to blame herself for her childish apprehensions.

"I will compose myself to sleep again," she said, in a low tone. "Yes, I will compose myself to sleep again, and all will be well."

She resolutely closed her eyes with this intention; but scarcely had she done so, when a low whispering voice in the room—yes, she felt certain that it was in the room—pronounced her name.

"Emma!" it said.

Had a thunderbolt fallen through the roof, it could not have had a greater effect upon the young girl. She started wide awake with a cry of surprise and fright.

"Who is that?—who is that?" she said.

"Hush! hush! hush!" said the voice.

Emma was silent from very apprehension. She held her hand clasped over her heart to still, by pressure, if that might be done, its wild tumultuous beating; and then she heard the voice proceed in the same whispering tones, saying—

"Emma, Emma, do not allow any needless alarm to get the better of your judgment. It is a friend who now speaks to you."

"Who are you?" she gasped. "Who are you? Oh! tell me who and what you really are!"

"Hush! hush! You will alarm the house, and what I have to say is only for your private ear. Do not doubt for a moment but that it is a friend who now addresses you."

"I will doubt—I must doubt," said Emma, "if I do not know who you are."

"You will soon learn, I say again, that I am a friend. Who but a sincere friend would address you in such a way as this? You are going, Emma, to embrace a hard course of life. You are going to be a domestic slave, possibly, to a tyrant who may return you nothing but abuse and hard treatment for all that you may do. You are going to sell yourself for the best part of your life to a state of servitude and degradation, and you who are so fair too."

"I will not listen to this," said Emma.

"Hush! hush! Only a moment. There is one in the world who loves you tenderly. He has the means of lifting you completely out of your present low state—of providing amply for your mother, and all that he asks in return is your gratitude."

"My gratitude?"

"Yes. That is all; and such dear companionship with him as will sufficiently show that gratitude."

"Begone!" said Emma. "I know your voice, now!"

"Indeed!"

"Yes; you are one of the two persons who came into the waggon during its journey. Begone, I say! Oh! how was it that you got into this chamber? I will call for help!"

"Nay; pause a moment. I am, indeed, one of those two young men who got into that waggon purposely to speak to you; but surely there was nothing in our manner or appearance at that time, to induce you to doubt the deep sincerity of what I now utter to you. I am he who is called Charles."

"Yes, I know your voice. Mother!—mother!"

"Confound it! do you want to raise the whole house, and ruin your reputation for ever by a lot of people—God only knows who—coming here and finding me in your bed-room?"

"I do not care! The shame be yours, not mine!"

Emma sprang from her bed, and made towards the door of the little chamber—that door which had proved no protection.

CHAPTER XVII.

A DISTURBANCE AT THE INN.—EMMA'S RESOLUTION.

EMMA would have reached the door in three steps across the floor of that small apartment, but she was interrupted by the person who had intruded himself into her chamber. He clasped her in his arms, and began covering her face with kisses, so that she could hardly cry for help: but she did manage, at intervals, to utter two such piercing shrieks, that if any one in the house were not awakened, they must be sleepers of a very uncommon character, indeed.

"D—n it!" said the young man; "who would have thought you intended to make half this fuss? You are as coy and skittish as a young colt! Hold your noise, do!"

Emma only screamed the louder; and then there was heard a tramping of feet upon the stairs, and a loud knocking took place against the door of the room. Emma was astonished to find that it was not open; and as her assailant had let her go, she flew towards it, and drew back the bolt, when it flying open, a motley group of persons appeared, bearing lights of all kinds and descriptions. Mrs. Lyon disentangled herself from the throng, and rushed into the room, crying—

"My child! my child! what has happened?"

One glance round the little attic told Emma that the intruder was gone; but how he had contrived to disappear was a complete mystery to her. She stood bewildered as the many lights flashed in her eyes. The landlady suddenly arrived in the room, and in a loud voice, began speaking:—

"Marry-come-up, and what's all this about?" she said. Can't one have a quiet night's rest, in one's own freehold house too, but one is to be woke up as if a thousand town bulls had broken loose? Dear me! what fine airs has somebody been giving themselves, I wonder?"

"Mother," said Emma, "help me with my clothes. We will leave this house at once."

"Leave it, my dear! Why—why, what has happened?"

"Some one has been in this room. I did not cry out, for the love of destroying my own or any one elses rest. But some one has been here, mother; and I will not stay.'

"Hoity toity!" cried the landlady; "a pretty joke, indeed. You have had a dream, my good girl, that's all; a dream, owing to sleeping in a stage cart."

"And a devilish strange bed it is too," cried a voice at the door.

"Now, Mr. Smithson," screamed the landlady, "nobody wants you to interfere. You go and mind your tadpoles, and your fishing, and all that sort of rubbish that you take such a delight in. I say the girl has had a dream: and so, poor young thing, she is not to be blamed, of course not. I will go down to the bar and get her a cup of my cherry cordial. Go to bed, my dear, again. Why, Lord love you, it's only one o'clock in the morning yet!"

"It was no dream," said Emma.

"No dream!" said the landlady, "no dream! How dare anybody say that anybody else has not been in the bed-room of nobody, in my house? Who dare say so?"

"Why, Mrs. Brown," said Smithson, "it would be rather difficult to reply to so complicated a question."

"And who asked you, with your gentles, and grubs, and worms, and frogs' hind-legs, and rubbish, to reply?"

"All I have got to say is," enjoined Mr.

Smithson, "that as I am staying at this Inn, I will do my best to protect any female who, by night or by day, calls for help. If this young girl says that some one has been in her room, I advise her to leave it, and the house too. She is the best judge as to whether she only dreamt it or not."

"And well, sir," said the landlady, "since you must take up the cudgels, you coughing, earth-worm looking individual, pray how do you account for the young woman's door being bolted on the inside, when you got to it first, as I believe you did."

"How do I account for that?"

EMMA DEFENDING HERSELF.

"Yes, you grub."

"Why, suppose that the intruder escaped as he got in, by the little square trap in the ceiling, which you may all see, is open now."

Everybody glanced up to the ceiling, and there they saw that same square trap door was staring open, and the ceiling was so low, that any man with ordinary agility could draw himself up through it, and so get away over the house top and in at the windows that opened upon a little balcony that ran round two sides of the building.— But whoever had made his way there, into the bed-room of Emma, must have been perfectly well acquainted with the route that way.

The landlady was thoroughly astounded at this unexpected visitation, for she had not happened to cast her glance upward, that for some few moments she had not a word to say, which was an exceedingly rare thing with her.

"Mother, I will leave this house," said Emma.

"And the best thing you can do, too," said Mr. Smithson. There's the Crown over the way, and I will go and knock up the landlord, who is a decent enough man, and get him to provide accommodation for you; and, as for myself, I shall pack up what this good woman calls my tadpoles, and go to the Crown, myself."

"Murder!" cried the landlady. "Am I to be enunciated only because a trap door is open."

"Serves you right," said Smithson.— "Don't you be long, my dear, in coming over to the Crown, and there you and your mother will have a welcome."

"A welcome, at the Crown!" said the landlady, clapping her hands together, with a blow that sounded like the discharge of a pistol. "A welcome, at the Crown! Oh, good gracious. Is it from you, Mr. Smithson, with your beautiful fishing line, and your fine, manly sport, that I hear such words?"

"Perhaps you'd like a tadpole," said Smithson, as he hastily descended the stairs to get what of his things together were in the house, and repair with them to the Crown.

The landlady took to tears, but Emma was resolute, and would not be stayed; so that she and her mother, in the course of a quarter of an hour, found themselves in the keen night air, at nearly two o'clock in the morning, in the High-street of Chorley.

Mr. Smithson, however, was as good as his word. He did procure them ample accommodation at the Crown; and the mother and daughter slept together in a bed wherein they could, indeed, find repose, after all their fatigue, and the disturbance of the night at the opposite Inn.

It was quite by accident that Emma peeped from her window at an early hour in the morning, and saw a couple of horses at the door of the Inn, where she had been so disturbed; in a moment the two within, one of whom had undoubtedly made the audacious entrance into her bed-room, came out of the Inn, and mounted their steeds. Emma saw them give money to the landlady, and then, with rather rueful countenances, for they had certainly made a failure of the whole affair, they rode off, at a great pace, down the little High-street, and were soon out of both sight and hearing of her whom they would fain have made the victim of their wild and lawless passions.

Emma would not disturb her mother, who was sleeping, to tell her of the departure of the two gallants; but she lay by the

side of her parent, revolving in her mind the occurrences of the last twenty-four hours, and thinking that there had been as much adventure compressed into that brief space of time as had occupied a good half-dozen years of her former life.

She thought of the village, too, and of the cottage, and of poor Edwin Lee, who loved her so dearly, and she thought of Horatio Nelson, who had rescued her from the fire, and who had promised not to forget her.

"I shall never forget him," she said. "No; in all situations, and under all circumstances, his image will cling to my heart. Heaven bless him, and send him prosperity and honour!"

With this, Emma fell asleep for another hour or so; and when she awoke again, she found that her mother was up, and that it was then broad daylight.

They easily found conveyance from Chorley, and then proceeded without any material accident to their journey's end, which, however, they did not reach until the evening of the next day. When they reached Hawarden, it had anything but an inviting appearance to them, for a misty thick rain was falling fast, and everything was sloppy and disagreeable. Of course, the first object was to find out the house of Mr. Thomas, to whom Emma had the letter of introduction from Doctor Lukin. This they found there was no great difficulty in doing—for Mr. Thomas seemed to be as well known as the parish pump, although certainly not one half so much esteemed.

"That's the old rascal's house," said one person to whom they applied; "that one with the green door there, and the little brass knocker. You will be sure to find the old villain at home now."

This was not a very promising beginning; but yet they had no choice, and accordingly they reached the door of Mr. Thomas's house, and made a timid appeal to the little brass knocker, which produced a miserable-looking girl, with an apron and sleeves of coarse canvas on, as though she had been doing the dirty work of the whole parish.

"Is Mr. Thomas at home?" said Emma.

"Oh, ah, rather!" said the girl. "Don't ye hear 'em?"

She gave a comical kind of jerk with her thumb over her right shoulder as she spoke; and then Emma heard a loud howl, and then a series of cries and shouts that filled the whole house with a hideous clamour.

"What is the meaning of that?" said Emma.

"Oh, he's only a whacking on 'em He always does when he's at home, and they sngs out a good un they does.'

"And who are they?"

"The young 'uns; missus has got what she calls the *wapons*, so she dose'nt interfere, and he whacks 'em like sacks—he does— don't ye hear 'um again."

Emma and her mother did hear them again,

for the shouts and outcries from the upper part of the house became more terrific; and then from the upper part of the stairs down rolled no less than five children, of different sorts and sizes, pursued by a short stout man, with a very shining bald head, whose face was blue with passion, and who had in his hand a riding switch.

"Curse you all!" he cried. "May the devil fly away with me if I don't be the death of some of you! Only let me catch you! Fire and fury! am I to be annoyed morning, noon, and night, by brats?"

"Somebody wants to see you," said the girl, with the apron and sleeves.

"What the devil do I care? I don't want to see anybody. The deuce take all the world! Brimstone and ashes! am I to be the victim that everybody annoys?"

"Ah!" said the girl, "there you go agin. You'll be laid up agin as sure as eggs is eggs, and no mistake! Lor! I would'nt have your temper, master, for the whole of Hawarden, that I would'nt. What a man you is."

"Si—lence!"

"Well, I'm sure! there's nobody a saying a word but yourself, master. Nobody can speak but you when you takes it into your head. Oh, what a face! You'll be busting the biler—I mean the blood-wessel, as they talks about, if you don't mind."

"Si—lence!"

"Sir," said Emma, "I have a letter for you from Doctor Lukin, at Preston."

Doctor Lukin? D—n Doctor Lukin! But don't stand there staring at me. Give me the letter directly. That will do. Sit down. Sit down, I say!"

"There are no seats," said Emma.

"Well, what's that to me? Am I to be crossed and wrangled with, and contradicted continually, because I don't choose to drag the chairs out of my drawing-room, or my dining-room, and stand them in a row in the hall, eh? Am I to be bullied and blackguarded in my own house, eh?"

Emma was utterly at a loss to know how to reply to such an unreasonable man as Mr. Thomas, and she, in her own mind, bitterly regretted leaving Preston to become the servant, in any shape, of such a being. Poor Mrs. Lyon trembled from head to foot, and durst hardly look at him. He nevertheless read the letter that had been sent to him by Doctor Lukin, and then in a voice of fury, he cried—

"Good God! what the deuce—the devil have I to do with the hiring of nursery maids, or any maids at all? What do the people write to me for? Don't I keep a wife to do all these odd jobs? Is one to keep a d—d great dog, half as big as a house, and then bark oneself—bow! wow! wow! eh? That's what I ask."

This was so truly ridiculous that Emma had the greatest difficulty to keep from laughing in his face.

"Sir," she said; "I will willingly speak to Mrs. Thomas, if you will have the goodness to permit me so to do."

"I permit you—I permit you! Good gracious! Here's a girl, who after goading me to death, and flying in my face like a gad fly, says she is willing to speak to Mrs. Thomas, if I will let her. As if she could not go up stairs to the first floor at once, and do so. Good merciful devils and gracious providence. Sticks and blood, who are you?"

"I am the mother, sir, of the young person recommended to you, by Doctor Lukin," said Mrs. Lyon, trembling all over like a piece of blanc-mange.

"Oh, you are the mother, are you?"

"Yes, sir."

"Well, what in the name of all the powers is that to me. If you are ten thousand mothers, I repeat, what the duce is that to me? Eh? Eh? Eh? I wonder what people see in me, that they torment me day and night, in this horrible way?"

CHAPTER XVIII.

SHOWS WHAT SORT OF A SITUATION EMMA HAD IN HAWARDEN.

NEITHER Emma nor her mother could help looking at Mr. Thomas with indescribable surprise. He certainly, to use the words of an erratic nobleman of the present day, was one of the most "cross individuals" that it would be possible to meet with. As, however, he had give Emma, at all events, an implicit permission to go up stairs and seek Mrs. Thomas, she thought she had better avail herself of it, particularly as Mr. Thomas suddenly bounced into a room that opened from the hall, and closed the door behind him with a vehemence and a bang that shook the whole house.

"My dear," said Mrs. Lyon, "I am afraid this will not be a comfortable place for you."

"I will hope, mother," said Emma, "that I have seen now the worst of it."

"Ah, my dear, I am afraid not. This Mr. Thomas is a man who would drive me out of my mind in a week."

"Well, mother, do you wait here while I go and speak to Mrs. Thomas; and if the lady be not more gentle than the gentleman, I shall, indeed, think with you, that it will not suit me, and I shall try my fortune elsewhere."

"And offend Doctor Lukin, perhaps?"

"Oh, no, Doctor Lukin is, I am sure, by far too just to wish me to remain where I should be unhappy. I am quite convinced, mother, he can have no sort of notion of what sort of man this Mr. Thomas is, or he would never have recommended me here; but perhaps the lady will make amends."

With this Emma tripped gently up the stairs and tapped at the first door that faced her on the landing-place.

There was no answer returned to this modest appeal upon the panel of the door, so after waiting a short, but a reasonable time,

Emma knocked again somewhat louder, and this time she heard a faint voice cry—"Come in."

She opened the door and found herself in a tolerably handsomly got-up drawing-room. On a couch, was half reclining, a lady in that slip-shod sort of costume which lazy people affect from morning until night, and which is composed of a great number of white garments, with an infinity of frills and little bits of lace-edging here and there. The lady was holding to her nose a smelling bottle, and looked the very picture of languor and fatigue from doing nothing at all.

As for taking the vast trouble and undergoing the serious fatigue of saying "who are you," to Emma, that was completely out of the question. She only turned her pale grey eyes upon her, and looked a faint inquiry, so that Emma was compelled to take the indicative, and introduce herself.

"I hope, madam," she said, "I have the pleasure of seeing Mrs. Thomas."

"Oh, yes, certainly. Ah, dear me."

"I have been recommended by Doctor Lukin to a situation, as Mr. Thomas has my letter, and told me I should find you here."

"Oh dear !"

"Madam."

"Oh dear, oh dear. Really, now, this is too bad of Thomas. He not only lets me have no peace in this world with his nasty, horrid temper, and the noises he makes in the house, but he nearly lays me up by making me go through the fatigue of having a servant. This is too—too bad. I am a suffering woman. I am, indeed. Oh, dear, I am."

Mrs. Thomas was so much affected by her sufferings that she was compelled to hold her handkerchief for a few moments to her eyes, and then to have vigorous resource to the smelling-bottle in order to recover her usual equanimity, if she usually had any equanimity at all.

Emma felt completely puzzled what to say or do in such an emergency ; but as the lady did not speak, she continued, after rather a prolonged silence, to say—

"Madam, do you think that I shall be able to suit you in the capacity which you require a person ? I will do my best to give you satisfaction, madam."

"Oh dear, oh dear. How can I take upon myself to say that you will suit ? Do I look like a conjurer, I should like to know; or a wizard, or I don't know what ? Six pound per annum, and find your own tea and sugar. Dear me, dear me, what a world this is. There's nothing in it but extortion. No followers allowed, and no holidays or any future pretence. Pleasure—pleasure—pleasure ! that's all people think of now a days."

What possible connexion, then, could be between the different sentences of Mrs. Thomas's speech ? Emma might truly have said that she was not conjurer enough to find out, but still amid the loop of disjointed sentences she could gather that her wages were to be six pound per annum, out of which she was to provide herself with tea and sugar if she should choose to require those luxuries, and that no followers nor holidays were allowed.

"I have no one in this place, madam," she said, "but my mother. She, of course, I should wish to see at times."

"Your mother. Oh dear—oh dear—what people the lower classes are, dear me, dear me. I suppose your prejudices in that particular must be given way to at times."

"Thank you, madam."

"You will—you will. Ah, me! You will go to the girl below, who will show you the dreadful children and everything else. I believe I shall have to retire to bed now, for, of course, after this, I am by far too much exhausted to keep up any longer. Can you make and alter dresses, and dress hair, and make pomatum, and knit and mend lace ? Oh, dear."

"Neither, madam."

"Dear me—dear me ! What could that Doctor Thingamy mean by sending such a handless creature here? Why there are only six children, and what can you find to occupy your time in this house, I should like to know? Well, well, don't say anything. I cannot really argue. Oh, mother, with you, I am exhausted, and must return to bed."

The lady let herself fall gently back upon the couch, and spread the handkerchief over her eyes, which Emma took as a sufficiently intelligible signal that the interview was over ; and so, finding that she was engaged, she went down stairs to the hall again, and told her mother so much.

"Then, my dear," said Mrs. Lyon, "I will go and find some humble lodging, in which I can remain until I can find something to do, which I daresay, in my humble way, I shall not be long in doing ; and let us hope that you will be more comfortable than things seem to promise. Bear with as much as you can, my child, and remember that this is your first place, and that, of course, things will seem very difficult to you to what they were at home."

"I will do my best, mother."

Poor Mrs. Lyon could not trust herself to say more ; but after kissing Emma, she left the house. Our heroine then made her way to the back of the house, where there was a large detached kitchen, close to the garden, and there she found the girl who had opened the door to her, and who was the servant of all work of the Thomas's.

"Mrs. Thomas sent me to you," said Emma. "I am engaged as nursery maid, I suppose I may call myself, for I am to have the care of the children, and she said that you would introduce me to them, and so on.'

"Did she ?" exclaimed the girl. "Oh, she's a harticle, she is, is missus. Has she gone to bed now, in what she calls a state of exhaustiwon ?"

"I think she is going."

"The deuce doubt her ! Well, if you can stand this place you is cast-iron, that's all."

"Is it uncomfortable?"

"*Unconformable?* Lor! it's everythink, it is. Don't you see as master is a wild beastes, and as missus is a—I don't know what, except it's a hyœnœ, or a crokindile; and as for the children. Oh, they is warments and fiends, they is."

"Bad behaved are they?"

"No. Oh, dear, no. They ain't behoved at all, they ain't. What a mercy it would be if they was all to go to glory some day; but they sticks to life, they does. Nothink kills 'em, not it. I wishes you joy, I does. As for master, you must give him as good as he gives you. It's the only way with him, I can tell you. And as for missus: the very best thing in the world is to say nothing to her, and to treat her contemptious. That's my advice. You can take it, or leave it, as you likes."

"I am much obliged to you for your advice; but in one respect, I am afraid I cannot follow it."

"As how?"

"As regards Mr. Thomas. I cannot reply to him in the way you recommend, although I can imagine that it might be the very best plan with such a man."

"Werry good. If you can't, why, you can't, and that's the long and short of it; but, perhaps he won t say things to you as he says 'em to me. The brats is in the garden, and if you'll only come with me, I'll shew 'em to you. The boys I calls 'wolves,' and the girls I calls 'Waspses.' Here they is. What's your name, though?"

"My name is Emma Lyon."

"Oh, Emma. Well, they calls me Sly."

"Sly?"

"Yes; that's my name. I was found in a basket at the door o' the workus, a matter o' fifteen years ago; and the *beetle* of the parish, as was the first person to see me, he says 'how sly she looks,' and from that time they called me Sly, and it stuck to me like pitch to a cat's back."

If Emma had been in a state of mind to be amused, this singular household would certainly have afforded to her ample food for laughter; but the circumstances of a serious character that had been mingled with her fate, so recently, as yet kept down a spirit of animation which was really natural to her. If Mr. and Mrs. Thomas, or either of them, fancied that in Emma Lyon they had got a poor, weak, submissive slave, they were much mistaken, indeed, for at the bottom of that young girl's heart there was a slumbering spirit, which only wanted the touch from outward circumstances to awaken to all its life and energy.

The introduction to the 'wolves' and the 'wasps,' as Sly called the boys and girls of the Thomas's family, was duly effected; and for the present, the only result was that the boys put their fingers into their mouths, and looked as stupid as boys usually do upon an introduction to any stranger; while the girls made whispered comments to each other upon the costume of the nursery maid.

It was a great point with Emma to get upon as good terms with the children as she possibly could; and she was so far in that respect successful, that before the day was quite gone she was deep in all their secrets, and began to fancy that even a sojourn at Mr. Thomas's might be endurable. But Emma had as yet had anything but sufficient experience of Mr. Thomas. He had left the house upon some business shortly after her arrival, and he did not come home until rather late. Sly sat up for him; and from the little room adjoining the nursery, which had been allotted to her use as a sleeping chamber, Emma heard the most violent altercation going on between those two worthies.

If any correct conclusion might be come to from the sound of the voices, Sly had certainly the best of the conflict, for her voice increased in shrill treble, while Mr. Thomas's decreased to a low bass growl. After awhile, Emma could hear him coming up the stairs, and as Sly slept in her own domain, the kitchen, a calm came over the household.

She heard the kind and gentle Thomas close his bed-room door with a bang that was enough to have awaked the whole street, and the six children all began to cry.

"Hush," said Emma, "it's only your father."

"Oh, is it pa?" said the eldest girl, from the next room. "Won't their be some jolly row soon?"

"And a bit of fun," said another.

"And we'll all get up and have a game with the pillows and bolsters," said a third.

"What do you mean?" said Emma.

"Oh, you'll see—you'll see!" was the only answer she could get from them; and then thinking that it was only the children's nonsense, and feeling very much inclined for sleep, she soon dropped off again to repose.

How long she had slept, Emma had not the least notion; for her repose had been deep and dreamless. No disturbing images had found a place in her imagination; and so she would have slept, no doubt, until the break of day, had she not been suddenly awakened by a noise, as singular as it was alarming.

A watchman's rattle was sprung with terrific vehemence within the house by some one.

CHAPTER XIX.

EMMA MEETS WITH AN ADVENTURE, AND THEN GIVES NOTICE TO QUIT.

EMMA started wide awake, and listened intently. The rattle went on at a prodigious rate, and she thought that, to be sure, the house must be either on fire or beset with burglars. She rushed from her bed in a moment, and began dressing herself with the most frantic haste.

Suddenly the rattle ceased, and then a loud, unearthly sort of voice, sounding as though it belonged to some giant, who was bellowing his words from afar off, cried—

"A flea! A flea! A flea!"

Then the rattle began again more vigorously than before ; and Emma, from the singularity of the announcement of " A flea!" began almost to doubt the evidence of her own senses ; but she still, with all the haste she could command, continued dressing herself ; and the children, she could hear, had risen, and were getting clamorous ; while, from the cries and tumult in their sleeping room, she could guess that the threatened game with the pillows and bolsters had begun.

The rattle ceased again, and again the deep preternatural voice shouted—

"A flea! A flea! A flea!"

"Good Heaven!" exclaimed Emma ;— "what can all this mean? Am I mad or am I asleep? or is this house haunted by some evil spirit? Oh! what will become of me now? If it be fire, I am lost, indeed ; for he who saved me once from the raging flames is not here to do so again He is far away. Yes, he is far away ; and if it be fire I shall perish!"

For the third time the voice, still awful and reverberating, shouted to her terrified ears

"A flea! A flea! A flea!"

All was then profoundly still, and Emma just rushed into the corridor into which her bed-room opened as she heard the loud bang of a door shutting. All was darkness and stillness now, for the children had had their game, and some of them whimpering from the blows they had received in the dark, crept to bed again. The mysterious rattle no longer sounded, and the awful voice that had proclaimed, or announced " A flea!" had ceased.

"Am I mad?" said Emma, " or is this real? and does it mean more than appears from it? Dare I sleep to-night again at the risk of being awakened by some dreadful noise similar to that which has only just now ceased?"

She waited upon the landing place for some moments, but the cold night air, that came up the staircase, made her shiver, and warned her that bed was the better place.— Yet, she did not like to retire again without making one effort to find out the meaning of the sounds she had heard, and as she thought she would find her way to the dormitory of Sly, and inquire of her, if such nocturnal disturbances were usual or explainable in that house.

Acting upon this idea, Emma crept carefully and noiselessly down the stairs, and so on, until she came to the kitchen, at the door of which she tapped, and was quickly answered by Sly, who said in her peculiar phraseology,

"Who is you?"

"It is I—Emma ; I have been awakened by a dreadful noise, and dare not go to rest again until I know what is the meaning of it. Can you tell me, Sly?"

"In course I can ; open the door and come in, I always sleeps on a latch only, I does.—

Come on ; there is nothing as I knows on to tumble over."

Emma was only too well pleased at this invitation of Sly's, and she, at once, entered the kitchen, when Sly added, " Well, you need never be afraid when you hear anything in the night. It's only master ; he's got a rattle, and a bell, and a speaking trumpet in his room ; and sometimes rings, and sometimes he gives us a little of the rattle, and then he always says something through the speaking trumpet. If he can't sleep himself, he takes care that nobody else shall. You see, to-night he pretended it was owing to a flea as he couldn't sleep ; so you see, he bawled it out in that way, to frighten everybody."

"But how very unreasonable to awaken every one in the house for such a pretence," said Emma.

"Oh, wery. You needn't mind him though ; you need never get up on his account. I'll speak to him in the morning about it, and let him know what's what."

After thanking Sly for the information which she had given to her, Emma retired to her own room again, thinking, as she went, that if her rest were to be continually disturbed in such a manner by Mr. Thomas, that the sooner she succeeded in providing herself with another place the better it would be for her. In this frame of mind she again sought repose, and as no further disturbance happened on that night, she soon fell again into a sleep, which lasted until the clamours of the children awoke her at an early hour in the morning.

After breakfast, Mrs. Thomas sent for her, and lying upon the sofa in the drawing-room, with a piece of gauze over her face, she said, in a faint voice,—

" Children well?"

" They are well, madam."

" Oh, very good. I shall, being of course, quite a slave to my children, make the same inquiry of you every morning, and you will, therefore, please to come to me, and answer it."

" Yes, madam. But I don't think they or I will be long well, if such disturbances take place in the night."

" Oh, dear! oh, dear! Now, you are going to attack my nerves. Good gracious, how can I help the disturbances? You should stop your ears with a quantity of cotton every night, as I do, and then you would not hear it at all. Oh, dear—oh, dear, what a dreadful fatigue."

" I doubt, madam, if any amount of cotton would save one from Mr. Thomas's annoyances."

" There—there. Oh, dear. Now there is nothing but wrangle jangle in the house."

Emma was not aware that Mr. Thomas was in the room adjoining, and had heard every word of this little dialogue, but she was made aware of it by his suddenly opening one of the folding doors, and rushing in with his features distorted by rage, and his eyes half starting from their sockets.

"And so," he cried, "you reptile—you wretch, I am to have my actions questioned by you. A million of devils, what do you mean by it, you wretched pauper? I ask you what do you mean by it, and how dare you say one word upon the subject? Confound you and all your race. Confound all the world. Curse everybody. You are a nice article to dictate to me the morning after your arrival here, you beggar—you slut—you troll!"

"Oh, dear—oh, dear!" cried Mrs. Thomas. "Child, hand me that hartshorn bottle. The blue one—oh, dear."

"You know perfectly well," roared Mr. Thomas, "and all the world knows perfectly well, that you brought the identical flea that would not let me sleep last night, all the way from Preston—d—n Preston—on purpose. You know you did, and you lay in your bed glorying and grinning at the idea of it, bite—bite—bite—biting me, and skipping over me, you did, you miserable pauper—you heartless, soulless wretch, you, you know you did."

Emma was terrified, as well she might be, at these terrific denunciations, accompanied too as they were by such violence of manner, that any one would have thought he must conclude by striking her; but Emma did not wait for the anger that was blazing away so fiercely to reach any higher point. She could not find courage at that moment to enter into any altercation with Mr. Thomas, and although she advice of Sly, she felt that she was not the person to carry it out, nor did she consider that she ought to humiliate herself so far as to enter into a wordy warfare with a man who could be so singularly abusive to a young, unprotected female. Controlling her feelings, then, as much as she was able, she retired from the drawing-room, and in the privacy of her own chamber she gave way to tears.

Not for long, however, was Emma permitted to be alone and to weep over her poor prospects. The six children—the wolves and the wasps—at once required attention, and with a broken spirit and tears in her eyes, she was compelled to turn her attention to her duties.

Mrs. Lyon called in the course of the day, to say that she had been fortunate beyond all her expectations, for she had not only got a kind of situation partly as servant and partly to assist in a shop, but she had been able to get a home for nothing by the promise of taking care of and keeping clean a little cottage of two rooms, that belonged to a family who occasionally came to it for the sake of its garden produce in the summer time, but who would now, that the winter was rapidly approaching, only now and then look in to see that all was right. All this was very felicitous, and Mrs. Lyon appeared so pleased, smiling too. for the first time since the father's death, that Emma had not the heart to tell her how wretched she was in her new place. All she said was that Mr. Thomas was a very bad temper; but Mrs.

Lyon on the day previous had seen quite enough of him to feel pretty well assured of that fact.

The story of the flea, Emma said nothing about.

"If, my dear," said the mother, "you can only for a time try to endure this situation, something better may turn up for you; but always bear in mind, my child, that until you can change for the better, you should put up with what you have got in this world."

Of course, Emma felt that no one who did not actually live in the same house with the Thomases, could know what there was to put up with; but she promised her mother that she would be patient and try to persevere in keeping her situation as long as it was possible so to do.

"I shall not feel pleased, mother," she said, "until I have seen your new cottage, and I must find time in the course of to-day to come to you. These people cannot be so barbarous as to deny me that poor gratification now and then."

"They will not, my dear. You may depend that they will not."

"Ah, mother, you don't know them so well as I do. The man is actually cruel and wicked, and the woman is indolently so. I do not know which is the worst, he who goes out of his way to make those about him unhappy, or she who is too much immersed in her own selfish mode of life to care about the happiness or the welfare of any one."

"Alas, my dear, the world is full of such people."

"Is it really, mother?"

"Yes, and the more you see of it the more you will be convinced that selfishness and passion are the two great rulers of the greatest number of people. Yes, my child, those are the twin demons who divide between them the care of this world."

"But all are not so. There is Doctor Lukin, and there is poor Edwin Lee, and there is the young man, who at the risk of his own life, rescued me from the blazing Grange. Ah, no. All are not selfish and full of rage."

"You are right enough, my child; there are many, many exceptions, but they are not as one to a million of others. See, however, if you can get leave to come to me this evening. It will be a great joy to have an hour's talk with you at my new home. Emma, you will be sure and come, if you can; and don't lose that little bit of paper that has the address upon it."

"I will be careful of it, mother; and you may expect me when the children are in bed, which is by eight o'clock, at the latest."

Emma did not, by any means, feel sure that she should get permission to go on this little visit to her mother, so she spoke to Sly about it; and after telling her the particulars, she said—"Do you think they will let me go for an hour, Sly."

"Not they," said Sly. Don't you *expectorate* any such a thing. Lord bless you, they find as your mind is set on it, they won't let you, so if you was to go for to ask 'em on your bended marrow-bones that they would'nt. I knows 'em."

"Indeed!"

"No. Missus would say as her nerves wouldn't let her even speak about it; and master, he'd scream like *Lucifer*, he would."

"What shall I do? Alas! what shall I do?"

"Do? Why go without asking of 'em at all, and blow 'em up well when you comes back. That's what you ought to do. That's what I'd do, pretty quick, too. I'll give a eye to the wolves and the waspses, while you is gone. So you be off, whenever you thinks as the old lady is waiting for you."

"Sly, I will follow your advice, and I thank you for it," said Emma. "It will not do to be completely a slave in this world. I will go."

CHAPTER XX.

THE OLD MANOR HOUSE.—A FRIGHTFUL ADVENTURE HAPPENS TO EMMA.

ACTING upon this advice from Sly, whether it was judicious or not, Emma did not say one word concerning her intention of visiting her mother in the evening; but at the usual hour she put the children to bed, and exhorted them to be quiet. Mr. Thomas was out, as it appeared he usually was of an evening; and as for any interruption from Mrs. Thomas, that was completely out of the queston, as that lady only migrated from the bed to the sofa, and the sofa to the bed.

Emma could leave her own room without going through the nursery; so she gently put on her things, and tripped gently down the stairs.

"I am much obliged to you, Sly," she said, as she peeped into the kitchen, previous to leaving the house. "I am going now, and I am so much obliged to you. The children are all in bed?"

"All's right," cried Sly. "I'll be among 'em if they so much as moves a little finger or a great toe, and they knows me. When I does go among 'em, they knows what they has to get."

"I thank you, Sly. I may possibly pay this visit to my poor mother, and no one know of it but you. I will come home very soon, indeed, and possibly Mr. Thomas may not have returned, and if he has, he may not ask for me."

"Certainly not," said Sly. "You go, and make your mind easy, and don't you go for to hurry yourself, for there ain't no sort of good in doing that."

Emma, with the direction of the little cottage on the outskirts of Hawarden, which her mother had the charge of in her hand, hurried from Mr. Thomas's house. It seemed to her, when she was in the open air once again, like an escape from bondage, and she could have ran along the streets in exultation at her renewed liberty, had she not feared to attract too much attention from the passengers, by so doing.

She had not the remotest idea of where the cottage was, except that her mother had told her to turn to the right, when she left the door-step of Mr. Thomas's house, and she knew that the cottage was called the "Rosery." Of course though, in so small a place, any one could direct her. She accordingly got the requisite information from a little girl in the street, and was soon at the little place, which, to tell the truth, was much more like a mere summer-house in a garden, than a cottage; but Mrs. Lyon had a cheerful fire blazing upon the hearth, and everything about her breathed an air of comfort, although the cottage—if cottage even by courtesy it could be called—was only built of weather-boarding.

In this interview Emma found the task of keeping secret from her mother anything that had occurred at the Thomas's much too irksome a one for her to persevere in, so she told her everything, the story of the flea occupying, as it well might, a prominent place in the narrative.

Poor Mrs. Lyon was perfectly amazed at the perversity of Mr. Thomas. She said she fully expected from what she had seen of him, that he would be a troublesome man by day, but she certainly had expected that he would let people rest in peace at night in their beds—which was not much to expect after all.

In fine, the mother and daughter passed an hour together in such discourse regarding the past and the present, and the probabilities of the future, as may be easily imagined; and when Emma rose to go, Mrs. Lyon said to her—

"No doubt, my dear, Doctor Lukin, to whom I have written to-day, will soon send the money that our few little things at the old cottage at Preston will produce; and with that and your own two guineas, we shall be quite rich, so that then, if this situation at Mr. Thomas's still remains so bad as it is, I shall be the first to advise you to leave it."

This assurance was a great comfort to Emma, and she left the cottage altogether in a much happier frame of mind than she had entered it.

She had, as she thought, taken sufficient notice of the route from Mr. Thomas's to her mother's cottage to know it again well, and so she might, had she been going again to it; but now that she was coming from it, every house that she thought she should be sure to remember so well, now that she looked at them under a different aspect, rather puzzled her. The night, too, was uncommonly dark, so that it was not much to be wondered at that Emma went down a wrong turning, and got into a long straggling thoroughfare that she knew nothing of. While she paused for a few moments, looking about her to endeavour to find her way, or to see some one who could direct her, a woman came out of a door in a very old garden wall, clustered with ivy. She went direct up to Emma, and said in smiling accents—

"Is your name Emma Lyon, my dear?"

"Yes, yes," said Emma.

"Then Doctor Lukin has just arrived in Hawarden, and has seen you from one of the windows of my house, and wishes to speak to you directly, if you will come with me. You know the doctor?"

"Know him? Oh, yes—he is mine and my poor mother's very best friend. I shall be delighted to see him, although I am surprised at his coming to Hawarden."

"It is very particular business," said the

THE MYSTERIOUS BEDROOM.

woman. "Follow me, and I will take you to him at once."

Emma did not entertain any suspicion. The name of Doctor Lukin acted upon her as a spell. There was absolute safety and protection in the sound of it; so she followed the woman through the doorway in the gar-t den wall with the expectation of, in a few moments, seeing the good doctor, who had been so true a friend to her and her mother, as well as to her poor father, who was gone.

"This way, my dear," said the woman, as she preceded Emma through a garden of some extent; "this way, if you please."

Emma followed her closely, but the darkness was so great that she could not see at all where she was going; she only felt that she was treading upon a gravel path; and presently a gleam of light from a window showed her that there were a great number of trees and shrubs about. The woman opened a door that was upon the latch, and held it open for Emma to pass through, which she did; and then, when the door was closed, all was darkness until another door was opened, and disclosed a comfortable enough parlour, upon the table in the centre of which, a couple of lights were burning.

A bright coal fire too, was in this room; and Emma noticed a decanter and some wine glasses.

"Where is Doctor Lukin?" she said.

"He will be here directly," said the woman; and Emma thought that her tone was very sharp and quick, in comparison to what it had been when she first addressed her. The door too, was shut sharply, and then something went with a snap, which sounded to Emma very like fastening it on the outside. A feeling of alarm for the first time, since the woman had invited her in, began to take possession of her. Her first impulse was to fly to the door, to ascertain if it was really fastened, or if her imagination only had deceived her upon this point.

No! It was fast!

The pang of apprehension that shot through the heart of Emma at this moment, nearly caused her to faint. She reeled back from the door, and was compelled to take refuge in the nearest chair to it, in order to rally her strength and spirits.

"What is the meaning of this?" she said. "Why am I decoyed hither? Is it for murder? Oh, God help me! How could I be so foolish as to listen to an invitation from a perfect stranger? and yet it was the name of Doctor Lukin that deceived me. How should this woman know that the use of that name would be to me any charm, any inducement to follow her. I am wrong—I am wrong—I am, perhaps, after all, not deceived; and I shall see him yet. Be still, my heart, all may yet be well. And yet, why do they lock me in?—Why should they lock me in?"

She thought that even in that she might be deceived, and she rose and tried the door again. She could not be mistaken now—It was fast, and no strength of her's could force it open. She then strove to reason herself into courage; and glanced round the room to observe its contents. It was handsomely got up, but everything was in the style of an age gone by. The apartment looked like the well-kept, seldom used, one of some old mansion, that was preserved in its integrity, out of respect for its associations; but Emma had not many minutes given to her for the purpose of examining the room. A door, that was so well fitted to the panelling at one part of the wall that she had not observed it, suddenly opened, and a person at once entered the room. Emma knew him at a glance. It was the younger of the two gentlemen who had spoken to her in the waggon. It was he who had assailed her in her bed-room at the Inn. It was, in truth, her persecutor.

The colour fled from the cheeks of Emma as she looked at him, and she could only stretch out her hands before her as though by this faint strength she could keep off the man who, with eyes of fierce passion, now regarded her. Thus, they stood confronting each other—the libertine and his victim; at least, he hoped that in that young girl, in all her maidenly youth and beauty, he saw his victim!

Not a word was spoke for several minutes. He, with the eyes of a miser gloating over his gold, appeared to regard her, while she was too deeply affected by the dangers and the terrors of her situation to be able to address a word to him.

———

CHAPTER XXI.

EMMA'S SINGULAR ADVENTURES IN THE OLD MANOR HOUSE OF HAWARDEN.

THE silence seemed to the young gentleman—if gentleman he could be called, who thus took such pains to compass the ruin of a then, at all events, innocent girl—one of the most puzzling things that could have happened. He did not like to speak first, for what had he to say, that had not much better have been left unsaid?

It was Emma, however, who at length broke the awkward stillness.

"Help! help!" she cried. It was not a cry, for she only spoke in a husky whisper. Her feelings were, just at that moment, too much wrought upon to enable her to cry lustily for aid, as she wished to do; and a choaking seemed to prevent her from so doing. But she had broken the spell of that awful silence, and now her persecutor could himself speak. That was something.

"Why do you cry for help?" he said. "Beautiful girl, who is there in all the world would fly to your aid, if you were in any real danger, more quickly than I?"

"Approach me not, demon, villain—approach me not!"

"Nay, Emma. What in the name of all that's wonderful, have you to fear from me? Do I not tell you—do I not swear to you that I love you? and is it likely I would injure her, for whom I entertain such a sentiment? Ah, cruel girl, can you listen unmoved to my declaration of fervent attachment to you?"

"You do not love me, sir."

"I swear it by the sun, the moon, the stars—I swear it by your own wondrous beauty.'

"No, sir; did you truly love me, my happiness would be your chief care. You would then permit me to leave this place into which I have been most treacherously decoyed, for here I am wretched. I shall go mad here if I am compelled longer to remain."

"Not so—not so, dear Emma. I shall be the one to go mad if you look upon me with so much disdain. Hear only what I have to say to you. From the moment that I saw you get into that odious waggon, which was all unfit for so much beauty, I was struck with love for you; I followed you as you know, and spoke to you. Then, unable to resist your commands, I left you, but I hovered near you, and ascertained that you slept at an Inn at Chorley. My ungovernable passion forced me to overlook the great impropriety of the act, and to intrude upon you in your bed-chamber; then I did, indeed, bitterly repent that I had so much offended you, and on the following morning I would have given anything for an opportunity of apologizing to you, and procuring your forgiveness; but I could not; yet I followed you here, and have been watching for you ever since. I was nearly mad with my disappointed feelings, when chance threw you in the way this evening. I sent out the woman with the name of Doctor Lukin upon her lips to get you into this house, Emma, so that I might ask your forgiveness of the past."

"If that be all," said Emma, "you shall have it the moment I am free from this place. How you became acquainted with so much of my history I know not."

"The landlady at the inn was communicative. Money will purchase most secrets, Emma. But do you—can you forgive one whose principal ever has consisted in loving you only too well?"

"When I am free, I can and will forgive all the past. Let me leave this place at once, and I will forget you as I hope you will forget me."

"Never—never! I forget you? Impossible! No, Emma, while life remains to me, I shall think of you by day and night! Oh! cruel fate, to make a nursery-maid of one who was surely fashioned to be a princess."

The language of flattery was not altogether unwelcome to the ears of Emma; but as yet she had not

"o'erstepped the modesty of nature;"

as yet she was pure and innocent; and as yet she had no thought but for the preservation of that purity and that innocence. She might, in after years, have smiled at her feelings upon this occasion; but at the time they were genuine, and she quickly recovered from the pleasing vibration of that fatal flattery, which has been the destruction of so many of God's fairest creatures.

"I will hear no more, sir," she said. "I wish to hear no more. My path in life is fixed. It is that of my own choice. Leave me to pursue it, and pursue you, yours. I demand my freedom."

"Yes," replied the young man. "Your path in life is fixed. It was fixed when Nature, from out her store-house of beauty, lavished upon you all that was most choice. It was fixed, then, that your path in life was

to love and to be beloved. I love you. Love, do I say? Ah! how cold a word that is to express the overwhelming passion that I feel for you, my charmer!"

Emma made another attempt at the door of the room. "This is insufferable," she said. "Help! Help! Murder!"

A change came over the face of the young man; but he still, by an effort of more self-control than he had managed to exhibit in the chamber at the little inn at Chorley, managed to keep up a semblance of courtesy.

"Listen to me," he said. "I am a nobleman, and can and will place you in a position to be envied by the proudest. I am, I tell you, a nobleman."

"You may, sir, have the name of nobility, but noble you are not."

"This is folly—madness. I tell you I can gratify every whim you may have—every possible caprice. You can, with me, if you please, lead such a life as in dreams never entered your imagination. My carriage is close at hand. Fly with me to the metropolis, Emma, and then, by the splendour of your beauty, which is on the increase rather than the wane, you will eclipse the proudest and the fairest of those who make beautiful the leisure of the noble and the wealthy. You are a country girl; but you must have heard of such affairs as what I propose to you. I only ask you to make your own terms."

"Help! Help!"

"Your cries are usless; I warn you of that. There are but three living souls, besides ourselves, in this house, and they are my creatures—my slaves—I have bought them at their own price—I have the means of so buying the very souls of human things.— Your cries will fall upon the deafest of ears, for they will fall upon those who will not hear. I tell you, Emma, you are mine."

"No—no."

"I say, yes. You are mine—you shall not —you cannot now escape me, girl. I would not be harsh with you; but it rests with you to mould me to what humour you will. If you defy me, you'll drive me mad, and you must take the consequences of your own indiscretion. Do not be so wilfully mad yourself, as to do so."

As he spoke these words, he made a dart towards her, but the table, which was between them, was a capital defence for Emma. She snatched up one of the lighted candles, and hurled it in his face.

Half maddened by his passion, and wholly infuriated by the blow which the candlestick gave him, he darted round the table after her; she fled before him. The little narrow but tall door, in the panelling, by which he had entered the room, yielded to her touch, and in a moment she was gone.

"Stop—stop!" he cried. "Not that way. Stop, you shall go! Stop! D——n where are you going now?"

He snatched up the remaining light and dashed after her, through the panel door.— He still called upon her to stop, and his voice sounded strange and hollow in the narrow passage that the panel door opened into.—She fled with the speed of a hunted hare; she knew nothing, she felt nothing, but that she was making way with headlong speed from that man.

"Stop—stop!" he still shouted. "Stop, you rush upon your own destruction! You know not where you go! Fool, that you are, you fly from me to a worse danger."

She did not heed him; she only felt that she was escaping from that room into which she had been so basely decoyed.—She only felt that she was distancing her pursuer.

CHAPTER XXII.

EMMA MEETS WITH A SURPRISE IN THE OLD MANOR HOUSE.

FOR a few moments after she had passed through the panel door, the light from the room had shed a faint radiance around her path. It had been sufficient to enable her to see that the walls on each side of her were within arms-length, and then, when he who pursued her with such hot haste came after her bearing the other light, she saw more clearly, and the passage she was in appeared to be of interminable length. It was clear to her, however, that she was distancing her foe, for the light grew more dim, and his voice sounded less distinct, as still in frantic and shouting accents he called upon her to stop.

Fear is more energetic, when it is not so intense as to lock up the faculties in frozen horror, than passion, and Emma was young and agile. No wonder that she outstripped her half-mad pursuer.

And now, suddenly, she came to the end of the passage. It terminated in a door similar to the one in the paneling of the room whence she had escaped with such precipitancy. It was half open as that one had been incautiously left.

To rush through the small apartment was the work of a moment, and then Emma found herself in a room, upon the table in the centre of which was a lamp shedding a bright light around it. By that light one glance was sufficient to assure her that there were two very heavy bolts upon the door through which she had passed, and with a cry of thankfulness, she shot them into their sockets. Then, exhausted by the race she had taken, she sank to the floor, and remained for some moments without sense or motion.

She had not fainted. It was, after all, only the exhaustion of the time that had come over Emma, and she could plainly hear some one knocking violently upon the other side of the door.

"Open, open," said the voice of her persecutor. "Open. You will in vain strive to fly from me; open the door, fool that you are. Why will you drive me to be violent when I would fain be gentle with you?—Open the door, I say, and you shall go in peace."

Emma sprang to her feet. She had no more idea of trusting to the promises of that man, than she would have had of trusting to the seductions of the Archfiend himself. She glanced hastily around the room in search of some other mode of leaving it than that by which she had entered it. She saw a door. To open it was the impulse and the work of a moment. It was only a cupboard full of a strange assemblage of articles.—Among the rest, Emma saw several swords. With a feeling of desperation she clutched one of them in her grasp, and, drawing it from its scabbard, she turned its point towards the panel door, which she could see was yielding and creeking beneath the pressure from without.

"What if I kill him," she said, "what if I kill him? It will be his own fault—almost his own act!"

As she spoke, she happened to cast her eyes upon yet another door in the wall of the room. It was in the same relative situation as regarded the fire-place, as the cupboard that she had already opened, but she flew to it notwithstanding—it might lead from the apartment, and, if it did, it was a chance worth the trying.

Yes, it was a door, opening to a room, and not to a mere cupboard; all was darkness beyond it, but, with the sword in her grasp, Emma sprang farward, and determined upon exploring it. She would have taken the light with her, but it was too heavy a lamp for such a purpose, besides, it might after all only be a guide to her presence if she did, so she thought she was better, after consideration, without it.

By holding the sword out before her she provided pretty well against the possibility of encountering any object against which she might do herself an injury, and so she proceed along the length of a very large room. She listened intently to hear if the panel door was broken in, but no such sound came upon her ear as yet. She began to breathe a little more freely; the violent beating of her heart had partially subsided; her temples no longer throbbed with the agony of fear. It was true that she was still beneath the roof of the house; but she had for the time escaped her great enemy.

Feeling her way carefully along a wall that she reached, she at length touched the handle of a door. Upon turning it the door yielded, and, in total darkness, Emma entered another room. She could feel by the tread that a carpet was upon the floor of the room; and that it was sufficiently furnished she might guess, by the numerous obstructions she found in crossing the floor of it. At the farther end of this room she fancied she saw a faint light; it was too ruddy to be the light from a lamp or a candle; it seemed much more like the pleasant faint radiance from a fire in a dark room.

As her eyes got accustomed to this dim light she found that it came through an opening left by a half-closed door; and she could see, likewise, that the apartment she was in was richly appointed, but all in the old style

—the magnificence of a former age. There were no sounds of pursuit behind her; all was as still as though she had made her way to some holy sanctuary, at the threshold of which evil passions were denied an entrance; and so, impelled by an irresistible curiosity so to do, and still holding the sword between her and any possible danger, she slowly advanced to the half-open doorway through which came the gleams of fire-light.

As she approached the inner apartment she found herself in a current of warm air that came from it; and when she entered it she saw, by the dim fire-light that came from a crimson, smouldering compound of logs and coal, that was upon the hearth, that it was a bed-chamber; and that in its fittings and appointments it was truly a place where luxury might lie down, satisfied that art had done its best to lend beauty to repose.

It was by the glitter of mirrors, and the faint shine of costly hangings, that Emma saw thus much; and then she stumbled against something that was lying upon the floor: it was a candle in a gorgeous holder, and both seemed to have been roughly cast down from a neighbouring table, upon which there was another of similar appearance.

Again Emma listened, to be sure that no one was coming stealthily upon her footsteps, but all was still as before; and then, stooping to the smouldering remains of the fire, she strove to re-light the candle. Her attempts were, for some moments, abortive, but presently a little flame gushed out from a portion of the wood not thoroughly charred, and she did succeed in lighting it. With a glance of intense interest she looked round the room, but in a moment all her attention was rivetted to the bed, where she saw a sight that might well enchain her faculties in one long look of wonder and terror.

Hanging half way from the bed, her hands and her long dark hair touching, and the latter trailing, on the floor, was the form of a young girl. By the delicate shape of the head and of the hands she seemed hardly to have reached that period of life which separates the child from the woman. The bed cloathes were much disarranged; and this apparition of youth and beauty—for beautiful she was—was perfectly still. Not the smallest vestige of a movement indicative of life was visible to the most watchful gaze of Emma.

There she stood, transfixed for several seconds, ay, for minutes, gazing on that silent and sad spectacle.

It might have been that some current of air had come into the room, or that the mere presence of Emma had made some change in the disposition of its atmosphere, or it might be that it was the will of Heaven a change should then take place, for suddenly the young girl slid entirely from the bed, and fell to the floor with a dull and heavy sound.

Emma utterd a shriek of dismay.

It was a wonder that she did not drop the light. She was sure to do so or to clutch it tighter with frantic vehemence. She did the latter; so she saved herself from the addition of darkness to the horrors of her situation.

There lay the young creature who had fallen from the bed. Her disarranged night clothing showed the pearly purity of the skin; and now that the face was turned towards Emma, she could see how young and how beautiful she was.

And yet it was a dead face!

Yes. The light of life had been extinguished. The more Emma gazed upon that being of beauty, the more she felt convinced that death had done its work, and that the young spirit had fled to its maker. Oh! what a world of sad and trembling fascination there was in that face that no longer was to be illumined by the soul's intelligence—in those eyes that never more were to look upon the world! With horror, with wonder, and with pity, Emma stood as though rooted to the spot, gazing upon the spectacle before her.

What was she to think? What was she to do? Was she dreaming, or had such things really taken place, and had cruel fortune compelled her to be a spectator of them? How was she to act in such a dreadful emergency? Had death, in the insidious guise of disease, claimed that fair victim to his dark dominion, or had the ruthless hand of nature sent the young spirit on its mission to another woald? Who shall say? And yet something lies by the body. By that huddled-up mass, which surely not many hours—perhaps not many minutes—since had been full of life, and hope, and fears, and wants, and aspirations, even as she, Emma, was, there lay a piece of paper half folded like a letter. Emma would fain have lifted it from the floor; but she dreaded to approach so very close to the poor remains, as it would be necessary to do in order to possess herself of it.

And yet what ought she to fear? That being, young like herself, was yet beautiful in death. Emma saw her

"Ere the first hour of death has fled,
The first sad hour of nothingness,
The last of sorrow and distress."

Yes. Emma looked upon that young girl

"Before decay's effacive fingers
Had marred the lines where beauty lingers;"

and why should she then dread to approach one fashioned like herself, but whose better and purer portion had cleared the night sky in search of that Home beyond the stars, where there is joy eternal and the sunshine of the soul?

Slowly she crept forward. The piece of folded paper lay close to the dead body. Emma touched it slightly, and then emboldened, she lifted it from the floor. By the light of the candle which she had placed upon the table, she read the following words:

"Farewell! I now know that you placed the poison in my way with the hope that I should take it. You no longer love me—you no longer wish me to live. God forgive you for all as I do. When you see this, if there be any potency in the drug you told me was so swift an enemy to life, I shall be with the dead. Lay me in the garden beneath the arbutus, where you first told me that you loved me, and would make me yours. Again, God forgive you. Farewell!"

Emma had scarcely finished the reading of these few words, so really expressive in their simplicity, and so awfully explanatory of the tragedy that had occurred, when she heard footsteps rapidly approaching, and the voice of him who had done her wrong by his solicitations, came upon her ears.

"Are you this way?" he cried. "Are you this way? If you are here come away. Come away, I say! You will plot mischief together!"

Emma would not reply. She stood by the table. The sword was in her hand, and she shook with emotion at the idea that he who spoke was the virtual murderer of the young girl who lay so still before her. Her indignation was mingled with terror now.

"Speak, speak: if you hear me, speak!" cried the voice.

That voice only came from the next room.

"Are you there, Kate?" said the voice again. "Are you there, Kate?"

"Kate!" thought Emma, as she glanced upon the dead girl. "Ah! they may call Kate now, but when will you answer them?"

In another moment, with an appalled look—with the dread of something terrible having happened, he who might be called Emma's persecutor, appeared upon the threshold of the room. He carried a light, and as he held it up some little space higher than his head, it cast strange shadows upon his face, and betrayed the agitation that had possession of every feature.

"You are here!" he gasped. "You are here!"

"Yes," said Emma, "and another."

She pointed to the corpse. The light he carried dropped from the hands of the destroyer. He half fell, half crouched down to the floor, and stretching out his hands, he yelled rather than spoke.

"No—no, I did not do it. Don't look at me, Kate, with those dead eyes. You cannot say I did it. Off—off; why is your gaze bent on me? Why do you lie there so cold and chill?· You are not dead—no—no—no you are not dead. Why should you, so young, be dead? I did not kill you. Why did you take the poison? I did not tell you to take it. Do not look at me as though I were a murderer. No—no! I offered you money if you would go in peace—in peace—yes, in peace. Turn those glossy eyes from me. God! she moves—she moves. I shall be haunted by the dead. Not by the spirit, but by the corpse itself, horribly verified to drive me mad—quite mad. Off—off, I say. I did not do it—I did not do it!"

CHAPTER XXX.

EMMA WISHES TO LEAVE HAWARDEN.—THE PROJECTED JOURNEY TO LONDON.

IT was almost enough to drive any one to the verge of insanity to hear that man thus

heap the burning coals of accusation upon his own head, and in every word that he uttered, pourtray his own guilt, and picture his own punishment.

Emma felt her very heart's blood run chill as she listened to him. When he did pause, it was from mere want of physical force to say more. The heavy beads of perspiration stood upon his brow, and he looked as though he too, from the emotion of that violent access of passion, was a fit candidate for the grave.

He suddenly sprang to his feet.

"Wine—wine!" he cried. "Ha! ha! The Lithe of the wine cup. The sparkling waters of oblivion, which the wise Persian could not find but in the poison bowl. Wine—wine—wine!"

Upon a side-table was a glittering array of decanters, and some massive silver cups. He drained one of the decanters of bright red wine into one of the silver cups. He placed it to his lips, and when he let go his hold of the cup, it fell empty to the floor of the room.

The draught he had taken, upon any other occasion, would have been more than enough to produce intoxication; but it failed in having such an effect upon him, in that season of mad and raging excitement. It only deadened his sense of right and wrong, and stupified those feelings of remorse, which had made him but a few minutes before utter such wild incoherences.

"Yes, yes," he cried. "The wine-cup has stilled the demon in my heart, and I breathe again. I did not kill her—I did not do it. It was her own act, and I will hold another to my heart, though all the fiends of a lower world should howl destruction in my ears. Emma, I love you—I love you as I have not yet loved any one. To my arms—to my arm. Queen of my best affections, come to me."

"Horror! horror!" cried Emma.

"No—no—love, not horror shall be our watchword. I am the master here. The king of all, and you shall rule as queen. We will lead a life of glittering pleasure."

"Help! Oh, help!"

"Nay, I have before told you that such cries in this place were worse than useless. Chance has made you acquainted with one of the secrets of this house, and further disguise is useless. You are mine, and nothing can save you. We leave the dead to the chamber of death, and in the wild frenzy of passion, we will forget that death has anything to do with the bright world of pleasure which we will create around us. Ha! ha! ha! Wine—wine! More wine. Blessed be the patriarch who first thought of the bright wine!"

Again, with now a staggering gait, that half-maddened votary of pleasure made his way to the buffet, where was wine in abundance; and again he quaffed deeply of the intoxicating juice. Then with a wild shout, he made a rush towards Emma.

Before this she might, while he was drinking, have escaped by the door; but a kind of benumbing sensation had crept over her, and held her in bondage. She felt as though she were suffering from the night-mare, and that escape was far beyond her power. But when, with mad gestures and furious exclamations, he who had caused the wreck that was within her gaze, made his way towards her, the spell that had fallen upon her powers seemed broken at once, and with a shriek, she fled towards the door of the room.

He tried to intercept her, but she was too quick for him. She passed into the outer room, but he pursued her quickly. She felt that he would overtake her, and she turned with the sword in her hand.

"Villain!" she said, "take the reward of your ill-deeds."

He rushed on. Emma felt that the sword penetrated his chest. He uttered a cry, and then she heard a heavy fall. Her first impulse was to drop the weapon; but how could she know what other dangers it might protect her from? She clasped it still in her hands, although she guessed that blood was upon its point; so she hurried through the rooms, calling aloud, as she went, for help.

Suddenly a flash of light came upon her eyes. A door had been flung open, and to her surprise, she saw the elder of the two gentlemen who had first made a sort of acquaintance with her in the waggon, standing before her. He looked pale and agitated.

"Good Heaven," he said. "What is the meaning of all this? Speak, for the love of Heaven, and tell me what has happened."

"Stop me not," cried Emma. "I will go from this place—I will go from this place. For your life's sake stop me not."

"Yes, yes, you shall go. I will myself show you the way; but tell me what has taken place. Believe me, you shall. I was alarmed by your cries, and coming to your assistance. Where is my friend?"

"I do not know. I cannot tell. Only show me how to leave this house, and I will bless you, sir. I shall go mad if I am condemned to remain here longer. I cannot endure such horrors."

"Do not speak in such a tone. I tell you that hearing your cries for aid, I have followed the sound for the purpose of rescuing you. If you will come with me I will show you the shortest route from this house. Do not mistrust me. I swear by all that's sacred I will not mislead you."

"I—I—know not if I ought to trust you?"

"Indeed you may, Emma."

"Lead on, I will follow you, sir. But I am armed, and the feeling of desperation that is at my heart, you will find is more than sufficient to move me to resist you. Weak, and a girl as I am, I feel now that I shall not fail for want of power to aid myself. Lead on, sir, I will follow you."

He did not make any reply to this speech of Emma's. He judged, and he judged rightly, that action could alone, in her state of mind, have any real effect upon her, so he led the way, and she followed him closely, still, however, retaining that sword which had already done her good service.

Emma did not trouble herself to look about her at the rooms through which they passed; she was only rather surprised at the number of them; and she guessed that they were taking a very circuitous route to get out of the building, which seemed to be of great extent indeed. At length, they suddenly came upon a hall with marble flag-stones, and scarcely had they reached it, than the woman who had played her part in inveigling Emma into the house, came through a door-way and confronted them.

"Save me from her," said Emma.

"I will," said her companion.

"What is it all about?" said the woman. "I have heard strange noises. Why, you are never going to let her go, sir? We shall be all ruined if you do."

"I have promised."

"And must, and shall perform your promise," said Emma.

"There is no occasion," he replied, "to speak to me thus. It is quite sufficient that I have promised; I do not break my word. You shall be free to leave this house."

"Then we are all lost," cried the woman. "You know not what you do, colonel; and I am quite sure his lordship would never for a moment consent to it. Of course we expect a little squalling, but we are used to that, colonel."

"Peace, woman," he said. "Peace. This girl shall not be detained here against her will. From my heart I begin to loathe these transactions. You can tell his lordship that I am gone, and you may add that I shall never again cross the threshold of this house; I have taken a disgust at it, and shall keep my word. Follow me, Emma, and I will free you."

The woman ran to the foot of a staircase and began calling out at the top of her voice. "My lord, my lord, we shall all be ruined. Come this way!"

"Let him come," said the colonel. "I will face him, and dare him to stop me. In an evil hour I consented to join with him in objects and designs that I am ashamed of. It was expressly understood that there was to be no violence, and I find abundance of it. Let him come. Let him come. Fear nothing, Emma,"

"He will not come," said Emma.

"Not come? How know you that?"

"I say he will not come. Do not ask me for a reason, but I feel and know that he will not come. Take me away at once, and do not wait for what will not be."

"Come then."

The woman darted up the staircase, apparently in very great surprise that he whom she called "my lord," did not make any answer to her calls.

"Come," said he who evidently was of rather too pure a nature to go all the way with his friend in his wild and lawless excesses. "Come, Emma, such reparation as I can make to you for the wrongs that I have been partially instrumental in inflicting upon you, I will make. I see at present no other mode of convincing you of my sincerity, but freeing you from this place in which you must have suffered much."

"That will be sufficient proof," said Emma.

The colonel, as he was called, undid the heavy fastenings of a huge door, and then the moment it was opened she felt a gush of cold air upon her face, that sufficiently convinced her the colonel was really keeping his word with her. She had not doubted him from the first. There is

"A divinity doth hedge the truth,"

which at once makes it impressionable, and distinguishes it readily from that feigning feeling which never can be but a faint approximation to reality. The most accomplished actor the world ever saw could not have told Emma he would free her with the tone that the colonel used, unless he had really and truly intended it.

The sight of the trees in the garden, and the soft, delicious odours of some flowers that came upon the night-air, produced upon the feelings of Emma a most turly unexpected effect. She burst into tears and sobbed as though her heart would break. At that time, nothing could have been easier than to have disarmed her of the sword, and taken her back to the house, but such was really not the intention of him who was styled the colonel.

"Comfort yourself," he cried in a tone of sympathy. "Whatever have been your trials to-night they are now over. I will lead you through the garden, and then you are at liberty; and as we go, if you will listen to me, I will make a confession to you."

"What confession?"

"A confession concerning myself and him who I fear kept not his faith with me, which was to use what acts of persuasion he could to induce you to become his, but to stop short of anything in the shape of violence, or even a threat of it."

"Ah, how much indeed then he broke faith with you; but what a cruel compact was that which in any way contemplated my undoing."

"Perhaps it was!"

"Perhaps, sir? Is there any doubt?"

"No—no. There can be none; and you, I admit, have much—very much indeed to forgive. The real truth is, that being both of us enamoured of you, we made a sort of agreement to take our turns in trying to win you. The only credit I will take to myself in the discreditable transaction, is that I proposed the clause in the agreement that prohibited any violence or threat of violence to you."

"That was something," said Emma.

"Yes. It was, as you say, something, but not much. When we were both repulsed by you in the waggon, we still followed you; and then we cast lots, or rather, we threw a main

with dice to see which of us should try his fortune first again with you."

"And your companion won?"

"He did. The result you know. He and I really quarrelled about that interruption of your repose upon that night at the inn; and then after we left in the morning we thought that it was a poor thing on both our parts to leave you so, and not make another attempt. We followed you, and again we threw the dice for you, and again my friend won the chance. By mere accident, you were seen to-night, and induced to come into the house you have just quitted. Now you know all. You have heard me say that I regret having anything to do with the affair, and now I make you the only reparation I can. You are free. Here is the door in the garden-wall at which you came in."

"I must thank you."

"No, I do not deserve thanks; but if you can feel sufficiently satisfactory at your deliverance to promise me that you will keep this night's adventure a secret, I will in return thank you, and you will save me much trouble and uneasiness."

"I promise," said Emma.

"Then, from my heart I thank you; and if I do not now urge upon you, that I love you, that I love you far better than ever he could from whom you have happily escaped to-night, it is because I think it would be ungracious just now to do so."

CHAPTER XXIV.

ANOTHER NOCTURNAL DISTURBANCE AT MR. THOMAS'S.

EMMA was struck in spite of herself by the candour, and the romantic generosity of the colonel, and she replied—

Sir—persecution, such as I have endured, is not the right path to the esteem or the love of a young girl."

"You are right. You will now no doubt for ever regard me as some monster in human shape, who goes about seeking only whom he may doom. You will perhaps do me the injustice to think that my liberating you from that house, was after all only an act of fear, and I must submit to the cruel injustice. Farewell Emma. I commend myself to your after-thoughts, not to your present ones."

"You mistake me," said Emma. "I certainly cannot forget what I have suffered, but with that remembrance will come the thought that you rescued me. Take this sword sir; I do not need it now. I only hope that we shall never meet again."

She turned away from the door in the garden wall, and walked rapidly on. The first person she met was a labouring man, and from him she asked the way to Mr. Thomas's house.

"You have only to go down the lane here," he said, "and you will see it right before you. It's ugly Thomas you mean?"

"Ugly?"

"Yes. We mean his temper only when we call him ugly."

"Thank you," said Emma.

She went down the lane, as directed, and sure enough, she there saw her home. She thought that if folks were to be called ugly on account of their tempers, that no one she had ever met with so fully and so justly deserved the appellation as her master, Mr. Thomas.

"Oh," said Sly, when Emma reached the kitchen, "where in the mortal world has you been?"

EMMA LYON WAKING FROM HER DREAM.

"I lost my way. Has any one missed me? Have the children stirred, Sly?"

"Why, the wolves has slept like churches, but the waspses snivelled a little about half a hour agone; but I walked into 'em with a switch, and they is as quiet as crumpets now."

"And Mr. Thomas has not come home?"

"Not he, and he won't for some time yet. Why, I expectorated you full a hour agone, that I did; but, howsomever, we aren't all lost as is in danger. Will you have anything?"

"No, only a glass of water."

"Don't say no. Here's a lovely bit o' pork, and all fat too ; and some cold taters. Don't say no, now, if you feels quite tempted, in a way o' specking."

Emma excused herself as well as she could from partaking of the tempting fare that Sly mentioned to her. Her whole anxiety was now to retire to rest, for the scene she had gone through in the wilderness of a house in the street to which she had so unwillingly wandered, had powerfully affected her spirits. She wished to be alone that she might take counsel with herself as to what she should do. She did not forget that she had bound herself by promise to say nothing to any one concerning the events that had transpired in that house, and that promise troubled her ; for, each moment, the question seemed to her of how far she was justified in withholding a knowledge, at all events, of the death of the young girl, who had been in her hearing named Kate.

"Will you excuse me, Sly," she said.— "I am very weary through wandering about to recover my lost way in the town, and would fain now go to rest."

"In course," said Sly. "There's your candle. I wishes you pleasant dreams, and lots of 'em. You go to bed. Lord bless us, you are a poor creature, after all, and isn't, by no manner o' ways, fit for sarvice."

"Good-night, Sly ; I thank you for all your kindness to me ; for, to tell the truth, no one in this house has said one kind word to me but yourself."

"Nor won't," said Sly ? "if you was to live here for a hundred years, and be as old as Matheuselum, I can tell you. I never had no kind words said to me ; and, I believe, if I was a dying they'd ask me to put it off to wash up the tea-things. Ellow! that's him."

A thundering knock at the street door at this moment, announced the arrival of Mr. Thomas. Emma thought that she should be able to get up stairs before he saw her, but, unfortunately, her foot caught in the front of her dress, and she stumbled before she could get sufficiently high up the staircase to be out of reach of his observation, as he came into the hall.

"A million of devils !" he roared. "This is always the way ! I employ a wretch—a debased pauper—to remain with my children, and when I come home I find her all of a heap in the middle of the staircase. Fire and fury ! Ten-penny nails and boiling brimstone ! it's enough to rouse the anger of a fish—it is "

Emma had seen enough of Mr. Thomas to know that anything in the shape of an explanatory reply to him, would be most completely thrown away, so she did not say a word ; but Sly took up the cudgels and shouted,—

"Do you think that nobody is to tumble up stairs but you, I should like to know ?— Marry come up ; who are we I wonder ?— Dear me, bless us, what great folks we are. What a tail our cat has got."

From long experience, Mr. Thomas knew that he was no match for Sly ; so after uttering an oath or two, he crept up stairs. As for Emma, she had recovered from her stumble quickly enough, and was by then in her own room, and the door locked. Mrs. Thomas probably endured the replies for Sly, because she was the only servant that had ever been induced to stay in the house longer than the month of trial for which they were engaged, and she evidently took a kind of warlike pleasure in her frequent freaks with "Master," and no doubt would have been quite disappointed if four and twenty hours had passed over without one of them taking place.

When Emma felt that she really was alone in her little chamber, and that she had time to think, she became perfectly astonished at herself, that she should have had the courage to go through the scene that had taken place in the mysterious house in the garden. When she came to reflect upon all that she had done and upon all that she had said, it really appeared to her as though she must have been walking in her sleep.

A great multiplicity of incidents compressed into a small space of time, are very apt indeed to have such an effect upon the mind ; and it was by actual strong reasoning upon the subject, that Emma was able to convince herself of the absolute reality of all that she had gone through upon that most eventful and extraordinary evening

But even then, when she had arrived so far in her mental examination, there was much to be done, for the occurrences were of by far too serious a character to be lightly disposed of. She began to ask herself if he who was called my lord, would abandon his pursuit of her ? She asked herself if she had killed him by the sword-thrust that she had given to him ? and she shuddered at the idea that she might have done so, and at the long and tedious course of judicial proceedings in which she might, as a consequence, be mixed up. No wonder that such thoughts as these banished sleep from her eyes, although she deeply felt the want of rest for a considerable time.

At length, exhausted nature claimed her due, and Emma, at what still hour of the night she knew not, dropped off into a slumber which could hardly be called repose, inasmuch as it was haunted by all kinds of incongruous shapes and fancies, having some strange relation to the events that she had witnessed and taken a part in, in the mysterious house.

At times she would fancy herself pursued up long winding staircases by malignant demons, and that she only had the power to go step by step at a snail's pace. Then again she thought she was falling down tremendous precipices, and she would in fancy feel herself swinging through the air in wild attitudes, and she should reach the bottom of the deep declivity, and then be dashed to pieces ; and throughout all, the dead face of the young girl who lay so calm and still in the gorgeous chamber of the old house, would seem to be close to her, and to be about to move as though instinct with a horrible life again.

Once she thought she was thrown to the bottom of some deep tube or well-shaped receptacle, and that very far up above her she could see the narrow opening at which a crowd of busy fiends, with burning eyes and chuckling visages, appeared casting feathers upon her—merely small feathers, and surely they could harm her not; but soon they came thicker and faster upon her, until she had to fight with them for breath. They covered her up, and still they fell upon her. She gasped in horror for the breath of life. She tried to shriek, but the feathers filled her mouth. Her eyes were closed by their pressure, and then she heard a dismal bell tolling clearly and distinctly.

She sprang, with a wild cry, from her bed, and stood in the centre of a broad moonbeam that had found its way into her apartment.

"Oh, God," she said. "It was but a dream!"

With a burst of hysterical weeping, she sunk upon her knees, and felt such exquisite relief from her tears, that it was some few minutes before she became assured that the sound of the bell was not a dream, but a distinct reality, which, like the imaginary voice that assailed Macbeth, said to all the house

"Sleep no more."

Yes, there could be no possible mistake about the bell. It was no faint echo of a dream—no continuation of a fancied sound, but a real veritable bell, which was being tolled rapidly on the landing-place of the second floor of the house. Suddenly then it ceased, and an awful voice cried in bellowing accents—

"A cockroach on the ceiling! A cock—roach on the ceiling!"

Then the bell sounded again, after which all was still, save the banging shut of a door, that made the house shake again from its foundation upwards.

It needed no ghost to come and tell Emma that this was Mr. Thomas's mode of annoyance for that night, and that having of course awakened everybody, he would be tolerably contented until the morning permitted him to commence the personal abuse with which he treated her, and which in all its intensity it is quite impossible for us to transfer to our pages. No wonder then that she began to have serious thoughts of leaving Hawarden. There seemed to be many reasons conspiring to induce her to do so.

In the first place she could not hope or expect anything now like the most ordinary comfort in the situation she held; and then she felt that she should be in constant terror of that man whom she had wounded with the sword, and who did not seem to be of a very forgiving or giving way disposition. And then, too, her imagination had always been warmed at the idea of seeking her fortune in London, that great city which, to the imagi-

nation of persons who have only heard of it through exaggerated and false channels, is one vast arena of enjoyment, and an El Dorado of wealth!

As she lay awake for the remainder of that night, she almost made up her mind to leave Hawarden, and she began calculating how she could be able with her disposable means, namely, two guineas, to reach the metropolis, from which she was distant so many a long and weary mile.

The morning dawned before she could make up her mind upon these most harassing subjects; and then she again dropped asleep, and this time, until the house was astir, she enjoyed a tranquil, and truly sweet, refreshing repose.

The noisy prattle of what Sly called the wolves and wasps awoke her to the duties of the day, and found her still in a state of indecision as to her future proceedings; and she was not likely now, with the many cares and duties devolving upon her, to be able, until night should come again, to give anything like a rational thought to her situation. But before that night came she had, to the full, abundant additional acquirements for action.

Mr. Thomas, twice during the day, loaded her with abuse, even threatening to strike her; but at that threat she felt her courage revive, and facing him, she said—

"If, sir, you dare to so much as lay a finger upon me, I will defend myself with what chance weapon may come to hand, in a way, perhaps, that may make you bitterly repent your unmanly violence."

There was that in the tone and manner of Emma that gave a deep sincerity to these words, and as, like all bullies, Mr. Thomas was specially careful of himself, he at once retreated to a safer distance, from which he continued his abuse in the wildest tones of invective that his imagination could suggest to him.

It was only by Sly coming to the rescue that Emma was able to get up stairs to her own room, where she threw herself upon the bed in a passion of tears. During the next half hour Emma made up her mind to leave Mr. Thomas's service and Hawarden.

After she had made this determination she was much calmer and happier in her mind, and she was able to rise and wash from her eyes the traces of the tears that had flowed from them. She set about at once packing into as small a bundle as possible the few things that belonged to her; and then she waited until dark in order to step out of the house unobserved; for she dreaded a renewal of Mr. Thomas's abuse, and did not feel quite clear as regarded the power he might have to force her to stay, since, at her first coming, she had agreed for a whole month on trial, at the end of which time either party could bring the engagement to a conclusion.

Yet Emma did not like to go without taking leave of Sly, and giving to that eccentric denizen of the kitchen a word of thanks for the kindness she had shown to her.

Accordingly, with her little bundle in her hand, Emma crept down stairs, about half an hour after dusk, and made her way into the kitchen. Sly was preparing the tea-things for Mrs. Thomas, but the moment she cast her eyes upon Emma and the bundle, she said—

"You is a-going, I know'd it. You is a-going."

"Yes, Sly, I am indeed going. I cannot remain in this house longer. It would break my heart to do so. Do not say anything to me, Sly. I must and will go from here."

CHAPTER XXV.

MMA COMMENCES HER LONDON JOURNEY, AND MEETS WITH STRANGE INCIDENTS.

SLY looked at Emma for a few moments in silence; and then she said, with a dubious look—

"Well, well, everybody to his taste, as the old woman said when she kissed the cow; but I would rather you stayed, and looked a little arter the wolves and the waspses. Besides, you was a little company now and then; but if so be as you feels in your in'ards as you can't stay, why there's an end on it. I wishes you all sorts o' luck, Miss Emma, with all my heart."

"I thank you," said Emma. "You at least have been kind to me since my stay here, Sly, and I shall never forget you."

With this Emma moved towards the door. She turned to give Sly another kind word or two, and a smile, and she saw that paragon of maids-of-all-work wiping her eyes with the corner of her apron.

"Good-by," said Emma. "Good-by!"

"Good-by," sobbed Sly. "Everybody goes but me, and I shan't go, I suppose, till I goes heels forerdest to the churchyard. Good-by."

The door closed, and Emma, with her little bundle, was in the High-street of Hawarden.

Poor Emma could hardly define the feeling of regret with which she left even the unhospitable abode of Mr. Thomas. There must have been in her disposition at that time a strong principle of home-feeling and lovingness, or she never could have given one sigh to such a place as that she was escaping from. But perhaps, after all, it was the parting with Sly that had touched Emma. She certainly shed some tears. Such transient feelings were sure, however, to give way, soon before the much more important feelings and thoughts that began to crowd upon her. There she was, in the wide world, a wanderer. Young and beautiful, with her future all to come. No wonder that her feelings were rather in a turmoil; but amid all, there rose uppermost the wish to go to London.

Yes, London, with its dim promises of wealth and pleasure, was to Emma the land of hope—the city of refuge!

Her first object was to reach the cottage of her mother, and, if possible, to obtain her entire sanction to the step she was taking. This she was not long in doing; and although Mrs. Lyon could not but be much affected at the perilous situation in which a young and beautiful girl like Emma would be placed in the great world alone, she reasoned upon the subject sensibly enough.

"My dear," she said, "go, for you have set your mind upon this London trip, and I will not say no to you, nor will I send you away with the sad thought of parting from me in anything like disagreement or unkindness. No, Emma. I say to you go, and may every good fortune and blessing attend you. I will stay here, and then you can always say to yourself—'Let what will come, my mother is still at Hawarden, and that for me is a place of refuge.' I have no doubt, my dear, but that with industry, and please God spares my health, I shall do very well here, and always be able to say to you—'Emma, here is a home for you.'"

"You are very—very good to me, mother."

"I wish to be, my dear—I wish to be, Heaven knows."

"And yet," added Emma with a shudder, as she thought of her singular adventure in the old house. "And yet, mother, I would rather you were anywhere than here."

"And why so, my child?"

"I cannot tell. Perhaps it is mere prejudice upon my part against a place in which I have not been able to be happy; but I do wish it. Do not let that trouble you, however, mother. No doubt it is one of those feelings which will pass away, and in a little time I shall think perhaps as kindly of Hawarden as of any other place. At all events, it cannot be so painful to me to think of as Preston."

"No, my dear," said Mrs. Lyon, as she wiped the tears from her eye, "that would be impossible; for although Preston is to us very sacred, as the resting-place of your poor murdered father—for as good as murdered he was—yet I feel that it would be too painful a place for me to live in again."

"And for me, mother."

"Well, well, my dear, we must dismiss such gloomy thoughts; and I would not send you into the world with sadness in your heart and tears in your eyes. I have heard from Mr. Lukin, and he has sent me no less than £8 for the furniture in the cottage. I am quite sure that is much more than it was all worth; but he is very good, and has taken this mode of making us a present, I feel confident, of nearly half the money."

"It might be so, mother."

"Well, my dear, it is a God-send in its way, for it enables me to give you means which otherwise would have been far beyond my humble powers. Take the money, Emma; you may have need of it, and it is almost impossible that I should. Take it all, and keep it, in case some evil hour should come, when it may be of use to you—ay, of more use than you can well be aware of, for money is a friend you may always turn to with a certainty of finding a welcome."

"Not all, mother. I will not take it all. Remember that I shall have the two guineas that Doctor Lukin gave me; so if I take half what you would give, I shall be rich; and who knows but you may want the remainder? No, mother, do not press me, for indeed I am resolute."

Mrs. Lyon knew quite enough of Emma's character to feel that when she said she was resolute, she really was; and that anything in the shape of arguing would not be of the slightest use; so the young girl, who was about so boldly to face the world alone, took four of the guineas, and carefully concealed them in her dress. The two that she previously had she kept handy for the purpose of aiding her in her long journey to London.

"Well, my love," added Mrs. Lyon, "and have you determined anything about the way in which you are to go?"

"Yes, mother, I have not been idle upon that point. I have heard how to go to London. In one hour from now I can, by walking a mile from here, meet with a coach that is going to Lichfield, and that will be some distance on my road. When I get there, mother, I can make further inquiries as to the best way of getting on."

"It is far—very far. Do you know, my dear, how far off London is?"

"Not exactly, mother—but I know that it is more than two hundred miles. I don't see why that should terrify me. Distance is nothing in itself; and although the distance may be long and weary, it must be traversed at last."

After this, they both felt that if Emma was to take advantage of the coach that was going to Lichfield, that it would be most imprudent to linger longer in the cottage. Mrs. Lyon, therefore, with a nervous, fidgetty manner, set about getting ready to accompany Emma to the coach. The active walk to the cross-roads, where the vehicle was to pass, had in some measure the effect of tranquillising the spirits of both mother and daughter; although to tell the truth, the adventurous and chivalric spirit of Emma did not by any means quail before the circumstances in which she was placed. Already she was beginning to give abundant evidence of that indomitable will which in after life made her the mistress instead of the slave of circumstances.

They had hardly been two minutes at the cross-roads when they heard the bugle of the guard of the coach, and the heavy vehicle in a few moments drew up as they hailed it.

"Get up, both of you," cried the coachman. "We are behind time already. Get up!"

"It's only me," cried Emma. "I want to go to Lichfield. What will you charge me?"

"Get up, my dear, and we shall not quarrel about the price."

There was one embrace between the mother and daughter, and then the guard who had alighted, assisted Emma up to a comfortable-enough seat behind the coach, and in another moment the vehicle was off again at a spanking pace.

"Farewell to Hawarden!" thought Emma. "Farewell to the wild disturbances at Mr. Thomas's house, and farewell to the dread of again encountering the inhabitants of that fearful house in the lane, the events of which even now at times seem to me as though they could be nothing but the fearful visions of a dream."

Suddenly, something came with a heavy dab upon her shoulders, and she heard the guard say—

"There, my dear, wrap that coat around you, and take this horsecloth and roll your feet well up in it. You will be cold enough unless you do so before we have gone many miles on to-night, for there's an east wind brewing."

"I thank you," said Emma. "You are very kind."

"Don't mention it, my dear—don't mention it. Are you going further than Lichfield?"

"Yes, to London."

"Humph! That's a long pull. Your best way will be to get on to Coventry from Lichfield. You will find lots of conveyances from there; but it's a deuce of a way for all that."

Emma thanked the guard for his information, and then as the coach rattled on through a remarkably barren tract of country for many miles, a death-like stillness was around her—that is to say, a stillness of human intercourse; and it was only when the short bustle that was incidental to a change of horses at inn-doors took place, that the sound of voices came upon her ear, and then away into the darkness sped the coach.

Emma had got into a kind of doze, in which fancy began to mingle things past with things present, when suddenly the coach stopped, and the cessation of the noise of the wheels, and the steady tramp of the horses, in a moment woke her up.

"Move another inch, coachman," cried a hoarse voice, "and I'll blow your brains out."

Emma uttered a shriek.

"What the devil is the matter with you?" said the voice again. "I don't meddle with outsides. Now ladies and gentlemen, your money or your lives!"

"What is that?" said Emma.

"Hush!" said the guard, laying his hand upon her arm. "It's only a highwayman. It's Tom King. He never had the confounded impudence to stop us before, and he won't again, I take it, after this bout."

By the light of the coach-lamps, Emma could see a man on horseback by the coach-door, and she could hear faint screams from the inside of the vehicle. A man's voice, too, cried out—

"What, are we to be robbed on the king's highway?"

"Pho! pho! sir," said the man on horseback. "It's no matter whose highway it is, your money or your life. That's my watch word, and you know your own value, sir. Quick, quick, or by G—d I'll soon send a brace of slugs into your stupid head."

"Mercy, mercy!" cried a lady, to which the highwayman replied, "that mercy might be d—d, all he wanted was their money and valuables, and those he would have." Emma felt something cold touch her shoulder, and looking round she saw the guard in a crouching posture on the roof of the coach with a blunderbuss in his hands, the hugs bell-shaped brass barrel of which had just touched her. He put his fingers on his lips as a hint to her to be silent, but she whispered, "You will not take his life?"

"Safe as bricks," said the guard. "If he hasn't made his will, he'll die what the lawyer's call, *detested*."

Bang! went the blunderbuss, with an awful report, and Emma fully expected to see the highwayman fairly blown to pieces, but instead of that, he looked up through the smoke, and shouted in a loud clear voice—

"It won't do, my man. Of course it's your duty to try it on, but it won't do. I drew the bullets out of the blunderbuss myself, as you stopped to change horses at Nantwitch. Catch a weasel asleep. It won't do. Only as you have had your try, it's only fair that I should have mine."

"Blaze away then," cried the guard, "and be hanged to you. Only don't be hitting this girl here instead of me."

"You have saved yourself, Bill Wiggins, by that speech," said the highwayman, as he replaced the pistol he had drawn from the holster of his saddle, and with which he could easily have shot the guard. "You have saved yourself. You are a bold fellow, and after all there is no harm done. Ladies and gentlemen, I have the pleasure of wishing you good-night and a pleasant journey, and let me beg of you to travel with better filled purses on this road again, for really it is hardly worth a gentleman's while to stop a coach now."

With this the highwayman patted the neck of his horse, and giving it a touch with the spur, off he went like the wind.

"Confound it all," said the coachman, "what an ugly job."

"Yes," said the guard, "and the idea of my blunderbuss being tampered with at Nantwitch."

"Ah," growled the coachman. "I saw a fellow get up, but I thought he belonged to the Green Dragon and Snuffer Tray, where we changed 'osses, and in course thought he was a sorting some o' the baggage. It wasn't that fellow on horseback though, but somebody as he paid well to do the job for him."

"Certainly not," said the guard: "but it can't be helped now, that's clear, so drive on, Joe—drive on!"

The coach was once more in motion, and Emma could not but thank her stars that she had been outside, for the loss even of the two guineas that she kept loose for her expenses on the road, would have been to her rather serious. On the whole, however, as no one was hurt and no mischief done, she could not help being amused at the adventure, although she did not say so, for the guard was anything but pleased at it, and kept casting the most awful looks at his now useless blunderbuss.

It was half past nine o'clock when the coach rattled along the market street of the old town of Lichfield.

CHAPTER XXVI.

THE PROGRESS TO COVENTRY.—AN INN ON FIRE, AND ITS ODD RESULTS.

EMMA'S fatigue was very great, and she was glad to lie down for a few hours at the inn where the coach put up at Lichfield. The landlady was a kind motherly sort of woman, and for the short time that our heroine was in her house, she behaved to her with the most exemplary attention. By inquiries which she made after she had rested for a time, Emma found that the distance from Lichfield to Coventry was estimated at about sixty miles, and that a waggon would start in the afternoon which would take her for six shillings. She was further informed that this vehicle was considered a very fast one, and that she would be only twelve hours upon the road, which would include all stoppages. Upon this she at once made up her mind to secure a place in the waggon, which, as it started from the yard of an inn opposite to where she was staying, was easily accomplished.

With all her strength recovered by the rest she had had at Lichfield, and having made but a very slight inroad into her finances indeed, Emma started at half-past two o'clock in the waggon for Coventry.

There were but few passengers in the vehicle, but it was pretty well crammed up with goods of one sort or another; nevertheless, Emma, having now had some experience of travelling, secured herself a comfortable place, and hoping that she should be able to cheat the way of its weariness by getting to sleep, she resolutely closed her eyes, after getting clear of the suburbs of Lichfield.

She was to some extent successful in shutting out a sense of the long journey she was taking, although she could not be said to go fairly to sleep. She got into that drowsy state between sleeping and waking, which, while it does not actually shut out a consciousness of all external objects and occurrences, yet covers them up as it were in a strange mist.

People got out of and people get into the waggon, and Emma could not be said to see them, but at length the tones of conversation between two persons not far from her made some more sensible effect upon her ears, and she began to be cognisant of some of the words they spoke. Suddenly one pronounced a name that made her start wide awake with a sudden cry.

That name was Horatio Nelson!

"What's the matter? What's the matter?" cried everybody in the waggon,

"Nothing. Nothing," stammered Emma. "I was asleep and dreaming, that was all: I thought I was falling. Did I cry out?"

"Indeed you did," said a woman, "and nearly frightened me out of my wits. Folks as is troubled with bad dreams, in course on account of their consciences, should not travel in waggons along with other folks as—as——"

"As has no conscience at all," put in a voice of a fine manly character. "Is that what you mean, madam?"

"No, sir, it is not; and I *petickler* desires as you wont speak to me; I aint a Gill to be spoke to by every Jack I meets."

"Perhaps the lady," said another voice, "has had a gill of something before she got into the waggon."

This not very brilliant joke produced a general laugh, which was so decidedly against the lady, that she thought it prudent to say no more, but wrapping herself in her dignity and her shawl, she strove to look the greatest piece of injured virtue and respectability upon record.

And now Emma would fain have asked, "who spoke of Horatio Nelson?" but a something in her heart kept her silent. She had a hope that whoever had pronounced that name would pronounce it again, and as that hope grew in her mind she forthwith banished all desire or inclination to sleep, and listened with the most intense eagerness to what was being spoken of in the waggon. She felt quite certain that the name had fallen from the lips of one of the two persons who had taken up her cause against the fastidious lady in the large shawl; and if she had required any confirmation of her belief, she now had it, for after a slight pause, they continued their former conversation.

"Yes," said one, "you would find the whole particulars in the *Evening Courant*. It was off Ushant the affair took place, and a very brilliant thing it was. You see the French frigate, Le Cerf, had been taken and a prize crew put on board of her; but in the gale which took place in the Channel, four or five of the prize crew lost their lives, poor fellows, mostly by being washed overboard, for the French prisoners on board would not assist in working the vessel, but when the gale was over, seeing that the prize crew were reduced in numbers, and that those who remained were in a state of thorough exhaustion by the struggle they had had with the tempest, they fell upon them and retook the ship, and hoisted the French flag again with great glee.

"I understand," said the other. "It was not a very honourable thing."

"Quite the reverse, I think. Well, you see, they had not enough hands to make it a safe thing to keep out at sea, for they could not have fought the ship, as a number of them, as is usual, had been drafted on board the English frigate, Juno, as prisoners of war, when she took Le Cerf."

"Exactly."

"Then their move was to reach a French port as soon as they possibly could, and with that view they made for Brest as hard as they possibly could get through the water; but to their horror what should they find half a mile only on their lee, when the day broke, but the English frigate, Juno. Well, the first thing the French did was to haul down the tri-coulor in a twinkle, and up with the Union Jack again, with the hope of being able to get clear of the Juno; but the look-out on the English frigate had seen the little delicate operation and reported accordingly. There was hardly a breath of wind stirring, for the old adge of 'after a storm comes a calm,' had been verified; so although the Juno fired a shot or two at Le Cerf, they could not get well at her, so a boat was well manned and sent to see what was amiss; and seeing this the Frenchmen dragged up one of their English prisoners, who was no other than the lieutenant commanding the prize crew, and brining him to the quarter, commanded him on pain of death to hail the boat, and say that all was right, and if it was commanded by an officer inferior in rank to himself, to send him back."

"And did he do it?"

"Not exactly. Lieutenants in the English navy don't do such things. The moment the boat come within hail, he sung out—'Boat-a-hoy.' 'Coming on board,' said a voice in reply. 'Come with your roughest side outermost,' said the lieutenant, 'for the French are masters of the vessel.'

"Well, it appears that the French just knew enough of the language to comprehend that the lieutenant was encouraging the boat's crew to board them instead of dismissing them; but they feared to carry their threat of shooting the lieutenant into execution. The officer who had charge of the boat, was a young man who had been made lieutenant on board the Juno, when she sent her prize crew to take charge of Le Cerf, and seeing, in a moment, how matters stood, he ordered the boat's crew to pull hastily to the ship; and cheering them all the way, Le Cerf opened the fire of grape-shot upon the boat which did great execution, but did not actually swamp it; and the crew—that is to say, those left alive, with this young fellow of an officer, fairly boarded Le Cerf, and re-took her, after a desperate fight against double their numbers, before another boat could be sent from the Juno.

"It was a gallant action, and this young officer's name you said, was——"

"Horatio Nelson."

Emma compressed her lips to prevent the cry of delight that was nearly, despite of her, coming from them, and her eyes overflowed with tears. She would have given worlds to have asked if in the fight *he* had been hurt, but she felt that she could not just then trust her voice to say so much. She hoped she might be able to do so in a little while, and, perhaps, too, she might hear more by listening. How she blessed the state of semi-darkness in which the interior of the waggon was, for she felt that to that alone could she owe her exemption from remark, on account of the agitation that might otherwise have been most powerfully visible in her face.

She was disappointed, however, in her hopes of hearing more of Nelson. All that was further said by the narrator of the story consisted of an assurance that the whole particulars were to be found in the *Evening Courant*, for that the Juno had brought her prize into the Southampton Water, and hence the full particulars had got to London.

This narration gave quite a new bias to the mind of Emma. Her own prospects, and hopes, and fears, seemed to her to sink into utter insignificance before her lover's, lest anything should happen to him who held the first and foremost place in her heart. The more she reflected upon his diposition and upon the nature of his profession, the more vividly alive did she become to the many dangers which he must hourly be encountering.

"The day will come when they will tell me he is dead!"

These were the words that appeared ringing in her ears, and again she blessed the darkness of the waggon that shrouded her emotion from the gaze of those who could not understand if they saw it, and to whom she could not and would not explain it ; and so the fat, lazy, horses of the waggon tramped leisurely on, going at, for them, really a great speed, for when in motion the vehicle really went at more than five miles an hour, so that with stoppages, they got on over the ground fairly at the rate of five miles, which, in those days, for a waggon, was really something rather tremendous. And then this vehicle did not put up at night, which was rather a rarity ; but it went jingling and plodding on its way with the intention of getting into the ancient city of Coventry by half-past two in the morning, which was not a very bad arrangement for the Innkeeper where the waggon was wont to put up, inasmuch as it compelled everybody to take a bed there for the remainder of the night.

To be sure, by the time the cumbrous vehicle got into the Inn-yard at Coventry, everybody had had snatches of sleep, and even Emma had yielded to the drowsy motion of the vehicle, full as her mind was of the daring achievement of Nelson.

Then, there was a sleepy ostler, with a miserable lanthern that only made darkness visible, and then there was a yawning girl, who showed the female portion of the cargo of the waggon to their slumbers ; and after ascending a flight of steps in the open Inn-yard, traversing a long gallery, Emma was shown into a room in which there was a comfortable-enough bed, upon which, after securing her door, she hastily threw herself, and shivering in the night air, she sought repose.

She slept ; but, somehow, she dreamt of glaring light, and to her bewildered imagination there seemed to be no end of the scuffling of feet in all directions. Suddenly she was aroused from this half dormant state by a rapping at her door. She sprang half up from her bed, and in a voice of alarm, demanded who was there.

" Fire !" said a voice.

" What ? What do you mean ?" cried Emma.

" The inn is on fire. Save yourself !"

That one word " fire " was likely, indeed, after what she had gone through at the Grange, to find a frightful echo in the brain of Emma Lyon. Not even the association that it had in her mind with Nelson, could hinder it from being the fullest word of terror that could be uttered to her.

" No—no—no !" she cried.

As she sprang up, she saw, coming through the window of the room, a red glare, and she could no longer doubt but that the words spoken outside her door were true. To fly to it, and open it, was the work of a moment.

" Not this way—not this way," cried a voice, and she found herself clasped in the arms of some one, who carried her back into the room again, slamming the door shut with his foot. " That way," he added, " is destruction. It is by the window only that you can escape, and I will save you or perish with you. Oh, Emma, you do not know how much I love you."

The stranger clasped her tightly in his arms, and began to kiss her vehemently. She struggled to free herself from his mad embrace, and they both fell together. There had been a something in his voice which sounded familiar to her ; and when he now spoke again she knew.

" Emma," he said, " I have set my life upon your being mine, and you shall be. I love you to distraction, and nothing shall prevent me from making you my own. Beautiful girl ! I have not lost sight of you. Let him who hitherto has had all the chances of bending you to his will, perish. The wound you gave him in the old house at Hawarden is serious ; but the only wound you have given me is in my heart. Ah, Emma, you alone can make me happy."

By this Emma knew that it was no other than the man who, with so much pretended contrition, had let her out of the old house in the lane at Hawarden. She began to suspect that even the fire at the inn was a mere *ruse* to get her to open her bed-room door, and she cried loudly—

" Help ! help ! help !"

" Your cries are in vain," he said. " I have set fire to a quantity of straw upon the staircase, and no one will come through these flames to your aid. It is impossible. You are mine, Emma. By this light you are mine. You shall have all that wealth can command. Do you think I have followed you thus far, and tracked your path, to be baffled now ? No—no—no."

Emma felt herself half stifled by his kisses. A film seemed to come over her eyes. She breathed with difficulty. She tried to cry for help, but her tongue refused its office.

CHAPTER XXVII.

SHOWS HOW EMMA WAS RESCUED, AND HOW SHE GOT TO LONDON.

CRASH went the door of the room, and a couple of men rushed into the little apartment. Emma fainted

*   *   *   *   *

Oh! what a fearful sensation the recovery from that state of syncope was! How tht blood tingled in her veins, and how her hear throbbed. With difficulty she opened her eyes. Some one was holding something very fragrant to her nostrils. It was daylight, too.

"She's coming to," said a voice. "What a while she has been, to be sure. Oh, she'll soon be all right. How do you feel, now?"

"Better," said Emma; "where am I?"

EMMA FINDS HER WAY TO THE THIRD FLOOR OF A LONDON HOUSE.

"Why, here, at the Peacock and Broccole, to be sure. You have been two hours in a sort of faint, and only just now have come to. Do you think you can take anything?"

Emma looked around her, and from the array of bottles, and the general appearance of the place, she guessed she was in the bar of some public-house.

"Good God!" she said. "Tell me how i all came about?"

"Oh, that's easy enough told," said a fat, good-tempered looking female. "You were in the waggon while I was a-bed, and you slept in 22, you know; and then somebody or another set light to the stairs, and you could not get out of the room till two gentlemen broke in, and saved you from the smoke and smother."

"Two gentlemen?"

"Yes, to be sure; and a very dangerous thing for them it was, too; but they told me to tell you that they were mighty pleased they had saved you, and hoped you were not hurt."

"Two gentlemen!" again said Emma, and she passed her hand across her brow, as if striving to recollect something. "Two gentlemen! Was there not a third?"

"Not as I knows of, my dear."

"Tall and thin, rather, with dark eyes, and an olive complexion? Did no one see any such person in the inn?"

There was a general shake of the head from all present, and as recollection returned to Emma, she began to feel sure that he who had, with such pertinacity, forced his unwelcome addresses upon her, had in the confusion effected his escape without being noticed. She trembled as she thought of how she was followed and assailed from place to place by one or other of these two persons, who seemed resolved to be her evil geniuses; and each moment, as she gathered strength, she began to be anxious about her immediate departure from the old city of Coventry.

"How can I proceed?" she said. "I wish to reach London as quickly as I possibly can. Tell me how I may reach London, and that quickly too."

"Why, there's no great difficulty about that," said the stout lady, who was no other than the landlady of the inn. "There's no great difficulty about that. The London coach starts at eleven o'clock, and you can get a place outside or inside, just as you may please to pay for it."

"I thank you," said Emma. "I thank you from my heart for all your kindness to me. Indeed I do. I will go to London by the coach. I have some money. Outside I will go. I am not rich. I am, indeed, a poor girl, but I have money enough."

"Come now, you are only flurrying yourself," said the landlady. "A cup of tea will set you all to rights, I daresay; and if you wish it, I'll send and have a place took for you in the London coach. Now you sit still, and you shall take a bit of breakfast and a dish of tea with me, my dear. I don't eat much myself, but you will perhaps peck a little bit. John! John!"

"Yes, missus."

"Tell Betsy to grill a couple of pounds of ham, and to boil a dozen or so of eggs. I fancy I could take a trifle in the eating way myself, though Heaven alone knows it's little I take. A pound of chops, or half a dozen devilled kidneys, or, may be, a cold shoulder of lamb, is the most I can ever eat at my breakfast, with a pigeon pie or two. My appetite's fell off ever since my poor man went to Heaven."

Emma was rapidly now recovering from the first fainting fit she had ever had in her life, and she was, now that the dangers of the night had passed away, rather disposed to be amused at the extreme delicacy of the landlady in the eating line. The breakfast was duly laid by John, who, with a broad grin, told his mistress that "if there *warent* enough she knowed there was more where that comes from," to which she replied by flinging a half-pint pewter measure at his head, and telling him "she didn't want none of his *imperence* there, not she."

Emma was perfectly surprised at the little bit that the landlady "pecked," to use her own phraseology; but, certainly, our heroine found herself the better for the substantial breakfast that she took at the Peacock and Broccoli, at Coventry.

The outside place was duly taken for her on the Highflyer coach from London to Coventry, and *vice versa;* and at half-past eleven o'clock she caught a glimpse of the wooden representation of Peeping Tom as she was rattled out of the city upon the well-horsed coach, that was not to pause, except to change horses, until it reached the great metropolis.

Emma glanced about her almost with an expectation of seeing her tormentor of the previous night following her still, but he certainly was not upon the outside of the coach. She had a legal complaint against this person that any magistrate must have listened to; but if she could avoid his importunities without having recourse to the law, she felt that she would be much better pleased so to do.

The fine fresh morning air, combined with the rattling pace at which the coach went, exhilarated the spirits of Emma considerably, and she found herself much more hopeful of the future, and regardless of the perils of the past, than she had been. There was on the coach besides herself, a female with a child at her breast, and two men, but they seemed all quiet, well-disposed sort of people. The woman spoke to Emma mildly, after which they got into a quiet kind of chat together. The landlady of the Peacock and Broccoli had, upon hearing from Emma what was her mission to London, given her a few lines of introduction to a Mrs. Wassail, upon whom she said she had a claim founded upon gratitude, for kind treatment to her, Mrs. Wassail, when once in Coventry friendless and without means. The address was London Street, Fitzroy Square, and Emma asked the female with the child if she knew of such a place.

"Oh dear, yes, certainly," was the reply. "Everybody in London knows where that is, miss, and you won't have to ask twice to find your way quite well and easy. It's near—bless me! what is it near?—why, it's not far off—well, I can hardly say what—it's not far off, but you won't find any difficulty in getting to it at all."

This was not, perhaps, very precise in

formation, but it so far satisfied Emma, that she was not directed by the landlady to any part of the city that had a disreputable reputation; and so on went the coach nimbly up hill and down dale, until afar off in the dim cloudy obscurity of the sky some one looked long and narrowly, and then cried—

" There is London."

Yes, Emma Lyon was now near to that city in which all her hopes and all her fears lay concentrated. That city which to the imagination of the young in distant places, is a sparkling romance, but which to the perceptions of many, who live and toil within its vast recesses, is in truth a dreary reality.

As the coach neared the mighty city, the vegetation lost its bright freshness—the country-looking road gave place to the straggling suburb; and finally came the roar and the shout of London upon Emma's ears. Confused and bewildered by the novelty of her situation, she at times closed her eyes to shut out, if it were only for a brief space, the mighty tumult; and then being, as she was, upon the outside of the coach, she could not divest herself from the idea that every rapidly driven vehicle that came dashing on must inevitably produce a collision between it and the coach. Indeed, to her the whole progress of the vehicle upon which she was, from the outskirts of the city to an inn-yard, in Holborn, seemed to be but a series of narrow escapes.

With a feeling almost of terror she alighted, and found herself in one of those large quadrangles that are yet to be found within the gates of some of the old inns in London, and which, notwithstanding the railroads, still continue to look bustling and full of life. After securing her small bundle, the first thing that Emma felt the absolute necessity of was for rest. The whole journey from Hawarden to the metropolis had been performed too quickly for her strength, and she felt as though she was sinking under the impression of extreme fatigue.

Of course at the inn there was every accommodation to be had for the paying for, and Emma soon found herself in a comfortable enough chamber. A good-tempered looking girl brought her a cup of coffee, and then she threw herself upon the bed and fell fast asleep.

How refreshed Emma felt when she opened her eyes again, and yet the incessant rumble of the coach was not absent from her ears, and for the moment she could almost fancy herself still upon it; but that illusion was soon dispelled and she arose. It was twilight, and yet she could see well enough everything in the room, and by dashing cold water upon her face she fully aroused herself and brought her thinking powers into activity. Of course, an inn was not the sort of place for her to stay in, and therefore the sooner she availed herself of the introduction to the people in London-street the better.

With this view she descended to the lower part of the inn, and having paid for such accommodation as she had received, she asked leave to let her bundle remain while she went to call upon a friend, and at the same time asked her way to London-street.

She received that common answer in London, to go straight on a long way and then ask again; so on poor Emma went, through what to her there was the most bewildering scene of chaos and confusion that ever she had beheld. It seemed to her as if everybody in the street must be by some fatality too late for something or another, for eagerness and hurry were depicted upon the majority of their countenances; and then the incessant roar, clatter, and dash of every imaginable description of article upon four or two wheels, that roared and tugged and shivered down the centre of the thoroughfare, made up a babel of sounds that forced Emma more than once within the shelter of some friendly doorway, thus to wait for a short time until the wild din had to some extent subsided.

And, at length, she did ask her way again, and then she was directed to go down a street which, for its gloomy quietness, presented a marked contrast to the bustling, abounding thoroughfare she had only just left. The houses were tall and black-looking. An air of faded gentility pervaded them. They looked like respectable failures.

The Londoner will easily guess that Emma was not far from her destination, and in the neighbourhood of Fitzroy-square.

At length London-street was reached, and Emma stood upon the door-step of the house to which she had been recommended.

It was like a tall spectre made of bricks, flat and dingy, with what is called an artist's light on the first floor, which is produced by ingeniously elongating some window there situated, till it looks as though it had run up in a consumption beyond its strength.

Emma was puzzled at the half-dozen bells that graced the doorpost; she did not know that they indicated that the house was let out in unfurnished lodgings, and that if she should pull the wrong one, there would be intestive brawls in the establishment; but she thought while there was such a choice of bells she had better, as there was but one knocker, appeal to that, and she did so there without producing any effect whatever.

The knocker was let to nobody, therefore nobody ever asked who was that knocking at the door.

At length, the door suddenly opened, and some one was coming out, to whom Emma popped the question, if Mr. Wassail lived there.

" Oh, yes," was the reply ; " second-floor front."

Emma stepped into the passage, and the door was closed by the person who had gone out. She fancied she was entitled to ascend the staircase, and find out the second-floor front ; so she commenced the navigation which was not a very easy one, for either from fashion or from a redundancy of furniture, everybody had something on the landing-place ; but by being careful of her route,

Emma reached the second-floor, and was about to tap at the door, when she heard a voice from within, in deep-toned accents, say—

"Not love—oh hate—oh horror—oh despair!
  Tear out the shrinking heart of destiny and fate;
  And breathing with a mighty roar in elemental strife,
  Fly shrinking to the depths of blue and blazing chaos!"

"Gracious Heavens!" thought Emma, "what can this mean? Have I hit upon the abode of some maniac? I will yet listen, ere I venture to knock for admission."

In the course of a moment or two, the voice continued—

"The day will come, malignant, squinting tyrant,
  When with rough shells, from out the roaring deep,
  Sometime the home of oysters, I thy column
  Vertebral will scrape."

Emma began to think it prudent to retire, and give up the acquaintance of the Wassails, if this was the ordinary mood in which the gentleman of that name was to be found in; but before she could come to any decision, he spoke again.

"Ha! ha! I'll pluck thee by thy gore-stained locks,
  From out the debris of a thousand crimes; and then,
  Filling thy mouth with frog-spawn water, I will sit
  Thee on the blazing furnace, till bubbling echo shrieks,
  'It boils! It boils!'"

Emma was ready to sink with alarm, when a mild voice said suddenly close to her—

"Do you want any one here?"

And upon turning, she saw a pale-faced, meek-looking woman on the landing.

"I wanted Mrs. Wassail," said Emma, "but there seems a mad gentleman in the room."

"Mad? Oh, no. That is my husband only. He is rehearsing. I am Mrs. Wassail."

——

CHAPTER XXVIII.

EMMA GETS A SITUATION, AND LEARNS SOMETHING OF LONDON LIFE AND MANNERS.

EMMA was as much in the dark respecting the occupation of Mr. Wassail after the explanation of his lady as she had been before. All she quite understood was, the comforting assurance that the gentleman had not positively taken leave of his wits.

The technical term rehearsing, carried no precise meaning to her ears, but it was quite clear, from the manner of Mrs. Wassail, that she thought she had been quite explanatory.

"You need not be at all afraid," she added. "Pray come in, if you have any business with me or Mr. Wassail."

The door of what to Emma was certainly rather a remarkable looking apartment, was thrown open by Mrs. Wassail, and Emma was requested to enter. She did so, and the glance she cast around her was one that reflected no small amount of astonishment upon her face.

The room was a large one; but anybody could see at a glance that it was "kitchen, and chamber, and hall," to the Wassails. In one corner was a sofa-bedstead that, no doubt, in bygone times, had been put up in the day-time, but which had at length got so intimate with the Wassails, that it lay upon the floor in all its sprawling length, without a thought of doubling itself up into a "fraudulent couch." A threadbare something, Heaven and the Wassails only knew what it is, covered the floor, and there were certainly tables and chairs; but the less that is said about them, is decidedly the better.

Upon the walls hung theatrical crowns, helmets, and caps, with gorgeous feathers and circlets, some of thrum merely; and there were shields and swords, too, in grim array. Across the back of a chair hung a glittering robe, glowing with spangles.

The proprietor of all this was in the middle of the floor with an arm extended, while in the other he held a scrap of paper, upon which his eyes were fixed with a horrible temporary obliquity of vision.

Emma had her letter in her hand, and Mr. Wassail took it with the air of some emperor receiving an autograph congratulation on the death of his wife from a foreign court.

"I pray you be seated," he said, in the true stage commentional tragedy voice. "Be seated, while I peruse this missive. Ah! From a friend, who, when the leaden clouds of dire distress and want of money were hovering o'er us, was most kind. Come to my arms."

Emma, before she was aware of what Mr. Wassail was about, was subjected to a stage embrace; and when she was released, he added—

"Thrice welcome—thrice welcome! We cannot ask you to partake of the cheer of a palace, or to repose in soft luxuriance upon beds of down. We cannot place at your disposal the rich and gorgeous banquets of——"

"Do be quiet, Wassail," said his wife. "We have got some eggs and bacon."

"I do not wish to give you any trouble," said Emma; "but it is a great thing for me, in this vast city, to have any one to come to whom I may call a friend."

"A friend!" said Mr. Wassail; and then he made a step forward, evidently meditating another embrace, but his wife pushed him aside, saying—

"Be quiet, Wassail, you know you are far from up in your part to-night, so you attend to your business, while I speak to this young lady.—Now don't you interfere, Wassail: we will imagine all that you ought to say, and would say if you had time, which you have not."

Upon this, Mr. Wassail betook himself to the bit of paper again that he had in his hand ; and Mrs. Wassail taking Emma to a distant window, said—

"I suppose you have no idea of the profession, my dear?"

"Profession?" said Emma.

"Yes: the stage I mean."

"Oh, no—no, I never had such a thought, indeed. My object is to get to service in London, if I can."

"Well, I don't know but you choose the wiser course. Only see what we have made of it, and we have been at it these fifteen years, ay, and longer too. There is Mr. Wassail, who is eminently qualified to take the 'first business' at a patent house, is condemned to 'general utility' over the water ; and I can hardly get an engagement at all, although nobody can come within a hundred miles of my 'chambermaids.'"

If Mrs. Wassail had uttered a sentence or two in Greek, they could not have been much more incomprehensible to Emma than this speech, which sounded to her very much like the ravings of some perfectly harmless lunatic. All she could say was, "Yes," and "Indeed."

"So you see, my dear," added Mrs. Wassail, "I don't at all recommend the profession to you ; and as you talk of service, I do think that we have an opportunity at this very moment of doing you some good in that way. Wassail! Wassail!"

"Had I three ears I'd hear thee," said Wassail. "What is it?"

"Did not that young girl who was with us at the Amateurs last Tuesday, say that somebody was wanted where she lived at as a kind of child's-maid or nursery governess?"

Mr. Wassail tapped his forehead for some few moments, and then he replied. "Thou speakest sooth. She did. It is at Dr. Budd's in Chatham Place, Blackfriars, that she fills the post of kitchen-deity; but she has that within which passeth show. Talent she hath, and where the stars not malignant, a name would she make in histrionic annals second to few."

"Well, then, my dear," said Mrs. Wassail to Emma, "if the place is not filled up, and your recommendations are good, no doubt you can have it, for they think very highly at Dr. Budd's of this young person we mention, and I am quite sure that she will do all she can, if you go there, to make you happy and comfortable ; and now, after the bacon and eggs, you and I will go and see about it at once."

It was in vain that Emma protested she required just then neither bacon nor eggs.— The Wassails would prepare both of those articles and place them before her, when, from courtesay, rather than from inclination, she was compelled to partake of the fare; but her attention was frequently attracted by the extraordinary speeches of Mr. Wassail, who was to perform that evening some outrageous tyrant at a minor theatre over the water; and who, as his wife said, "truly was anything but up in his part, which he would have to rehearse in a couple of hours."

When the bacon and the eggs, and a pot of porter from a neighbouring public-house, which Mr. Wassail did not disdain to fetch "in his own mug," had been discussed, Emma set out with Mrs. Wassail to Chatham Place, Blackfriars, while Mr. Wassail, having buttoned a remarkably seedy-looking light-comedy-coat right up to his chin, and put on a pair of wofully defective light kid gloves, started to rehearsal.

"Let us see you often," he said to Emma. "You cannot take us amiss or unprepared, for we never prepare for anybody; so that whether bright Phœbus be refulgent in the heavens, or chaste Luna be looking down with a silvery eye upon the earth, you will be welcome. Adieu until we meet again."

Mr. Wassail, although they were in the open street, showed strong symptoms of being about to perpetrate another stage embrace, but Mrs. Wassail interposed and pushed him on his route, observing, "There, you will be too late and get fined, as you are continually doing, and I am quite sure we can't afford that. Get on with you, as quick as you can."

Emma and her new friend made the best of their way to the house of Doctor Budd, in Blackfriars. Fortunately, the doctor was at home ; and after a perusal of the highly satisfactory letter that Emma had, in the shape of a testimonial from Doctor Lukin, at Preston, and hearing from her own lips the reasons of her leaving her first situation at Hawarden, she was at once engaged in Doctor Budd's service, and told to go to the kitchen and make her own arrangements with the servant, whom she would find there.

And now, reader, picture to yourself the kitchen of Doctor Budd's house, containing two such occupants as Emma and the servant who was there previous to her arrival, and ask yourself by what freak of fortune two of the most beautiful women the world ever saw —possessed, likewise, of great talents—ever got together in that region of servitude! The one, our heroine, destined to occupy a large space in the world's observation, and to rule kings and courts, as well as heroes, while the other became, ultimately, the well-known, and charming actress, Mrs. Powell!

Emma was received by this young person, who then bore the name of Mary Ann Layton, with every kindness. Doctor Budd might have, at times, beauty and fashion in his drawing-room ; but what was it compared to the beauty and brilliancy he had in his kithen?

"You may be happy enough here," said Mary Ann, "if you can so far acquiesce in the situation in which fortune has placed you, as to cast no glance upon any other; but I am wretched. I fancy that, by embracing the stage as a profession, I might emerge from a condition of servitude. Perhaps my ambition blinds my judgment, but here I should die soon if I had no hope of some day releasing myself."

A flush of colour came across the face of

Emma, as she said, in a slightly tremulous voice—

"And I, too, will confess that I have had thoughts that would lift me far above this condition. I should, indeed, feel sad to think that there was no hope for me but that of a life of servitude. But I will not believe that such is to be the case. I will at least dream of happier fortune, if the reality should never come at all. I will please myself with imagining all that is great, if in truth I am condemned for my whole life to be all that is humble "

"Well," said Mary Ann, with a smile—that smile which afterwards was the delight of thousands, as it beamed from behind the foot-lights of the *great houses*—"we will be waiters upon Fortune, then; and if any opportunity does come to her, we will not send it away again. In the meantime, let us do what we have agreed to do here with as good a grace as we can; but I predict that the day will come when this kitchen will only be a laughable recollection to us both. You are very beautiful, Emma."

"And you," said Emma.

They both laughed, and involuntarily cast their eyes to a small piece of looking-glass that was nailed to the wall. Then they laughed again, and then they set to work cherrily.

A week passed away, and nothing disturbed the even tenor of Emma's life at Doctor Budd's. She had communicated with her mother and with Mr. Lukin, and she had received both their congratulations upon her good fortune, in so speedily getting a respectable situation. Mrs. Lyon's letter had one expression in it which brought a slight look of disdain into the face of Emma. The expression was simply this:—

"And, now, my dear, your great object should be to remain as long as possible in one place. A lifetime, if you can "

"No," said Emma. "No, mother, you do not know me; I am not doomed to spend a lifetime in servitude, and I will not. No. It is not the prophecy of the gipsy that affects me; but it is the prophetic feeling of my own heart that tells me I am formed for something different from this life that I am now leading. I—"

Emma was interrupted by the sudden entrance of Mary Ann, who, with a face beaming with joy, flew to her crying, "congratulate me, my dear girl, congratulate me. I think that the hour of my triumph and of my emancipation from this state of servitude is near at hand,"

"Indeed!" said Emma, while her heart sunk within her at the thoughts that, as yet, she saw no opening by which she might herself escape the chilling thraldom of personal ervice.

"Yes; I have just had a letter from Mr. Wassail, to say that he has secured for me an appearance this night week at a small theatre, where he wishes me to show what I can do. I am to play Ophelia in Hamlet, or I know the part well. It is the same I read to you last night, and I shall succeed. I feel that I shall: I am confident of it. I have a voice and—and I am sure I shall play Ophelia well."

"Happy, Mary Ann."

"Yes, I am happy now—I am very, very happy."

Tears started to the eyes of Mary Ann, and she was compelled to call to her aid all her fortitude to prevent herself from subsiding into an hysterical passion of weeping.

"And I," said Emma, mournfully, "I must remain here, and not even have the joy of seeing your triumph."

"Not so, Emma. Not so. That must not be, indeed. It would be to deprive me of more than one-half of my pleasure if you were not there. Indeed you must come."

"But how can we both leave ?"

"Oh, we must manage that in some way. Where there is a will there is a way. It shall be; so we will consider it to be quite settled. You shall ask leave to be away for an evening, and you will get it; and then I will take leave; so we shall both get away; and if anything comes of it, it will do you no harm then."

"That is true," said Emma, with a sigh. "Ah, I wish I could play Ophelia likewise."

"And who knows, Emma?—who knows ? Cheer up my dear friend. Your day will come, rest assured, and all will be well yet. Remember how much longer I have been waiting to what you have. Come, I will sing you all my bits of songs in my part, and you shall be my audience; but you must not be too indulgent to me or you will spoil me."

CHAPTER XXIX.

EMMA AND HER FRIEND BOTH MAKE A FIRST APPEARANCE.

MARY ANN was quite right as regarded Emma easily getting leave to be away for an evening. The permission was asked for and readily obtained, and the important day came.

Now, Emma," said the debutant, "you had better go at once to the Wassails, and they will take charge of you, for, otherwise, ignorant as you are of London, you may soon lose your way, and I would not have anything malapropos occur to-night for worlds. Wassail plays Hamlet for the first time, and I do hope he will succeed, with all my heart."

"And I, too," said Emma. "We shall meet again at the theatre ?"

"Certainly, my dear girl; I could not do without you. You will be with me, and not in the front of the house, Emma. I should be miserable if I did not have you to speak to at times; so now go at once, my dear friend, to the Wassails. I will be with you in an hour. Do—I—look well to-day, Emma ?"

"A little flushed, but more than well."

Mary Ann thanked her friend for the compliment with a smile, and in the course of the next quarter of an hour Emma was on her road to the Wassails, who still occupied their old apartments in London Street, Fitzroy Square. Notwithstanding the time that she (Emma) had been absent from that room, she might well have thought that but a few moments only had elapsed. There was the fraudulent sofa—there was the general litter, and there were the properties hanging to the old walls; and there was the odour of eggs and bacon.

"Triumph," exclaimed Mr. Wassail, as he advanced to welcome her. "Triumph is in my eye. Do you not behold it? I and the world have been at jars; for society too long has been—

"A little more than kin and less than kind."

But to night I rather think I shall astonish the town a few."

"I wish you all manner of success," cried Emma.

"I am beholden to you, gracious lady; but the time has come when I must render up myself to businss. Mrs. W. don't forget the black bottle."

Accompanying Mr. and Mrs. Wassail, Emma soon found her way to the theatre, which was one of those apologies for a Thespian Temple, which are to be found chiefly eastward of what is considered the fashion, and over the water. Emma, who was upon this occasion making decidedly her first appearance behind the curtain, was perfectly astonished at the dirt and squalor of everything. She had fancied that surely she was about to be introduced to something like a fairy-land of beauty and romance; for since from the front of the house in a theatre all was so bright, and beautiful, and resplendent, she conjectured that when she was at the back, she would be in the midst of such a combination of gorgeous things, that she would be perfectly bewildered which to admire the first.

Alas! Emma was soon undeceived: she found, indeed, that it was—

"Distance lent enchantment to the view;"

and that she was in a world of the unreal, where everything was made to seem what it was not, while upon a close inspection the deception was anything but a deception. Everything was rude and rough, and commonplace; and tarnish and decay seemed to hold a joint lease of the premises, and all that they contained.

"Is this indeed a theatre?" said Emma.

"Yes," said a voice at her elbow. "Don't you like it?"

She turned, and then indeed she saw a transformation. Her friend Mary Ann had suffered not a sea change, but a land change—

"Into something rich and strange."

The maid-of-all-work of Doctor Budd had become the gentle Ophelia—the beloved, wronged, played with a neglected toy of the Prince of Denmark; and radiantly beautiful she looked.

"And so you are disappointed at the theatre?" said Mary Ann.

"Not now," replied Emma. "Not now that I see you."

"Ah, you are a flatterer; but come this way, Wassail is dressing, and Mrs. Wassail is with him. You will feel strange if you are not with me. Come into the green-room."

Emma did go into the green-room which would have much more appropriately have been called the mouldy room; and there she found rapidly collecting the characters of the drama; and so gradually that sense of desolation, dirt, confusion, and wreck which the penetration of a theatre presents to the eye, wore off with Emma, and she was able to enjoy all she saw and all she heard.

The play began and proceeded, and to Emma's perception the Hamlet of Mr. Wassail was perfection itself. She thought him gorgeous in his princely suit of sable; and as from the wings she watched the progress of the play, she felt that that night was an epoch in her existence.

But Ophelia's best scene was coming on, and finally, with those wild snatches of song wrung from a mind disordered, the fair rose of the state entranced the audience. Through her tears only could Emma see what was doing, but she heard the thunder of applause from the front of the house; and finally, near the end of the scene, she saw, through a small orifice in a wing, the pit rise tumultuously, as though swayed by some irresistible impulse; and then she glanced upon the stage. The Ophelia of the night, completely overcome by her feelings, had fainted.

Without a thought of where she was, or of what she was doing, Emma rushed to her friend and supported her in her arms. The noise and tumult in the house was terrific. The light whirled for a moment before the bewildered eyes of Emma, and then she knew no more.

* * * * *

"She is better," said a voice. "She is better now, and will soon be all right again."

"Thank Heaven," said another.

Emma knew this latter voice. It was that of the Ophelia of the evening. Opening her eyes, she encountered those of Mary Ann, who immediately exclaimed—

"Speak to me, Emma, speak to me, and tell me that you are well!"

"Yes," replied Emma. "Oh, yes. But what has happened?"

"Never mind that now. All is well. It is very late, and we must attempt to go home; at all events, whether we shall at such an hour be received or not, is quite another question."

These words opened quite a new sort of alarm to Emma, and starting up, she cried—

"What is the hour?"

A clock in the green-room, for that was where she was, answered her, by striking "One!"

"So late!" exclaimed Emma. "Oh, what will become of us, Mary Ann? We shall never be received at home."

" We can only try, my dear Emma, if you are able to walk. For my own part, I—I think that I have this night begun a new career. Mr. Wassail tells me that I have been successful in Ophelia; but perhaps he speaks from the partiality of his feelings towards me only."

" In sooth," cried Wassail, "that do I not. You will do, and no one can prevent you. You were born to be an ornament to the stage. It must be so, and it will be so. But come, both of you—I will walk as far as Chatham Place with you, since you seem to entertain some doubts of your reception at Doctor Budds, and if things should go crossly, we must think of what had better be done."

This proposition was accepted by the two young girls, and Mrs. Wassail proceeded onwards towards home, while the Hamlet of the night escorted Ophelia and Emma to their place of servitude. It was quite evident to Emma, who, by the by, felt perfectly relieved upon getting into the fresh air, that Mary Ann's destiny was fixed from that night, and that she would not have been long for a companion, even if she, Emma, should stay at Doctor Budd's, which was a very doubtful proposition indeed.

The nearer they got to what they still called home, the more doubtful regarding their reception did they get; and finally, when Emma tried to let herself in at the area gate, and found that there was a chain and padlock upon it, she found that there was no longer any doubt about the fact of Doctor Budd having made a determination to keep his two servants out for the night.

" We will not be discouraged," said Mary Anne. "It is better that we should fully and clearly know our master's intentions, so I shall insist upon awakening his attention."

Emma shrunk back, and so in truth did Mr. Wassail, while Mary Anne perpetrated some hard single knocks upon the door, and some loud peals at the bell. A perseverance for about three minutes in this course forced the doctor to put on an appearance, and accordingly a nightcapped-head looked out at a window of the second floor, and the doctor, to whom it belonged, said—

" Ladies—I am quite convinced of the injustice I have hitherto done you in confining you to the kitchens of my house. You are both of you much too fine for me, therefore, with all due deference to you, I shall do myself the pleasure of considering you both discharged. At any reasonable hour tomorrow you can come or send for your cloathes and your wages."

" Noble   sir!"   exclaimed   Wassail. "Though rude in speech I yet venture——'

Bang went down the window.

" Humph!" said Wassail. "The learned doctor is determined to do the heavy old man with a vengeance. This is what may be called rather a fix—Eh, what's that?"

One—two! struck St. Bride's clock, and the solemn echo floated sonorously in the night air.

" This is a sad thing," said Emma; "what shall we do?"

" Upon my word," said Mary Ann, "I hardly know."

Mr. Wassail paced the pavement, and tapped his head a great many times; and then, at length, he said—

" Ladies, allow me to state that I can think of nothing but going, all of us, to London Street, and putting upon the consideration and resources of Mrs. Wassail. This brute of a doctor will not open his portal tonight. I never knew a man speak in a more determined way in all my life. But yet, before we go, I will give him a parting salute. He may have dropped off into a comfortable nap by this time, which it would be a thousand pities for us to leave him in."

With this, Mr. Wassail executed a furious succession of double knocks upon the street-door, calling out as he did so—

" Awake! Arise! Wassail doth murder sleep!"

" Does he?" said a watchman, suddenly pouncing upon poor Wassail and collaring him. "You shall come to the watch-house."

Wassail, for a moment or two, looked petrified; and then, in the words of Hamlet, he said—

'I pray thee take thy hand from off my throat,
For, though I am not splenetic nor rash,
Yet is there in me something dangerous
That I would have thy wisdom fear.'

" None of your nonsense," said the watchman. "Come on—come on. This way.— I'll soon lock you up."

" My friend," said Wassail, "I have knocked up Doctor Budd."

" I know you have.—Come on, come on."

" And now," continued Wassail, "I knock you down," and, suiting the word to the action and the action to the word, Wassail sent the watchman, who did not at all expect such an attack, rolling into the road. Catching, then, Mary Ann by one hand, and Emma by the other, he said—

" Off—off. Blow wind! come rack! At least we'll die with harness on our back! Let's run up Fleet Street as if the devil was behind us. The watchman don't seem able to find his rattle, and we shall be off and away before the enemy can mark the route we take."

Fortunately for them they found a disengaged hackney-coach at the corner of Fleet Street, into which Mr. Wassail at once pushed them both, and just as the sound of the watchman's rattle began to echo from Chatham Place, they were rolling up Fleet Street at as good a pace as two blind and lame horses, whose collective ages were about fifty, could take them.

" This is an escape, indeed." said Wassail. "It will go hard, but Mrs. W. will find you some sort of accommodation for the night. For you, Mary Ann, I can see a bright destiny; but for you, Miss Lyon, it may just now be a matter of dire import to lose your place."

"It was got easily," said Emma, "so let it go easily. I do not yet despair of emerging from my present position. I am young and hopeful, and shall not take much to heart my discharge from Doctor Budd's. Oh, if I could only hit upon some mode of making my living that would keep me out of a kitchen, I should be happy."

"You are thinking of the stage?" said Wassail.

"I own it," replied Emma. "I am thinking of the stage. It is but natural that after the triumph of Mary Ann, that I should turn my thoughts that way. Tell me, Mr. Wassail, do you think I have any chance of success in such a profession?"

EMMA AND MARY ANN SEARCHING THE ATTIC.

Wassail was silent for a few moments, and then he said—

"Emma, you have talents—you have beauty—and you have ambition. I do not, myself, know of anything in life in which you might not succeed, if—if—if——"

"Ah, that if," said Emma. "Go on,

Mr. Wassail, go on. Why do you stop at that ominous word, if?"

"Perhaps I shall offend you if I proceed."

"No, Mr. Wassail. The frankness of a friend can never offend me. I know that let you say what you will, it is said not with any feeling of unkindness to me ; so say freely what you think of me."

"Then I say, Emma, you would succeed, I think, in anything, if you only had a little more education."

"Education !" said Emma, clasping her hands. "Education ! Yes, I am wofully deficient, I know it and feel it. I am indeed most wofully deficient there. I can only just read and write—a little."

CHAPTER XXX.

EMMA MEETS WITH A NIGHT ADVENTURE AT LONDON STREET.

FOR a short time after Emma had spoken these words, there was silence in the old rumbling hackney-coach. Mr. Wassail did not know very well what to say, and Mary Ann felt rather distressed to think that the player had been so needlessly sincere in his opinion to Emma of her great disqualification for the stage; a disqualification which she, Mary Ann, had not failed to notice; but which, with that nice tact which belongs to some persons, she had forborne to hint at.

It was Emma herself who first broke the silence, by saying—

"I am very much obliged to you, Mr. Wassail, for what you have said, and I will begin to-morrow. None but a real friend would have said such a thing to me, and it has awakened in me thoughts and feelings which I will not lightly let go to sleep again. Yes, I will begin to-morrow, a course of such self-education as it may lie within my power to avail myself of. I am glad that the only disqualification you think I have is a recoverable, one for it gives me every hope. I will bide my time."

After this the conversation flowed much more freely, and by the time the coach stopped at London Street there was no sort of embarrassment about either of them, on account of the somewhat rare sincerity of the actor to Emma.

"Don't say a word," cried Mrs. Wassail, when they entered the room; "don't say a word about it. I fully expected you. It was only, after all, just what might very well have been looked for. How could any of you think of anything else? Doctor Budd won't let either of you in to-night."

"Nor to-morrow either," said Emma, "except for our wages and our things, for both of which I dread to go. Indeed, I don't suppose I am entitled to any of the former."

"Well, well, my dear, that can be all settled to-morrow. Now, we must find you some mode of passing the night. There is an attic to let up stairs, furnished; and I see no harm, as the people of the house are gone to bed, in you two occupying it, and paying them for its use in the morning. What do you say, Wassail ?"

"Why, nothing," replied Wassail, "only that it is *the* attic."

Mr. Wassail placed so much emphasis upon the *the*, that it was quite evident something very peculiar belonged to the attic; and the curiosity of both Mary Ann and Emma was strongly excited They both looked the inquiries they did not make.

"Oh, it is all nonsense," said Mrs. Wassail. "It is all stuff. I am quite vexed with Wassail for mentioning it; but some silly people who have lodged in that attic, will have it that it is haunted."

"Haunted !" exclaimed both Emma and Mary Ann in a breath. "Haunted! a haunted attic !"

"Just so, my dears; so if you are superstitiously inclined, you had better not think of resting in the attic, and we will do the best we can for you here."

"Is it haunted with the ghost in Hamlet ?" said Emma, "for, if so, I do not think I shall mind it much. What say you, Mary Ann? Are you afraid of ghosts ?"

"Certainly not," replied Mary Ann. "I am only quite delighted at the idea of sleeping in a haunted room, whether it be an attic or any other; so, Mrs. Wassail, I will not be deterred from taking possession of the lodging. At the same time, Emma, there is no occasion for you to come with me unless you like."

"But I do like," said Emma.

"Then let us go at once. The only pity is that it is past the witching hour of night; and I am afraid that the ghost, or ghosts, of the attic, will begin to

'Sniff the morning air,'

and so be off before we can have anything like a fair opportunity of seeing them. Come, Emma, come along. Surely we can find the way without troubling Mrs. Wassail ?"

"No, no, it is no trouble," said the good lady. "I will show you to your chamber; and I have no doubt you will both of you sleep too soundly to think of anything in the shape of either good spirits or bad.—This way—this way."

In the course of the next five minutes, Emma and Mary Ann found themselves the tenants of a tolerably large-sized attic, in which there was a comfortable enough bed, with all such appointments as could be, in any way, contributory to comfort. Indeed, for an attic, the room was very well got up indeed. Perhaps it was temptingly arrayed to induce persons to take it, in defiance of its supposed ghastly visitant.

The candle that Mrs. Wassail had accommodated them with, was none of the longest, and as it flickered on the little table by the window, it cast strange shadows upon the yellow-washed walls of the apartment. The two young girls looked at each other in silence, and then Mary Ann said—

"How odd it is that since I have been in this room a kind of shuddering fear has come over me. Do you feel it, Emma ?"

"I do," said Emma, in a low tone.

"Then," added Mary Anne, as she took the light in her hand, "I will not leave a hole or a cranny unsearched in this room before we lie down to rest in it. From my soul I discredit this idle tale of a spectre."

"And yet I wish we had heard the full particulars," said Emma, "of its supposed visitation to this place. My curiosity has been strongly excited. Let us, however, Mary Anne, be especially careful to secure the door and window, and let us see that there is nothing in the shape of a trap-door in the roof of the room or anywhere in the floor. Ah, is that a cupboard in yon corner?"

"Yes," said Mary Ann, shading the little light with her hand, and slightly trembling. "It looks like one. I—I almost dread to open it, for fear some horrid sight should meet my eyes."

"Give me the light, then," said Emma, and taking it from the passive hand of Mary Ann, she walked to the cupboard and flung the door of it open at once. There was nothing there but some old clothes and a hat.

"You have real courage, Emma," said Mary Ann, "or you could not have done that. Let us to bed at once, and in the morning no doubt we shall laugh at all the idle fears of to-night. I ought to say my idle fears, for you have none."

"Yes I have," said Emma, "but if I think there is anything fearful or dangerous at hand, I would rather take a step to meet it face to face than live a moment in suspense of its coming upon me."

"That is true courage, Emma. And now I think I have fully secured the door and the window, suppose we leave the candle and let it burn at all events as long as it will, which cannot be half an hour at the utmost?"

"Yes, I should prefer it," said Emma; "and I begin to think with you, that in the morning we we shall laugh at our fears of to-night."

They both got into bed with that nervous activity which people exhibit whose imaginations are sensibly affected by any unknown danger, and they felt then a much greater sense of security when they had fairly lain down for the remainder of the night.

"Good night and good rest," said Mary Ann, "I shall cover my eyes up, so don't say another word to me for mercy's sake. I feel half dead with fright already."

"But," began Emma.

"Not another word," said Mary Ann. "Not another word if you love me. I am asleep now."

Mary Ann was as good as her word, for she did cover up her face with the bed-clothes in right earnest, and there she lay, all the external world shut out, as it were. Emma kept her regards fixed upon the candle, which each moment was getting lower and lower, and betraying the most unequivocal signs of dissolution. She still could not get rid of the strange, uneasy feeling that had been creeping over her for the last half hour, and yet she could not be said to give way t it actually, inasmuch as she felt herself able to reason upon it and to treat it as an infirmity of nature merely, without, in her mind, connecting it with any supernatural events as occurring or likely to occur.

Still she kept her regards fixed upon the candle, and it was not without something approaching to a shudder, that she saw the last remains of the wick gradually sinking into a little pool of fat, preparatory to going out altogether. It was then that, in the faintly luminous disc that surrounded the little flame, she thought—nay, at that moment she more than thought—for she felt sure she saw *a face*.

At the moment that this most strange, startling, and unexpected of all phenomena, made itself apparent to her, she felt as though a sudden rush of blood to her brain was about to overwhelm her reason; but it did not do so, and she remained after a moment or two preternaturally calm, looking at that strange face, which, in its horrible luminosity, had a hot and glossy look about it.

She could not have spoken if her life had depended upon the utterance of one word, and she could not move so as to give the least intimation to Mary Ann of what was taking place. There she lay, spell-bound, and as still as though death had already made her its victim.

The light went out, but the luminous face did not go out with it. On the contrary, there it remained, as luminous and as bright as before, and, for a time, in the same spot, too. She could not then or afterwards take upon herself to say what expression that face wore. It was rather one of those impassable kind of expressionless faces that may belong to a higher order of intellect than we can very well imagine to be the attribute of anything in the shape of frail mortality, or very well comprehend in its entire passionless appearance and aspect.

Oh, what would she not have given at that time to have been able only to utter one cry! She felt that if she could but unloose the bondage in which all her senses were wound up, she should be free from the contemplation of that fearful vision.

But no, it was not to be done. She could not move—she could not speak. She could only watch that face, and in a confused manner speculate upon its doings. She had soon ample food for such speculation, for the face began to move towards her, and then she saw a hand, in which was a something that looked like a small hand-mirror, which had the same luminous character as the face and the hand that held it.

And now, in the course of a few minutes, hand, and face, and mirror, had all reached the side of the bed close to her, and the mirror was held before her eyes. She seemed to understand that something was to be shown to her by its instrumentality, and she fixed her gaze upon it. At first she could see nothing distintly; but presently two figures appeared to grow out of the kind of mist by which the mirror was obscured. One was that of a man in a rich naval uniform. One sleeve of his coat was fastened to his breast, and no arm was in it.

The other figure was that of a female, attired in costly apparel. She was keeling at the feet of the one-armed naval officer, and looking up in his face with an expression of intense affection.

In the features of the naval officer she recognised those of the hero of her dreams—Horatio Nelson. In the features of the female, she saw herself!

She tried to speak, and again succeeded in uttering a faint sigh. In an instant the objects in the mirror assumed an aspect of confusion. It seemed as though some subtile vapour was sailing between it and her eyes; but then, as she continued gazing at it sternly, a sort of form and shape grew out of the chaos, and she became conscious of a great change of scene in the picture that was presented to her observation. A crowd of figures, generally in costumes of blue and gold, intermingled with others in plain cloathing, and some without coats, met her gaze. The place in which they seemed all to be was but dimly lighted by oil lamps.

At times the crowd of persons swayed to and fro, as if actuated by some very extraordinary impulse; and then suddenly it opened, and she saw upon a low couch a figure lying half undressed. The face was very pale, and there was blood upon the cloathing, and upon the sheet that covered the lower limbs. She knew that face again, although the agony of death by violence was upon it.

It was the face of Horatio Nelson!

Fain would Emma have uttered now a cry of dismay, but she could only, as before, sigh faintly, and that sigh seemed as though it were the signal for the disappearance of the vision in the glass. Again all was dim confusion in the face of the mirror, but it was still there, and something in an audible voice to her heart seemed to tell Emma that she had yet more to see before the revelations were all over.

She continued gazing at the glass, and as before, the misty appearance continued for a little time and then slowly cleared away, and she saw a poor small miserable-looking room. Huge blackened rafters crossed the roof, and the wretched plaster of the walls was falling down in many places. Upon a little truckle-bed, infinitely inferior to the meanest that had ever been in the cottage at Preston, lay an emaciated form. One look at the face was sufficient to assure the fact that she who lay there was dying. Another look was sufficient, changed as the lineaments were, to let Emma see that the face was her own.

This time she found her voice.

"No—no!" she cried. "Help! Have mercy, Heaven!"

Face, hand, and mirror, in a moment disappeared, and nothing but blackness was in the room. Emma sprang from her couch in a state of terror that was difficult to control. She was amazed that Mary Ann did not move; but she flew to the door of the attic, and opened it in a moment. She could not be said to have any fixed purpose in what she was about; but she descended a few stairs,

and then she paused in horror, for the luminous face was not above five paces from her.

"More! more!" she cried. "Tell me more, or assure me that this is nothing. Speak to me again—oh, speak to me again with the mute but terrible pictures."

The face disappeared, and then, as if from some one upon the stairs, there came such a howling, shrieking, roaring laugh, that it made the blood run chill in the heart of Emma. The demoniac sound appeared to thrill through her; and overcome by her feelings, she dropped upon the topmost stairs in, for the time, a state of insensibility.

She had not absolutely fainted, so that this condition into which she was thrown did not last long, and she rose shuddering, and made her way back to the attic again. Groping her way as best she could, she found her route to the bed. Strange to say, Mary Ann was sleeping profoundly, and on Emma getting into bed again, did not rouse her in the least. The first idea of our heroine was to awaken her; but upon second thought, she abstained from so doing.

"No," she said. "No, I will not rouse her, for by so doing I should have to tell all that I have seen, or that I fancy I have seen, and that I do not wish to do. Oh, God! if it be really true—if it be really a picture of what I may in time to come go through!"

She wept bitterly at the supposition, but yet those tears were to her very welcome. They much relieved her perturbed spirit, and she found herself much better after they had flowed for a time.

"I will strive," she said, "to banish the remembrance of this night from my mind—I will not think of it —I will not dwell upon it—or it will make me miserable in time to come."

It was a long time before sleep visited the eyelids of Emma, but at length she did drop off into repose, although as might have naturally been expected, it was anything but a sound or quiet slumber that she had.

A bright sunshine was streaming into the attic, when she was awakened by Mary Ann saying—

"Why, Emma, have you been crying in your sleep?"

"Crying?" she said, starting awake.

"Yes, your eyes look red with weeping."

"Ah, I must have had a bad dream," said Emma, "but I will not strive to recollect it now. Have you slept well?"

"Unusually, Emma, I dropped off to sleep at once, and woke not till now."

CHAPTER XXX.

EMMA TAKES A SUDDEN START IN LIFE, AND BEGINS A NEW CAREER.

It was from this time that a remarkable change took place in the habits and in the feelings of Emma Lyon.

Up to this night upon which so extraordinary a vision was represented to her—a vision which she never forgot even amid all the luxuries and romances of her future career ; she had cherished notions of ambition, but she had never pictured her path to greatness, otherwise than by the high-road to virtue. Now, however, she contracted a notion, which of all others, is and was likely to be subversive of good intentions, and of that integrity of mind which battles with circumstances and conquers the dread to do that which is evil.

She became a convert to the theory of fatalism.

" Yes. After the strange vision that had appeared to her with that mirror in which it had professed to depict to her certain scenes in her future life, or in the future of life of him whose image lay at the bottom of her heart ; she began to call herself the creature of destiny—she began to yield to impulse instead of setting up reflection against its dictates, and yet she was herself hardly aware of how strong a hold such a feeling had got of her.

Whether this vision of the night was real, or only one of those vivid and remarkably coinciding dreams that do at times occur, we are not in a situation in this place to decide, but that Emma fully believed in its really supernatural character has been amply proved by several passages in her after life.

That she thought much more of it than of a dream, was upon the morning of her awakening amply verified by her keeping it a profound secret from her bed-fellow, the lovely and accomplished actress that was to be.

Her manner had undergone a great change, and at the humble and rather discussive breakfast-table of the Wassail's, she was at times silent and abstracted. This might be truly termed an epoch in her existence.

Upon that very day Mary Ann obtained an engagement at a minor theatre, and Emma found a situation in the house of a market gardener in St. James's Market, but in her places she was destined to be the farther removed from this most congenial one, as her removal happened then. Indeed it was in a manner greatly to add to her belief in the fatality to which she was subject, and to confirm her in the idea that she was in the hands of a destiny who would carry her on in her career without her greatly troubling herself about the matter.

One day a lady made her appearance at the shop of Emma's new master, and at once, after taking a good look at Emma, said to her—

" Are you not the young person who was at a private theatre, and who came abruptly upon the stage on account of the fainting of her friend who performed Ophelia?"

" I am, madam."

" I thought I could not possibly be mistaken : and I am sorry to see you in such a situation. Should you be dissatisfied, you have only to apply to me, and I dare say I shall find you a position such as your appearance merits."

With this the lady handed Emma a card, and disappeared in her carriage.

We may easily imagine how, under any circumstances, such an offer as this would have been tempting to one so buffeted by fortune as Emma was ; but with her then thoughts and feelings, it seemed to her like only a further development of that destined career which it was her fate to follow. She did not wait, but presented herself to the lady the very next day.

The address upon the card was Sackville Street, Piccadilly, and the lady's name was Villar's. Emma did not know that Sackville Street had then rather an unenviable notoriety as being a street in which some persons resided who were anything but ornaments to society, a reputation which it has not lost now ; and she went full of hope to wait upon this lady of fashion, expecting, in a vague manner, much advancement, but in what shape it was to present itself, certainly Emma had no sort of idea at that time. We may be a little more explicit regarding Mrs. Villars, as it was decidedly by becoming an inmate of her house that Emma made that first false step which may not be recalled in this world.

Mrs. Villars, then, was a lady of fashion, at whose house a number of persons, of by no means unimpeachable morals, were wont to congregate. Her saloons were certainly tolerably brilliant. Her little suppers were well attended, and her card table had devotees of the most aristocratic character. It was necessary that she should make her rooms attractive, as like the German dukes who live upon the *rouge et noir* tables, where silly Englishmen lose their money, she might find that the very bad lot that were her visitors, might be tempted elsewhere ; for in London there are a great many ladies of quality and fashion who get a living in the same way.

Now, the lady of fashion, herself, was of that age usually denominated uncertain, and however un-certain may be the number of years it signifies, it is quite certain to mean an age at which the personal graces have fled, and as the lady of fashion, in common with most ladies of fashion, had no mental resource to fall back upon, she could not depend upon herself as an attraction, and in fine she was compelled to have some young and attractive person about her in the quality of a companion, whose beauty should create a little *furore* among those in habitual attendance upon the saloons and her card tables.

Mrs. Villans had only recently parted with a personage of considerable attractions, who had been with her a year, but of whom a certain general had become enamoured, and given Mrs. Villars a " consideration " for making the sacrifice of parting with an eligible companion. The moment Mrs. Villars saw Emma Lyon, she felt that in her she had a friend—could she but secure her—the most attractive and really beautiful person she had ever had the good fortune to place in her brilliant and profligate saloons.

So much for Mrs. Villars.

"Ah, and so you have really sought me, so soon?" she cried; upon Emma being introduced to her in her boudoir. "Come, this is really good of you. But you shall say nothing of yourself until you have answered me categorically, one question, and that is, 'Have you come to stay?'"

"Yes, madam, if agreeable to you."

"Agreeable? My child, I should not have said what I did to you, if I had had the smallest doubt upon the subject, or the least mental reservation. Now, as briefly as you can tell me, who and what you are, and what you have been about since first your gloss told you were beautiful."

Emma was quite charmed with this reception, and Mrs. Villars soon knew all that she cared to know of her young protege, to whom she then said,—

"Very well, my dear, I am quite satisfied, and you shall be here as my companion, and confidential waiting maid. Nothing menial shall be required of you, and you shall be introduced to my visitors, and in every respect have the life of a lady. You must do the best you can by reading to improve yourself on current subjects. That is to say, you must be able to talk of dress—dancing—music and theatricals, for these subjects comprise all that a really fashionable person is expected to know anything of. But above all things, keep the men at a distance, and whatever any of them may say to you, or whatever tempting proposal may be made to you, tell me of it, and you shall have my most disinterested advice upon the subject. You will soon have plenty of money for your dress and other expenses."

"Shall I, madam? How?"

"Why, this way. You will be asked to play at cards, and, of course, you will always have a gentleman for your partner. We have very rarely, indeed, any ladies here. I hate the sight of them. But, as I was saying, you will play at cards with a gentleman for your partner. If you lose, of course he pays for himself and you likewise. If there be any winning, you take it all."

"That is quite clear, madam."

"Very good. I shall now provide you with everything requisite to enable you to make a first appearance; and from your quick winnings you can easily rapay me the £40 or £50 it will cost me. Are you satisfied?"

"Abundantly, madam," said Emma. "I should, indeed, be ungrateful, to be otherwise."

Mrs. Villars was as good as her word;—people, even of fashion, generally are when it suits their purpose—and Emma was presented in the saloons with great *eclat;* and, from her first night, there commenced for her a life which, truth to say, was not without its wonders and its fascinations. The few scruples with which she at first heard the bold language of gallantry, as it was called, soon died away. The trashy novels of the day supplied her leisure with such mental food as enabled her better, each time, to understand her position; and in the vitiated atmosphere of Lady Villar's house, the last remnants of gentle feeling and clinging sense of right and wrong, were dissipated to the winds.

The card tables were nightly crowded; and, in plain language, Mrs. Villars was driving a roaring trade by keeping Emma as a bait for the crowd of profligates and coxcombs who were in the habit of frequenting her house.

None had found favour with Emma sufficiently to induce her to keep a secret from Mrs. Villars, until a Captain Payne, of the Roayl Navy, made his appearance, and he succeeded in touching the heart of Emma. It was quickly enough understood by the guests of the house that "Payne was the happy man," and a general falling off in the number of visitors and in the profits of the card table took place, to the great chagrin of Mrs. Villars. It became necessary for that highly politic lady to take some step in the matter.

Adjoining the principal saloon in the house was a small apartment known as the "blue chamber," from its hangings being of pale azure satin; and one evening, when quite infatuated with the charms of Emma, Captain Payne followed her into this room, and in explicit language he declared to her his passion.

"My dear girl," he said, "I cannot live without you. Trust me. I am not one who would say this much to you, if I did not feel it. I have seen enough of life to be able to compare you with the best and the fairest; but no one can come near you in the magic power of your fascinations. Emma, I love you—I adore you. Only consent to be mine and you may name your own terms.— Publicly you shall be acknowledged by me as the queen of my affections, and all that my not inconsiderable means can do, to make you happy, shall be done."

This was the first explicit offer of—we must write the word—baseness that Emma had received. It struck a pang to her heart, even through the immense mass of frivolity with which it was crammed, and for a few moments she felt as though sensation was leaving her. When she moved she found herself in the arms of Captain Payne. She disengaged herself from him, crying—

"Leave me, sir! Leave me!"

"No, my angel," he said. "No, I cannot —I dare not leave you. If I loved you less than I do, I might, indeed, leave you; but I cannot now do so. Emma, Emma, why are you so beautiful?"

"Unhand me, sir. Unhand me. I will think of what you have said, and another time I will give you an answer."

"Nay," he cried, dropping upon one knee and intercepting her retreat from the room. "There is no time, Emma, like the present. Only consent to be mine, and I will realise any wish that your ardent imagination could picture. Sit by me upon this couch and tell me that you will try to love me."

"Let me go, sir. Oh, let me go!"

He would not let go his hold of her hands and she was compelled to sit upon the couch with him. He clasped her closer at each moment, and covered her face with kisses. She thought she would scream, but she found that she could not command breath to do so. A strange bewildered feeling crept over her—She could feel his burning kisses upon her lips.

The light went out.

CHAPTER XXXI.

EMMA SOON MAKES A CHANGE OF PARTNERS.

THERE was rather an unusual bustle in the hall of Mrs. Villars' house in Sackville Street, the next day. A handsome town chariot stood at the door, and sundry packages were being transferred to it by Mrs. Villars' footman. In her bed-room Emma Lyon was putting on her pelisse previous to leaving. In Mrs. Villars' boudoir Captain Payne was in deep conversation with Mrs. Villar; and if at precisely a quarter past twelve you could have looked into that little boudoir you could have seen him handing a bank note to the lady, with the words " five hundred " at the corner of it.

" That will do," said the lady.

" Good-morning," said Captain Payne.

" Good-morning, my dear captain. I will go and see if Emma be quite ready. Really it is enough to break my heart to part with her, but we must have these trials in this world."

" Certainly, madam," said the captain, " especially when we manage to sweeten them a little."

" Exactly, my dear captain. You are so very sensible."

In the course of the next ten minutes Emma and the captain sallied from the door of Mrs. Villars' house, to a fashionable suite of apartments that the captain had hired in Bond Street, for himself and Emma, who now found herself as regarded every imaginable luxury, in the full possession of all her desires. But did no thought of the old house at Preston now obtrude itself? Did she now think of Edwin, who truly loved her? Did she quite forget Doctor Lukin and her mother, and last, though not least, had she no remembrance of him, the gallant Horatio Nelson, who had snatched her from death in the fire of the Grange? Alas, at that time, in the wild intoxication of a life of lawless pleasure, all was forgotten that did not minister to the gratification of the moment.

The Emma Lyon of this time was not the Emma Lyon of our early pages.

Theatres, balls, concerts—routs—card-parties—pic-nicks—masks—every frivolity that London life could offer to one who was disposed to plunge headlong into the wild career of dissipation, was offered to Emma; and her transformation from what she was once to what she was then, appeared to her

to be to the full as great as that which attends the change of a grub to a butterfly, and truly it might have been said of her that she had now found the wings of pleasure, and with untiring perseverance used them. Her equipage in the park surpassed all others, and the life of extravagance that she led for the space of six weeks, went far towards embittering the life of her protector for the remainder of its continuance. And upon her part all this was done from an utter ignorance of the value of money, or of any idea of what might or what might not be his resources. That was a subject upon which she knew nothing, and concerning which she never enquired. Whether she was ruining him or not, never entered into her thoughts for one moment; but the end of her association with the gallant captain soon drew nigh.

During a slight absence of her protector for a day and a night, Emma was taking in the afternoon her accustomed drive in the park, when she found her carriage face to face with that of Mrs. Villars, who with nods, and becks, and wreathed smiles, invited a closer approach.

" My dear girl," said that lady, " how charming you look. Do you know that I am quite dying to introduce you to a gentleman who is really mad about your bewitching eyes. Now don't laugh, for it is really true."

" I do not laugh at that, Mrs. Villars, but at the idea of your presenting me to a gentleman, when you know that Payne is one of the most jealous men the world ever saw, and that he will be back to-morrow."

" Excuse me, my dear, Payne will not be back to-morrow."

" Indeed ?"

" No, he is at Boulogne, to get out of the reach of his creditors."

" His creditors ! I hardly comprehend what creditors are, Mrs. Villars; surely they would not, if they are mere tradesmen, be so insolent as to interfere with Payne, who is a gentleman ?"

Mrs. Villars laughed. " I am afraid, my love," she said, " that creditors are capable of anything, when they are tradesmen; from the lowest and most servile cringing when they think, in their own phraseology, all is right, to the most rampant insolence when all is wrong."

" You astonish and afflict me."

" Very probably, my dear Emma, very probably. My opinion is that you will not see Payne for some time, and I think it is a scandalous thing that he did not tell you. I could forgive a man anything but want of confidence in me. Come now, I have an engagement to a supper to-night at a pretty villa near Richmond. Will you cheat time of some of its weariness, by coming with me? Don't say no, for I am quite sure you will be delighted.

" Yes," said Emma, in a low tone, as if communing with herself. " Yes, Payne ought to have had confidence in me. Without confidence there can be no affection. I will come, Mrs. Villars."

"Very good, my child, I will call for you at seven. Adieu!"

*   *   *   *   *

It was a brilliant evening as the chariot in which were seated Mrs. Villars and Emma drove through a shady avenue of limes to the villa at Richmond, where the little supper was to take place. Emma was all life and spirits. Captain Payne and his real or supposed difficulties were alike forgotten. She heard the sound of music as the carriage stopped at the handsome portico of a brilliantly-lighted house, and a retinue of servants appeared to welcome them.

"Tell me now whose place this is," said Emma. "You need not keep the secret any longer, surely? Be confiding, my dear Mrs. Villars, and tell me at once."

"I will tell you. This is one of the little places renowned for its elegance that belongs to Sir Harry Featherstonhaugh, Bart. His estate is Up Park, Sussex, and he is as rich as he is liberal. He has seen you, Emma."

"Well he has seen me? What then?"

"To see you, Emma, is sufficient. I thought you could have no difficulty in guessing that the result of seeing you must be to love you, for who can compare with you."

When such a woman as Mrs. Villars flattered, the tempter was indeed at work—the serpent was in the boquet! The flash of conscious pleasure lit up the eyes and cheeks of Emma—she made no reply to the well thrown out insinuation of Mrs Villars, and they entered the villa together."

For the next few hours all was life and gaiety. Rich wines flowed in abundance, and the dance enlivened by strains of the most entrancing music, whirled the hours away. Suddenly then, in a pause of the dancing, Mrs. Villars whispered to Emma—

"Come with me and see the Oriental Conservatory?"

"Willingly," replied, Emma. "I shall not be surprised at anything here, for it is all enchantment, I never could have supposed that such places could exist in England."

"You like the villa?"

"Like it? It is a palace in miniature. It is charming, delightful."

"And its master?"

"Oh, he is a very proper sort of man, indeed. You are sure Payne cannot venture back to England, Mrs. Villars. Do not deceive me upon that point?"

"I would not for the world, but what do you think of this for luxury, Emma?"

They had been traversing a kind of corridor, and Mrs. Villars had suddenly touched a spring in the wall, which opened a door that admitted them to a place which for elegance combined with the greatest amount of gorgeous display could not be surpassed.

This room or conservatory, for it was both, and yet neither, was fitted in what is generally received as the oriental style of finishing and adornment. The walls were covered with rare plants. The floor was one mass of rich ottomans and gold-spangled cushions.

"Oh, this is delightful," said Emma.

"I am only too happy," said a man's voice "to find that it meets with your approbation."

Emma turned quickly at the unexpected sound, and found herself face to face with Sir Harry Featherstonhaugh. Mrs. Villars having vanished as mysteriously as she had entered the oriental conservatory.

"Ah, this is a plot," said Emma.

"It is, charmer," cried Sir Harry. "It is a plot, but let it have a delightful close by giving me the joy of calling my own the friend and most enchanting being that ever the sun shone upon. Miss Lyon, can you make yourself happy with me? If so, you will have no desire ungratified. Look around you, and ask yourself if the owner of even this place may not be able to attract your nature. You know who and what I am. Will you be mine, Emma?"

"Emma smiled. I think, Sir Harry, I will take you a little while upon trial only."

In a moment he clasped her in his arms. Her head sank upon his breast.

*   *   *   *

"Humph!" said Mrs. Villars, as she went home, that might alone. "A £1000 from Sir Harry is a pretty good consideration. If I mind what I am about, this girl may be a mine of wealth to me yet. I will most assuredly not lose sight of her, for either Sir Harry will be tired of her, or she will be tired of Sir Harry before many months have passed over their heads, and then I must introduce her to some one else. Oh, what fools these men are!"

Mrs. Villars was tolerably correct in her anticipations. Emma thought that while she had been with Captain Payne she had lived right royally; but she opened her eyes to a much wider sphere of expense when she became the mistress of Sir Harry. In an incredibly short time, what with her love of play, and her generally lavish expenditure, she had brought him to the verge of ruin. She reigned supreme at Up Park, Sussex, to which its owner had the bad taste to take her; she, in a short time acquired the most wonderful skill as a horsewoman, and had in the stables, at one time, for her own use, eight saddle-horses, that together cost £4,000. The stumps of her saddles were set with brilliants, and she gave £280 for a hunting whip, in the handle of which was set an emerald.

Sir Harry was ruined, and fled! Emma made her way to London, with £3 8s. in her pocket, and audaciously called upon Captain Payne, who had returned, and put his affairs in order again, they having been not even so seriously damaged as Mrs. Villars, to suit her own purposes, had represented them to be. The gallant captain sent down word to his Hall, that "he knew no such person as Miss Lyon."

Burning with rage, shame, and indignation,

Emma rushed from the door-step of her once ardent admirer, and calling a hackney-coach, she went direct to Sackville-street, ordering the driver to stop at Mrs. Villars' house.—Hastily alighting, Emma knoked and rang for admittance. A man, whose face she did not recollect as one of the old servants, replied to the summons.

"Is Mrs. Villars within?"

"Yes, ma'am, she is within; but she is dead."

"Dead? Dead?" Emma reeled off the

EMMA AND MR. GREVILLE.

steps—she paid her fare to the coachman, and dismissed him. Then in a state of mind, bordering upon distraction, she wandered on until she found herself in St. James's Park, upon one of the seats of the Grand Mall, in which she sat for more than an hour ruminating over her situation and prospects. Both were gloomy enough. The money she had might, with strict economy, last her a week; and then—she shuddered at the prospect that opened itself before her.—She was hardly aware that a man of vulgar mien and appearance was staring at her, as though he would devour her with his eyes.

CHAPTER XXXII.

EMMA GETS HER LIVING BY ATTENTION TO THE FINE ARTS.

AT length this person stepped up to her. "I beg your pardon, Miss," he said; 'but I make free to speak to you, because it really seems to me as if Providence itself had thrown you in my way this morning.— I was in a quandary from which I do believe you can free me if you like, and to convince you that I am a person of some standing, and of undoubted respectability, there is my card."

He handed her a card, upon which she saw engraved amid a vast number of flourishes the name of "Dr. Graham."

"Well, Sir," she said. "What can you have to say to me?"

"I will soon tell you. I am the celebrated Dr. Graham, who is now giving lectures in the Adelphi, upon health and beauty; I want a kind of model to illustrate my lectures—and somebody, who in appearance, should combine both health and beauty, and by George, you are just the person. There is not your equal in London; I have been looking at you for this half hour from behind that tree."

Emma looked at the man for some few moments, as though she doubted the evidence of her own senses to the effect that in the hour of her distress, and all but destitution, she was offered such a resource. The earnestness of the man did not permit her for a moment to doubt the truth of what he said, and she at once replied—

"I will accept your offer; for to tell the truth, I am glad of any mode by which I can earn a livelihood that may not be too degrading."

"This is not degrading at all," said the doctor. "You will be the means of assisting in diffusing the light of genius, and as my lecture will hand me down to posterity as one of the most eminent men that ever lived, so you will be likewise spoken of as having, by your beauty, illustrated those subjects that—that—without—you would be—a—a—that is, would be——"

The learned doctor's eloquence was rather at fault, and Emma replied with a smile—

"I shall be content with the profit, leaving to you, sir, all the fame. Only say where I shall call upon you, and when, and you will find me puntual."

The doctor gave his address, and he and Emma parted with a clear understanding that she was to be his model at his forthcoming lectures in the Adelphi. She hired a humble lodging in Savoy Street, Strand, and began to feel more cheerful, notwithstanding what had occurred to her, and the bitter feelings to which she had been the prey, after leaving her splendid house at Up Park.

Emma kept her word with Doctor Graham, and at the first lecture made such a sensation that she could have largely increased her terms to her employer, if she had felt so inclined; but she was too generous to do that, so that she was filling his pockets without doing more than obtaining a subsistence for herself, which is frequently the case between the employed and employer in London, although not so frequently as many persons pretend, for they are apt to forget that employers run all the risk, and provide all the capital, and have a full share of the anxiety.

But brighter days were in store for Emma Lyon. Some very eminent persons attended from motives of curiosity, to see Emma, whose beauty was much talked about in conjunction with the additional interesting lectures of Doctor Graham. Among them were to be found Romney, the royal academician, and Hayly, the poet and biographer. Both these persons were quite charmed with Emma. Romney employed her as a model from which to draw forms of loveliness, and Hayly made her the beau ideal of his poetic inspirations. Her fame spread far and wide, and if at that time she had been content with such a situation, she might have settled down into the quiet of domestic life with sufficient means for that real happiness which is only to be found in serenity; but her disposition would not let her do so. At the bottom of her heart lay the germ of a thousand passions and feelings which had hardly as yet shown themselves.

A love of luxury—a love of extravagant expenditure—a love of power, and a spirit of revenge prompted her to look around her for some other protector, who, like her two former ones, might be pleased to be moved by her bright eyes. She was not long in finding such a one.

Mr. Charles Francis Greville, the nephew of Sir W. Hamilton, and a young gent of those days, with extensive means, was charmed by the syren, and she, after a little inquiry, was graciously pleased to bestow her smiles upon him. That for a time Mr. Greville loved Emma to distraction there can be no doubt. He gave up his whole future time and talents to her, with an idea that he would pass his life in her delightful society; he provided her with the most accomplished masters in every branch of information that could lend new graces to his idol.

She sang—danced—played upon several musical instruments, and in fine, became a truly accomplished as well as a lovely woman, and each day endeared her more and more to Mr. Greville.

The principal visitor of Mr Greville was his uncle, Sir William Hamilton, then upwards of sixty years of age.

"Charles," said Sir William one day after the illicit connexion with Emma had gone on for three years. "Charles, I am really very much shocked that you should keep this woman, and not marry in your own sphere, as you might fairly do. Really, your immorality is too glaring, Charles. It is, indeed, and this Emma what's her name will be the ruin of you."

"Why, uncle," said Charles Greville, "have you only just found that out; but don't call her Emma. You know she has changed her name, and chooses to go by that of Ann Hart."

"The name of any one," said Sir William, with a severe air, "is of little consequence. It is their actions that are only of moment, and I urge you to put an end to this disgraceful connexion."

"Ah, uncle, the hey-day in the blood may well be tame, and wait upon the judgment at your time of life; but if you were forty years younger you would look upon that fair creature with very different eyes than what you do now."

"S' blood, sir," said Sir William; "what do you mean by my time of life? Eh? Eh?"

"I mean no insult or reproach, uncle, unless you will, of your own accord, take my word as such. We must all get old or die young, I suppose. I believe that that is a proposition you will not dispute."

"Sir, I will dispute anything," said Sir William, trembling with passion, and the only terms upon which I will be reconciled to you, are that you discard this Ann or Emma, or whatever the devil may be her name. Will you do it, sir, at once, and retain my favour?'

"I would not do it, uncle, to save your life as well as retain your favour. Why, one would think you wanted me to discard her in order to take her yourself, only that in a man of your age it would be too absurd."

Sir William Hamilton was in that agony of rage at this little hit of quite accidental home truth, that he flew out of the house without venturing upon a reply; and screaming with laughter, Mr. Greville sought Emma to tell her what had taken place

"Well," said Emma, "now that you have quarrelled with him, I have no hesitation in telling you that he has made me an offer."

"He? My old uncle?"

"The very same. I only laughed at him; but I suppose he thought if you discarded me I should think better of it."

"The old rascal! Now if I had only known that, he should not have got out of the house so easily. The old hypocritical goat! Well, well, he is not worth a thought. We will be off to Raneleigh to-night, if you feel inclined."

"With all my heart."

Raneleigh was unusually brilliant upon that evening. It would have been so if our heroine had not been there; but with her the enchantment of that favourite place of resort, was, indeed, complete. Carried away by the enthusiasm of the time and place, she volunteered a song, which she actually sung in the public orchestra of the gardens, while Mr. Greville looked on with amazement.

That night he informed Emma that he highly disapproved of any public display, and, in fact, that such another act might—he did not say would—lead to their separation.

"And yet you love me?" said Emma.

"I do love you, Emma, and I have given you many proofs of that love; but I have yet lingering in my breast some regard for my name as well as for your character. When some one asked this night who was the fair and exquisite singer, another replied that she was Greville's kept mistress."

"Very well," said Emma;" and she immediately left the room, while Mr. Greville continued pacing with unequal steps, pining and fretting himself into a matter that, after all, compared with other things, was of but trivial moment. Suddenly he paused. Some one tapped slightly at the door of the apartment.—"Come in," he cried;" and Emma, but not the Emma who had so recently left him, made her appearance. The exquisite face and form were there; but in place of the gorgeous satin robe, and the brilliants, there only appeared a plain stuff gown.

"Sir," she said, "you are displeased with me. Let me go now, taking nothing with me but my broken heart and my poor children. All that you have given me in the shape of jewels you will find in my room. Farewell, Charles, and may you find some one whom you can love better than your poor discarded Emma."

"Discarded!" he cried. "Oh, no—no. A thousand times no. Perish the word. Emma, you are dearer to me than ever. You are all perfection—all excellence and fascination."

He clasped her in his arms, and from that moment she reigned supremely over his heart and fortune. But alas! although the former might know no change, the latter did. The expense of Emma to him was something positively enormous. The fame of her mode of life had reached Hawarden, and exposed her mother to many an insult; so that Emma had persuaded her to come to London, and under the name of Mrs. Cadogan, she inhabited a pretty little house, paid for out of Mr. Greville's pocket. But as we say, all this was coming to an end. Ruin, like a thunderbolt, fell upon Mr. Greville. The last night of his stay in his voluptuous home arrived. Emma had gone to the theatre, whither he had promised to join her in the course of the evening, and he was opening a dressing-room that was then not his own, when, to his surprise, his uncle, Sir William Hamilton, was duly announced by the footman in attendance.

Notwithstanding the very unexpected nature of this call, Mr. Greville desired that his uncle should be shown in, and he reasoned with himself very justly that as it was Sir William Hamilton, K. B. who had taken offence at him, and not he at Sir William Hamilton, he might very well afford to show no resentment. His reception of the old man was, therefore, just the same as though they had only recently parted, and were the best of friends.

"Well, Charles," said Hamilton. "Contrary to my expectations I am once more within your doors. Eh? If all I hear be right, you are a ruined man, Charles. Eh? Eh?"

"Sir," said Mr. Greville, "if that be all you come to say, I think you might with great propriety keep without my doors."

CHAPTER XXXIII.

EMMA BIDS FOR A TIME ADIEU TO ENGLAND.

INSTEAD of taking offence at this, Sir William merely nodded his head several times, and took a seat as though nothing particularly offensive had been said to him. Mr. Greville, after regarding him with a look of surprise for a few moments, was about to leave the room, when Sir William stopped him by saying—

"Charles, I have not come here without a motive. I am your uncle, and as such, may probably take a kind of liberty that might fairly enough be denied to a stranger."

"Well, sir," said Charles, somewhat impatiently, "say your say. What is it? I am not in the most pleasant and complying of tempers, and I tell you frankly that if you have come to preach to me any sermons about prudence and so forth, I am by no means in a state of mind to listen to them, and I assure you that they will be completely thrown away upon me at this time."

"Listen to me, for ten minutes," said the uncle, taking out his watch and placing it upon the table between them. "Will you do so, Charles?"

"I will. Go on. I pray you to go on."

"Very good. I will not keep you in suspense, Charles. You are, however you may dislike to hear it, a ruined man."

"Not quite, uncle. I intend to realise my remaining property, and after I have settled everything I shall have something left."

"But you have debts."

"Yes, they are about £8000, and I can pay them, uncle."

"Have you counted in that amount the sums that your Lady Emma, or Ann, or whatever you may choose to call her, owes, and which debts she has entirely contracted in your name and upon your credit, if not entirely with your sanction. Charles, are you sure you have counted those amounts?"

"Yes, I have made a rough estimate of them. I dare say she owes £500, for I gave her leave to get any little trinket or other matter in the way of woman's gear that took her fancy, and to have the same put down to me."

"Well, Charles, I think I am better informed of your affairs than you are yourself. I have taken the trouble to make the enquiry, and I can tell you for a certainty that her debts, principally for jewellery, which she has given away with a lavish hand, amount to more than thousands, where you thought they were only hundreds."

Mr. Greville shrank back at this information and then in a faltering voice he said—

"Are you sure of this—Are you quite certain? Because if so——"

"If so, what?" cried Sir William, with eagerness. "If so, what?"

"Why, if so, I am a little worse off than I thought I was—that's all."

"Well, Charles, I suppose you call yourself a philosopher, and pride yourself upon looking ruin calmly in the face; but yet there is a resource."

"And pray what may that be? A pistol, or the King's Bench, uncle?"

"Neither. I can get you an appointment as Attaché to the St. Petersburgh Embassy. I will pay your debts, and take the management of your property, until, by degrees, I am repaid again."

"Will you, indeed, uncle?"

"The children you have by this Emma, or Ann, shall be provided for."

"This is kind, indeed."

"And—and—I will take Emma to Naples with me!"

Charles sprang from his chair, and stared at his uncle for a few moments in silence; and then, with a loud peal of laughter, he sank back into it, roaring out—

"This is capital! Ho! ho! This is capital! Sir William Hamilton, Bart., Trustee of the British Museum, K.B.F.R.S., Vice President of the Society of Antiquaries, Member of the Delettanti Club, Ambassador to Naples, &c., &c, &c., and sixty years of age only, is smitten by the charms of Emma Lyon, and will pay some £10,000 down for her! Ha! ha! ha! ha! 'Goats and Monkeys!' as *Othello* says."

The countenance of Sir William turned purple with passion, and rising, he screamed, rather than said—

"You shall repent this! You shall live, sir, to feel that this is the most imprudent speech you ever made in your life! By Heaven, you shall repent it!"

"No, no, uncle. No—I consent——"

"You—you con—sent?"

"In good faith, I do, uncle. I consent. Hark you: if the lady have no objection, and your statement concerning her debts be borne out by the facts, I consent, fully and freely to the whole of your conditions—so there is no offence."

"No—no," said the old man, softening down, "not there; oh, no. There is no great offence if you consent, but there was no manner of occasion to make such a speech as you did, Charles. Not the least."

"Perhaps not, uncle—but it is past now. Forget it. Words are but words after all. Remain where you are, and I will send Emma to you. If you can gain her over to your plans, take her in the name of all that's—that's—good, bad, and indifferent, and you will hear no more from me upon the subject.

Emma had a long interview with Sir William. She parted with him with a written agreement in her pocket to the effect that he would marry her within two years, or pay to her the sum of £10,000. Upon that, she consented to accompany him as soon as he chose, to Naples.

Her old lover—really very nearly old

enough to have been her grandfather—was anxious to get away from England before their infamous story got current, and he made the most hasty preparations accordingly for departure. Within three weeks of the morning upon which the memorable conversation took place between the uncle and the nephew, Emma was upon Neapolitan ground as the avowed mistress of the ambassdor.

The code of morals in Naples is not a very strict one, and she at once, after finding herself fairly installed in a magnificent residence, threw off all restraint, and commenced a career of reckless extravagance and, we must say, vice. Folks, after all that had taken place, are not now to expect that Emma Lyon is to be very particular. She revelled in the full blaze of her charms, and with a conviction that the old ambassador was quite infatuated with her, she did exactly as she pleased.

We cannot help saying, and we feel that our readers will agree with us, that the former acts of Emma sink into insignificance before this glaring sale of herself to a man whom she must have detested and despised. From that time goodness and her parted for ever. The last spark of holy or tender feeling went out in her mind, and she became the debased being that to the end of her eventful history she remained.

CHAPTER XXXV.

EMMA'S DOINGS AT NAPLES.—HER MARRIAGE. NELSON, THE HERO.

FROM the more sterile and uncongenial clime of England we now invite the attention of the reader to the sunny skies and soft influences of an Italian landscape. The cool freshness of the vegetation of a more northern region no longer salutes the senses of Emma Lyon, but she looks upon the land of fruit, of flowers, and of song—

"Birth-place of beauty and the vine."

Sunny, lustrous Italy, with all its varied charms and seductions, is about her, and the last finishing touch is given both to the charms and to the passions of Emma, by a residence in the city of licentiousness and intrigue—Naples.

As the wife—no—no—not yet—she called herself the wife—but wife she was not then —of the British Ambassador, she certainly found herself in what to very many would have been an envied position. The loose morals of the Neapolitan society were not very much shocked to be told by the English who occasionally took up their residence in the sunny city, that the fair lady who did the honours of the British Embassy was a mere adventuress, and not by any means entitled to the name she bore. And so to a certain set she was received with acclamation.

Many lovers soon sighed at her feet; and if the old superanuated ambassador had had the eyes of Argus, he would have needed them all to watch his precious bargain that he had paid so dear a price to his kind nephew for. But if love be blind, dotage is so most certainly, and Sir William Hamilton did not, or would not, see that he was the silly dupe of the woman who made havoc with his wealth, and who scarcely affected to conceal the contempt she could not help feeling in her inmost heart for such a man.

This state of things went on for a considerable time, until one day it happened that a certain Count Villair, who had been distinguished by Emma from among the crowd of her admirers, exclaimed to her with rapture in his eyes—

"Ah, my beautiful Inglese, the time has come when you will show how much beauty and how much wit you really possess. The time has come when not only those who have the happiness of knowing you in the palazzo will bend the knee of homage to your charms, but the whole of Naples will acknowledge that you are without compare."

"And pray, count," said Emma, "in what manner am I to make this wonderful sensation?"

"At the approaching *fete*. There is to be an *al-fresco* masque in the gardens of the palace; and there in carriages, there will be a progress through the principal thoroughfares of the city, and you as the impersonification of the Queen of Love herself, will cast into the shade all minor beauties. Only say that you will be there, my charmer?"

"I will," said Emma, her lips curling with the conscious beauty that she felt had but to be seen to eclipse the fairest and the proudest dames of Naples. "I will be present at this *fete*, count. I have said it, and I will."

"Oh, what delight—what joy. But—but there is one very little preliminary—one little overture."

"What mean you?"

"Nay, fair one, it need not be a difficulty, for I think, that is, I hope, I have sufficient influence at court to get you introduced under some other name—say as an English lady upon her travels—for if not introduced, it will not be possible to be present at the *fete*."

The colour came and went upon the cheeks and brow of Emma, and finally with a face as pale as monumental marble, she said in a low voice—

"Count, you know that I have been refused admittance to the court circle here, at Naples, because the ambassador had scruples."

"Perfectly, madam. The ambassador had some scruples about pledging his honour to the chamberlain that madam was his wife."

"His honour!" ejaculated Emma, with a look of the most inconceivable scorn. "His honour! Well, count, it is so. Get me introduced at court, and depend upon my gratitude."

"And love?" said the count, bowing low.

"We shall see. I do not bid any one despair who can do me so great a service."

" Then, madam," said the count, " I am the happiest of men, and shall be your humble cavalier. Of course the old imbecile, Sir W. Hamilton, need know nothing of this interview between us?"

" Not unless you fail, count, and then I must take steps to accomplish my wishes myself. But I will first make trial of your skill and deplomacy. By when can you let me know decisively upon this subject?"

" By to-morrow, madam, at mid-day. If I succeed I will be here myself. If I fail, I will send by my page a heron's feather."

With this they separated, and punctual to the hour of noon on the following day the count's page made his appearance in the private saloon of Emma and laid before her a heron's feather. He had failed, and failed most signally. Emma sat for the space of about twenty minutes without moving a limb, but during that time her face was

" A tablet of unutterable thoughts."

Then rising, she at once made her way to the cabinet of the ambassador.

What passed in the half hour's interview that followed, no one could ever tell. Once she rushed from the cabinet: but the old dotard, as fast as his infirmities would let him, was after her. None are so easily caught as those who wish to be overtaken, and he had the satisfaction of leading Emma back again to that cabinet which was supposed to be devoted to affairs of state.— When she came out again a triumphant smile was upon her lips, and her step was like that of some empress upon the first day of her exaltation, to be the observed of all observers.

The events that followed rapidly upon that interview were sufficiently explanatory of its subject matter. Sir William Hamilton sent an express courier with dispatches to London, requesting of the minister leave of absence from his mission for a time on his own business in London. The leave was granted as a thing of course. The affairs of the embassy were left in charge of a couple of senators, and Sir William and Emma landed in England on the 1st of September, 1791.

On September the 6th, Emma Lyon, spinster, aged 27 years, was married at St. George's church, to Sir William Hamilton!

Human infatuation—human dotage could not get beyond this; but the strangest part of the affair remains to be told. The fashionable world of London, which knew perfectly well all about Lady Hamilton, and who and what she was and had been, all at once forgot what may be called her antecedents, and was quite cordial to the wife of the ambassador. Nobody would know anything but that Sir William Hamilton, a very rich man, had married a highly fascinating and beautiful personage ; and the new Lady Hamilton found herself all at once welcomed with open arms by the very people who, for twelve months before, had spoken of her in whispers, and greedily listened to, and circulated the most extravagant stories of her mode of life in Naples, as the mistress of the ambassador.

Intoxicated by her reception in the fashionable world, Emma would not hear of an immediate return to Naples, and poor Sir William was kept in London for the full round of a season, during which his wife was the star of what is miscalled society, and the centre of attraction. There was one thing, however, in which Lady Hamilton failed. For a sum of money *down*, an old Dowager Countess was prevailed upon to be the sponsor of Lady Hamilton, at the last drawing-room for the season, which was given by Queen Charlotte ; and according to custom, the two cards bearing the name of the presenter, and the to-be-presented, were sent in three days before to the office of the Queen's Chamberlain.

Both of the cards were sent back under cover to the old countess !

This was tantamount to a direct denial, and the rage of Lady Hamilton knew no bounds. She roared like a maniac, and for a whole day and a night kept her bed. She would neither eat nor drink, nor would she see any one Sir William, at last, forced his way into her room, and falling upon his knees, asked her what he could do to please her, and divert her from her chagrin.

Emma—we beg her pardon—Lady Hamilton pondered for a few moments over this speech. Perhaps she was very well pleased that there was somebody in the world who would take the trouble to persuade her not to be sulky too long.

" Start for Naples within twelve hours," she said.

" I will—I will. I will go at once and get my despatches and credentials, and be off."

Sir William had been led such a life during the London season, that he was, in truth, heartily glad to get away again to Naples, where he was, in truth, a much greater man as the English Ambassador, than he was in the saloons of the metropolis, where he was completely lost amid a crowd of far brighter stars than he.

He knew the imperious character of his lady too well to tamper with her in any way after she had fairly given expression to her will ; and, within the time specified, a travelling carriage was carrying Sir William and his fair wife to Southampton, there to embark for Naples, which city was reached in an extraordinarily short space of time.

It now became a serious question with Sir William whether, as his wife had actually been refused presentation at the English court, the Queen of Naples would feel that she could, with any propriety, be more indulgent ; but Maria Caroline, the Queen of Naples, was not troubled with many scruples. She had heard much of the abilities and of the fascinations of Lady Hamilton, and she, like the fashionable world of London, quite forgot all about the lady, but that she had just arrived as the wife of the English

Ambassador, and was entitled to a presentation at court, of course.

The reception that Lady Hamilton met with at the court of Naples was sufficient to obliterate from her mind the sting of her disappointment in London; and never had she been so enchanting, or looked so radiantly beautiful, as upon that occasion. With very few exceptions, and only one of any moment, namely, the family of the Caracciolo, she found the doors of every palazzo in Naples open to her; and she found means, in the course of time, to avenge herself upon those few that were kept closed upon her fascinations and her iniquities.

The Queen of Naples was not one of the most scrupulous of her sex. In Lady Hamilton she found a kindred spirit, and within three months of the date of her ladyships reception at the Court of Naples, she became the bosom friend and chosen intimate of the queen.

The king was a Bourbon, and, therefore, as history has taught us to believe, necessarily, a rogue or a fool. Fate made him the latter, and Neapolitan affairs stood thus:— The king was supposed to rule Naples— the queen ruled the king, and Lady Hamilton, the late nursery-maid, who started from Preston to seek her fortune with a few guineas sewn in her stays, ruled the queen!

For two years Lady Hamilton ruled in Naples as despotically as any sultan; and during that time not the far-famed Catherine of all the Russia's carried on so many intrigues with such a happy nonchalance and heedlessness of public opinion; and all this while Sir William was perfectly satisfied. Happy man! How delighted Sir William Hamilton's descendants must be with the great achievements of their ancestor, the ambassador!

It was at the end of these two years that the most important period of the life of Lady Hamilton began, that period which entitled her to some of the pity if to none of the respect of Englishmen; and which has made for her an historical reputation along with the name of Nelson!

CHAPTER XXXXVI.

NELSON A CAPTAIN.—HE AND EMMA MEET AT NAPLES.

"My dear," said Sir William Hamilton, one day as he hobbled into the presence of his beautiful wife. "My dear, will you be so good as to receive a visiter to day."

"Who?" said her ladyship.

"Oh, nobody of any importance just now, although I have some hopes of him if he be not cut off early in his career. This is only the captain of a frigate."

"You know, Sir William, that I am always glad to see any officers of the marine. They are frank and manly spirits. I shall give him a reception."

"You will much oblige me; and if I am

not very much mistaken this captain of the Agamemnon will be a hero yet."

"What is his name?"

"Nelson!"

Lady Hamilton uttered a slight cry, and then pressing her hands upon her breast she assured the terrified Sir William that she had suffered from a sudden spasm; and at once retired to her chamber. "Nelson! Nelson! My Nelson!" she cried, as she flung herself upon a couch, and wept. "He has come at last."

There was some feeling yet in the heart of Lady Hamilton, and with a pang of regret she now felt that in pursuing the object of her ambition, she had put it out of the power of him whom she had loved to make her his. But these thoughts were but the faint yearnings after that virtue which had long since ceased to consort with Lady Hamilton.—"It is enough," she said. "He will come; and he will recollect me, and we shall yet be happy. If he be not utterly insensible to all the influence of—of—" She rose and looked at herself in a full-length mirror; and then she added the word "beauty—he will be mine, and mine only."

Hastily ringing for her favourite attendant, a sharp unscrupulous Neapolitan girl, Lady Hamilton ordered her to procure all the information she could regarding the Captian Nelson who was to dine at the embassy that day. The attendant understood her mistress perfectly well, and performed her mission well. Lady Hamilton was duly informed that Captain Nelson was a tallish thin man, of remarkably vivacious manner, and that he was married.

The news produced another revulsion of feeling in the bosom of Lady Hamilton.

"Married! married!" she repeated; "and does he love his wife? That is the question. Well, well. No matter. If he love her as never man loved woman, he shall love me better, or I will give up for the time to come all faith in myself."

The embassy visitors have arrived, and in a robe of pearl-white satin, Lady Hamilton made her appearance. Nelson was in the room, and bowed low to the ambassador's lady.

"You are very welcome," she said, in a low tone.

He started, and then smiled as though amused at his own credulity in fancying he had heard that voice before, and seen that face. How should he? and yet the more he looked upon her, the more he seemed to feel that she was a reminiscence, gorgeously beautified, of some one whom he had seen before. And she, what did she think of him?

Nelson was not handsome. He was not commonly well looking, and yet there was that in his appearance, and in the expression of his face, which was more than beauty; and this something, combined with the prestige he had acquired in the eyes of Lady Hamilton by his conduct upon the occasion of the fire at the village of Preston, was quite sufficient to make him in her eyes the hero that, in the altitude of his character, was far above all ordinary attractions. Her pride—her feelings, good, bad, and indifferent, were all enlisted in the one pursuit—to captivate Nelson; and she fully succeeded.

The dinner, according to the Neapolitan method, went off rather formally, and Nelson had but little opportunity of saying a word to his charming hostess; but when that meal was over, and some of the guests were enjoying that calm rest which is so much esteemed in the afternoon portion of the day in warm climates, Nelson alone sought, by a stroll in the gardens of the embassy house, to wile away the time, and to give his thoughts free play regarding his lovely and accomplished hostess. He felt certain that he had seen her previously, but where, and under what circumstances, he could not say. The reminiscence was present to him, but yet it baffled all his exertions to put it into any form or shape.

Suddenly as he stopped to look at an orange tree of great beauty, he heard a light footstep near him, and upon hastily turning in the direction from whence it came, he saw Lady Hamilton advancing towards him with a smile.

"Horatio Nelson," she said, "does not recollect all his friends."

"He strives to do so," replied Nelson; "and of all others he would be the least likely to forget the one before him."

"And yet she of all others is forgotten. She who should never forget one to whom she owes her life——"

"Your life—your life! Impossible!"

"There was once a fire in a village, and a young girl crying for aid, and there was a young sailor on a coach-top, and——"

"No more—no more!" he cried. "I know you now. You are Emma Lyon, of whom I have thought many and many a day when tossed on the billows, and when in the battle's strife. Oh, how I have wished to see you once again. You are Emma Lyon."

He sprung towards her, and clasping her in his arms, he kissed her twice before she could be aware of what in the vehemence of his recollection he was about. She gently then disengaged herself, as she said—

"I am not Emma Lyon: I am Lady Hamilton."

Nelson shrunk back, but she reassured him by a smile; she held out her hand towards him in token of reconciliation. He devoured it with kisses.

"You can then, love," he said, "and I may hope?"

Another smile from her, and that bond of union was sealed between them which lasted until death. Nelson forgot that he had a wife who was indifferent alike to his person, and to his comforts; and Lady Hamilton, perhaps with still greater ease, forgot that she had a husband whom she despised.

*   *   *   *   *

The stay of Nelson at Naples was upon that occasion short, but he left his heart behind him; and many a time, although fortune rained successes and honours upon him, he would have given them all for one day in the ambassador's garden with the lovely Lady Hamilton.

No less than five years elapsed before he again set his foot upon the shores of Naples, but what a five years had they been! He came to Naples a Peer of England, and with a reputation that extended over the world. He was by Lady Hamilton received with open arms. The world's blazon had not yet stamped their intrigue with notoriety, but it was very soon understood at Naples, and Lady Hamilton spent whole days on board his vessel, at which Sir William Hamilton only declared himself "highly flattered."

The stay of Nelson, however, was again but short, and in the pursuit of that everlasting fame which he achieved, he was once again compelled to tear himself away from Lady Hamilton. It was in June 1798, that Nelson, being in pursuit of the French fleet, sought food and water at Naples for his men, and was refused it upon the ground of a treaty with France that expressly prohibited it. Lady Hamilton, in despite of that refusal by the king in council, procured from the queen an order under her own hand that supplied Nelson all he required, and the result was the annihilation of the French fleet on the 1st of August succeeding.

On the 20th of September, with all his wounds upon him, for he had suffered severely in the recent action with the French, Nelson again reached Naples. He found a home in the house of the obliging ambassador—he found a tender nurse and an attached mistress in the person of his lovely and now most accomplished lady.

But the assistance that had been given to the French fleet, raised the ire of France. A rupture between Naples and that state ensued. Affairs became so critical that the royal family were compelled to escape from Naples by a subterranean passage leading to the sea, and to take refuge in Nelson's ship, the Vanguard, in which they were in perfect safety all transported to Palermo. But fortune was rapidly decreasing the standard of the French both by sea and land, and the royal family of Naples were shortly enabled to return, and a system of rancorous hostility commenced against all who had offended the court. The most distinguished victim was the Count Caracciolo, who was actually hanged at the yard-arm of his own frigate, with the connivance of Nelson, at the instigation of Lady Hamilton. This circumstance is the flaw, the blot upon the escutcheon of the hero, and the darkest passage in the not very luminous career of Lady Hamilton. From that period Nelson and the ambassador's lady lived openly together, in defiance of the opinion or of the censures of the world.

It was probably a natural result of all these transactions that induced the English cabinet to recal the ambassador from Naples, and Sir William Hamilton, after being refused all compensation for his heavy losses at the time he fled with the Royal Family rom Naples, lived in London upon a sadly diminished income, with the respect of no one, and the contempt of many, while his wife, as the mistress of Nelson, was the observed of all observers. But the day of retribution was coming.

On the 30th of January, 1801, a daughter was born to Lady Hamilton. The infant was

LADY HAMILTON IN THE KING'S BENCH PRISON.

named Horatio, the feminine of Horatio, the christian name of Nelson, her father. And now the eventful year, 1805, arrived. Lady Hamilton was at the height of her ambition. She was surrounded by every luxury, and although the better portion of society said "Nay," when she made attempts to intrude upon their circles, she found many in a dissolute city like London, especially in what is termed "high life," to give her abundance of countenance and support. Nelson was with her as often as his duties permitted; but at times the war waxed fast and furious, and then, with his ships, he proclaimed England mistress of the seas.

But the time was rapidly approaching when his last battle with the French was to be fought, and when Lady Hamilton's first battle for many a long year with adversity was to begin. It was a battle, with him, that lasted his life out, and it was the same to her.

It was on the 21st of October, and long before any news of the Fleet could reach England, that Lady Hamilton, upon walking carelessly to the window of her drawing-room, saw two persons on the opposite side of the way. A couple of females who were in the room with her saw her change colour, and grasp the back of a chair for support, and they hastened to her aid, eagerly inquiring what ailed her.

"Look! look!" was all she could say for some time: and she pointed to the road-way opposite the house. "Look! stop them—stop them!"

The ladies looked from the window, but they could see no one, and in a few moments Lady Hamilton fainted.

Upon her recovery later in the day, she said she had seen Mr. Lukin, Edwin Lee, and Lord Nelson, standing together opposite the house, and that then they all three walked across a meadow close at hand, and that she fainted upon suddenly recollecting that both Mr. Lukin and Edwin Lee were dead!

This was the strange story told by Lady Hamilton, and a belief in which she cherished to her dying hour: and that was the day upon which was fought the Battle of Trafalgar!

CHAPTER XXXVII.

THE LAST ACT IN THE HISTORY OF EMMA LYON.

FROM the state of despondency into which this vision threw Lady Hamilton, those who were about her found it impossible to rouse her. They endeavoured in every possible way to lead her into a confidential statement of who the Mr. Lukin and the Edwin Lee—whom she professed to have seen there after their deaths—were; but she resisted all attempts of the kind. She only answered by floods of tears, and by saying—

"I knew them well! I knew them well!"

To the readers of this narrative they are likewise known well. Mr. Lukin will be remembered as the village doctor at Preston, who had been so sincere a friend to Emma, and Edwin Lee will be recollected as her first, her best, and her most sincere lover, and one who had gone to the grave with a broken heart, when he heard from common report of Emma's—his Emma's—mode of life.

* * * * *

On the 21st day of October, 1805, and on board the Victory, "then in sight of the combined fleets of France and Spain, distant about ten miles," Lord Nelson retired to his cabin, and made a codicil to his will. He recorded the services performed by Lady Hamilton (the reader is acquainted with them), and then wrote as follows:—

"Could I have rewarded those services, I would not now call upon my country; but as that has not been in my power, I leave Emma Lady Hamilton, therefore, a legacy to my King and country, that they will give her an ample provision to maintain her rank in life.

"I also leave to the beneficence of my country my adopted daughter, Horatia Nelson Thompson; and I desire she will use in future the name of Nelson only. These are the only favours I ask of my King and country at this moment when I am going to fight their battle.

"May God bless my King and country, and all those who I love dear. My relations it is needless to mention: they will, of course, be amply provided for."

Within a few hours of his signing the document, Nelson lay upon a bed, stripped of his clothes, and covered with a sheet. A shot from the mizen-top of the Redoubtable had done its work. As the men placed the wounded hero on his back, he looked round for Doctor Scott. "Doctor," he said, "I told you so—I am gone!" And after a short pause he added, in a low voice, "I have to leave Lady Hamilton and my adopted daughter, Horatia, as a legacy to my country."

An hour and a quarter afterwards Captain Hardy was at his side.

"I hope," said the dying man, "none of our ships have struck, Hardy?"

"No, my lord," replied Captain Hardy; "there is no fear of that." Lord Nelson then said, "I am a dead man, Hardy. I am going fast—it will be all over with me soon. Come nearer to me. Pray let my dear Lady Hamilton have my hair, and all other things belonging to me."

Another hour elapsed, and Hardy was at the bedside again. He told the captain "he felt that in a few minutes he should be no more; and added, in a low tone, 'Don't throw me overboard, Hardy.' The captain answered, 'Oh, no; certainly not.' 'Then,' replied Nelson, 'you know what to do. *Take care of my dear Lady Hamilton; take care of poor Lady Hamilton!*'"

A few minutes more, and Nelson breathed his last.

* * * * *

Lady Hamilton still resided at Merton House, but her difficulties increased fearfully upon her. She yet could not, however, divest her mind of the hope that the government would do something for Nelson's legacy; but in this hope she was doomed to all the bitterness of disappointment.

One morning her attendant, the only one remaining about her in personal service, came into her bed-room with tears in her eyes, and terror in her aspect:—

"Oh, madam," she said, "an execution is in the house."

At the word execution, Lady Hamilton turned pale. Did she at that moment think of Caracciolo? Recovering, however, her presence of mind, she commanded the girl to explain herself fully; and then she found that everything the house contained was seized for debt.

That evening she removed to a lodging at Richmond, from whence she removed to another in Bond Street. Debt and poverty tracked her steps; she—the spoiled child of fortune—found herself exposed to all the petty insults of those who, while her star was in the ascendant, would have kissed the ground she trod upon, but who, when the heavy cloud of misfortune lowered upon her, blessed themselves that they were not as she was.

For a time she certainly contrived, by the sale of a few jewels, to keep not only herself from starvation, but one attendant. That was a resource, however, which, although it might provide for current wants, could not be supposed to be sufficient for heavy debts, incurred during the lifetime of Nelson. One creditor, and only one, who had no grain of feeling for the woman, who, whatever might have been her faults, did not owe her inability to pay him to any one of them, went the length of arresting her. She was cast into the King's Bench Prison; and there she parted at the gate of that dismal home with her attendant. The fair and much cherished Lady Hamilton was now in the world alone.

That night she wept bitterly; and in the long dreary hours she thought over the busy past, much of which appeared to her more like a dream than a reality. She thought of how many friends and how many foes the grave had closed over, and she wished from her inmost heart that her brief and bustling career was over.

It was a dreary time that she lingered in the prison; and then one who had known Nelson paid the debt, and the poor mourner was free. At the gate of the prison she met her old domestic, who, with tears in her eyes, addressed her:—

"Fly, madam," she said; "fly from here. There is no safety for you in England. Others, now that it is found there are hearts that feel for you, will try the same course, and soon the prison will open its doors again to receive you."

"I know it, I feel it," replied Lady Hamilton. "Alas! what will become of me, now I am homeless and friendless?"

"No, madam, no. Take this purse. There is not much, but I am told it will enable you to reach France. In a lodging belonging to my sister in Soho you may wait until you can start, and then let me pray you to go far from here."

Lady Hamilton could not speak. Leaning upon the girl's arm, she was led to the place mentioned, in Soho; and there, after an illness of a week's duration, her passports were procured, and with the poor servant's purse in her bosom, she landed at Calais, a friendless and forlorn wanderer upon a foreign shore.

By the kindness of the English interpreter,

she was secured a respectable, though a very humble lodging, in a mean portion of the town; and there, day by day, her little store wasted, until famine stared her in the face. Her friend, the interpreter, from his slender resources, did what he could for her, but that was too little to support life—Lady Hamilton was starving!

* * * *

"Now, my good man," said an English lady to one of the butchers of Calais, "you must let me have some tender pieces for my dog. The poor thing has been so long petted and spoiled, that it may well be so now while its short life lasts."

"Certainly, madame," replied the butcher, with true French politeness, "certainly, madame. A feeling for the dumb creation is glorious."

M. De Rheims, the interpreter, was making a purchase at the shop; and when the tender pieces were duly selected for the dog, he pointed to them, saying—

"Madame, there is a lady, and one of your own countrywomen too, would be glad of the worst of those pieces of meat which you provide for your dog."

Mrs. Hunter, for such was the English lady's name, called hastily after M. Rheims, for, with a bow, he was walking away—

"Tell me, sir," she said, "who is this lady in distress you speak of?"

"Madame," he said, "I am forbidden to mention her name; but destitution needs no name."

"That is true," said the lady. "It does not. Let me beg of you, as you know the sufferer, to supply her with what is necessary. Here are two five-franc pieces, and here is my address. Come to me when you please, and let me know more of this sad case."

The interpreter called upon Mrs. Hunter on the following day, and assured her that her charity had been well bestowed, but that he yet, although he was charged with thanks and blessings, could not prevail upon the sick and destitute lady to permit him to name her to her friend.

"Very well," said Mrs. Hunter; "let her keep her secret as long as it shall please her so to do, and to the extent of my means I will supply her wants. But tell her that when she will permit it, I shall be happy to see her by calling upon her."

"I will, madame; and that time will soon come, for, poor lady, it is quite impossible she can live long."

Things continued in this state for some time. Mrs. Hunter, by a daily sum to M. Rheims, supplied the wants of the unknown sufferer; but one evening the interpreter arrived at Mrs. Hunter's house.

"Madame," he asked, "are you a titled lady in England?"

"No. But why do you ask?"

"Because, not being such, my poor sick friend, who, I fear, is dying, will see you, to bless you before she leaves this life."

The curiosity of Mrs. Hunter—a pardonable feeling, under such circumstances—had been strongly excited to know who the unknown one was to whose wants she had administered; and she at once accompanied the interpreter to a miserable lodging, up three pairs of stairs, in a wretched house. A girl was at the door of a room, apparently looking for some one; and when she saw M. Rheims, she said—

"Ah! have you brought the good lady?"

"I have—I have!" he said. "She is here. How is poor Madame?"

The girl shook her head, and M. Rheims, followed by Mrs. Hunter, entered the room. Upon a couch lay a female figure. The eyes were still lustrous, but it was the fast-fading fire of life that was there. The cheek had a preternatural bloom, and the dying one raised her gently upon her arm.

"Support me, Emile," she said.

The young girl held her up; and then, stretching out both her wasted hands to her visitor, the dying creature spoke—

"My friend—my dear friend, pride—sinful pride, of which God knows I have had my share, has prevented me from asking to see you until now. I—I—am faint."

"Do not exhaust yourself by speaking," said Mrs. Hunter. "You will do yourself harm."

"Bear with me for a moment. I am past all harm now. My race is run. God—God, in his justice and his goodness, bless you for your charity to one you knew not."

"But you will let me bring you a physician?" said Mrs. Hunter.

"No, no. It is useless. I am dying. It is God's will, and my hour has come. But you shall know to whom you have been so good—so very good. God will reward you,

for he will not weigh your goodness by my deserts."

"Nay, cheer up. You are yet young. Tell me, now, who you are, and think better of your condition, I pray you. You take by far too desponding a view of your condition. Believe me, you do. Who are you?"

"I am—Lady Hamilton!"

"Lady Hamilton?"

"Yes. Nelson's Legacy!"

Her head drooped upon her breast, and when the girl spoke to her she made no answer. They thought that she had fainted, and they brought restoratives to her; but all were in vain. The girl and Mrs. Hunter unfolded their arms from around her, and Lady Hamilton fell back a corpse!

*   *   *   *   *

Mrs. Hunter desired to bury the remains according to English custom. She was laughed at for her importunities upon the subject, and Emma Hamilton was placed in a deal box without inscription, her pall being a black silk petticoat stitched on a white curtain. No English Protestant clergyman could be found in Calais, but an Irish half-pay officer was sent for, and he read the burial service. The ground in which the body lies interred is now a timber-yard; it ceased to be a public cemetery in 1816, and Lady Hamilton had found her resting-place in the January of the preceding year.

"The Earl of Nelson" (Mr. Pettigrew informs us) "went over to demand Lady Hamilton's property, but found only the duplicates of trinkets, &c., pledged, and which he wished to take away without payment. He declined repaying any expenses that had been incurred."

Does our Tale want a moral?

www.ingramcontent.com/pod-product-compliance
Lightning Source LLC
Chambersburg PA
CBHW081211170626
46811CB00010B/3244